WORLD ENOUGH AND CRIME

WORLD ENOUGH AND CRIME

a multi-author anthology brought to you by

and the

Edited by:
Donna & Alex Carrick

World Enough and Crime

An Anthology of Crime Stories

Edited by Donna and Alex Carrick

Cover art by Sara Carrick

Kindle Edition ISBN: 978-1-927-114-92-6

Print Edition ISBN: 978-1-927114-91-9

Copyright Carrick Publishing 2014

This book is intended for your personal enjoyment. If you did not purchase this book, or it was not purchased for your use only, then please visit Amazon.com and purchase a copy. Thank you for respecting the hard work of these authors.

This is a work of fiction. No real people or situations are represented in these stories. Any resemblance to real people or situations is unintentional.

Contents

Crime…Noun, Michael C. Slater	1
Doctor Shediac, Donna Carrick	3
The Case of the Carriageless Horse, Steven M. Moore	23
Cover Girl, Melodie Campbell	35
The Prime Suspect, Rosemary Aubert	47
What Fresh Hell Is This? John Thompson	55
The Savages Among Us, Bianca Marais	71
Antonia, Rosemary McCracken	77
Delights in Novelty, Brad Ling	89
Runaway, Joan O'Callaghan	103
Live Free or Die, Judy Penz Sheluk	117
Writer's Block, Kevin P. Thornton	127
Belief, Jane Petersen Burfield	147
Ghost Protocol, Angie Capozello	157
The Angels Wait, Ed Piwowarczyk	171
The Ultimate Mystery, M.H. Callway	189
An Inexpensive Piece, C.A. Rowland	205
A Locked Room Puzzle, Anne Barton	217
Danger by Moonlight, Anne Barton	221
Leverage, Andrea Kikuchi	237
Potluck, Lynne Murphy	241
Easter Aches, Jayne Barnard	253
The Peace of Mind Thief, Alex Carrick	267

Had we but world enough, and time,
This coyness, Lady, were no crime…

To His Coy Mistress
Andrew Marvell (1621–1678)

Crime...Noun
Michael C. Slater

Editor's Note: Michael C. Slater's poetry appeared in our first multi-genre anthology, EFD1: Starship Goodwords. We were delighted when he offered to contribute Crime...Noun to kick off our 2014 crime anthology.

Crime *noun:* \ˈkrīm
: an illegal act for which someone can be punished by government
: activity that is against the law : illegal acts in general
: an act that is foolish or wrong (but not necessarily illegal)

you see it your way
all pompous and self-righteous
like you ever had a hard day
in your life
you have no clue
what it's like to be starving
to have needs
that no-one cares about
the world through your eyes
is a nice Summer picnic
that would have been sweet
when I was twelve!
but my pain never ends
cuz it's not about the "tokens"
or chasing "rabbits"
it's about calming the voices
you don't even hear
and stopping the pounding
by making me tired
so I can sleep
my heart vibrates
they are coming again
I leave your window,
but I'll watch you soon
until then, sleep tight!

Michael C. Slater loves words. It all started in grade school with vocabulary tests. Sometimes, it was augmented by having to copy the dictionary when "in trouble" and even more words were learned. Currently, Michael tries to capture emotions he sees on display with words instead of a camera.

Visit Michael at Facebook
or Tweet with him @MikeCSlater

Doctor Shediac

Donna Carrick

Editor's Note: When a thirty-year-old murder drags Detective Mallory Tosh back into a past she'd prefer to leave buried, she is forced to choose between childhood loyalties and adult conscience, in the case of Doctor Shediac.

Some mysteries are better left unsolved.

Detectives aren't supposed to think that way. We're taught to uncover secrets, to desire the truth, for its own sake.

It's not our job to adjudicate, to navigate the intricacies of crime and punishment, rather to ask questions and follow evidence. And we are expected to do so without reason, purely for the satisfaction of reaching a solution.

But we are human, after all.

Almost every cop has, at one time or another, imagined a case through to its *preferred* conclusion. Allowed himself to fantasize that he is judge and jury—that he knows best what the outcome should be.

But I digress. I'm not here to explore the endless spectrum of evil deeds encountered by the average cop.

I'm here to tell you about only one felony, and one outcome.

I'll happily leave the greater world of crime for others to ponder, and focus instead on the death of a doctor.

He died long ago. It's hard to say, after so many years, whether justice serves any tangible purpose.

But that's not my concern. I'm a cop, not a philosopher.

***

White sand scorched my fingertips.

It was impossible not to gaze at the shimmering length of beach. I found my sunglasses in the pocket of my tailored cotton shirt and settled them onto my nose.

Parlee Beach. Keeper of my earliest memories, both the good and the...well...less fortunate ones.

I'd forgotten some of the details, like how damned hot the sand was, and how the roaring waves threatened to muffle all other sounds, except for the piercing squawks of overhead gulls.

In one regard, at least, my memory had served me: the lacy trim of blistering sand really *did* stretch for miles.

"Where was he found?" I stood and brushed my hands, opening my nostrils to the salty breeze.

The young Mountie from Southeast Division, Shediac Detachment, straightened herself. Rhéanne Blanchette was on the short side for a cop, but had that strength of bearing they train into all new recruits, especially the females.

"There's a grassy knoll farther up, well past the high water mark."

Grassy knoll. I liked the phrase. I looked in the direction of her pointing finger, and could just make out a tail of yellow crime tape fluttering above a ridge.

She puffed her chest and started toward the scene.

I hesitated, reluctant to leave the water's edge. If I hadn't been wearing my good Italian leathers and black wool pants, the crease freshened that very morning by the hotel's dry-cleaning service, I'd have been tempted to walk in the opposite direction. The frothy lure of the whitecaps was powerful.

Instead, I turned and followed the officer.

We crested the ridge, stepping over a short clump of bush. The scene was laid out before us. A handful of RCMP officers from the Cold Case Division in Fredericton milled around a trussed up hole in the sand, about seven feet by five. As we approached, I could see it was deep, dropping approximately ten feet.

"He must have been near the surface, right?" I said, to no one in particular.

A detective in scruffy-looking plain clothes extended his hand. We shook as he answered.

"He might've been planted as much as four or five feet down," he said. "It would've been hard to go much deeper using a shovel, without hitting packed dirt and rock."

"Tosh," I said. "Mallory Tosh, Toronto P.D."

"François Jobin. Fredericton MCU."

"I have to say up front, I'm not here as part of the investigating team."

"No worries. Blanchette filled me in." He nodded at the officer who'd accompanied me to the scene. "She's with the Shediac Detachment, Southeast Division."

I nodded. It had been Rhéanne Blanchette who'd first contacted me through Toronto's 52nd Division. When they found a small, thick leather-bound journal nestled amongst the bony remains, with my mother's name and childhood address printed on the final page, Blanchette had done the legwork, tracking my late mother, and myself, to the Little Apple.

Toronto.

A driver's license recovered from the burial site revealed the victim to be Dr. Jean-Paul Leroux, a Shediac local, who was reported missing in 1981.

My mother's name might not have raised any questions—might have been mistaken for patient information—except for one thing: it was printed in black, firmly pressed ink, a tidy script that indicated frustration to the handwriting experts. Furthermore, her name had been underlined three times with an angry red pen, circled twice by the same pen, and appeared in the calendar notebook on the day before his reported disappearance.

To add a layer of damnation, a note had been scrawled by the same hand, also in red, under her address: *Make her see reason!*

It might not mean anything, but to the eyes of a detective, it screamed of conflict.

And, since Leroux's skull had been brutally smashed in, "conflict" seemed to be the word of the day.

Blanchette hadn't given me much information over the phone. She had a long conversation with my boss, who advised me to fly to New Brunswick and offer my help as a civilian.

My mother, Naomee Tosh, had kept close ties with her Maritime family right up till her death in 2010.

When we were little, Mom took me and my identical twin, Moraine, and much later our youngest sister Grace, "down home" every summer to be with her family. Our mother was a volatile woman, most often reticent and sometimes angry, who likely suffered from a bi-polar disorder. The only time we ever saw her happy was during those summer visits.

My father, Derek Moody, was a Toronto boy. They met in 1981, when Mom came to the city. They never married, but lived together in Wilson Heights area until he died in 2001.

My father was difficult to live with. I can't say he was missed—let's leave it at that.

In my memory, Moraine and I raised each other. She was lovely, feminine, stylish and demure, while I was the tomboy of the family. When Grace came along, we quickly took over her basic care, leaving our mother to tend to her demons.

"Blanchette tells me you've offered to drive up to the Tosh farm with us," Jobin said.

"When do you want to go?"

"This afternoon would be good. Before word gets out. You know how quickly bad news spreads."

He gave me a sideways look, and I hurried to say, "Blanchette asked me to keep it to myself. I haven't contacted any of my relatives."

"Good. Since you're here as a civilian, I'll ask the questions."

"Of course. I'll make the introductions and let you take it from there."

Jobin wasn't being a bully. He was following protocol. I had to be careful not to be perceived as inserting myself into the investigation. After all, my mother, Naomee Tosh, was the only POI we had at the moment.

My capacity had to be strictly off-the-books.

Having a cop on hand who knew the Tosh family well enough to encourage open dialogue, but not well enough to suffer from misguided loyalties, could prove useful for Jobin.

I followed him to the parking lot. I'd rented a Focus—not much muscle, but great on gas. It had been more than fifteen years since my last visit, and I wasn't sure I'd be able to find the farm on my own.

"I'll drive," he said. "We'll come back for your car afterward."

"Good." It made sense, but I missed my Wrangler.

"When was the last time you were at the farm?"

"Jeez, it would've been sometime in the late '90s. My grandmother Bessie Tosh was still alive at the time."

"Was your mother close to the family?"

"Yeah, very close. She brought us home every summer. Her oldest brother, George, took over running the farm. He still lives in the old house, along with his sister, my Aunt Zelda. Uncle John and his wife Tillie have a new house on the property. They have two grown kids, about my age. Stacia and Robbie. I'm not sure where my cousins live."

"Any other cousins? Aunts or Uncles?"

"Not that I know of, at least not in the Shediac area. Mom did have a younger brother, Harold, but he died in the early '80s. She didn't talk about him much."

I stared out the window, watching the cottages of Vista Street give way to Gould Beach Road, and on to Main Street, past the fried clam stands and the Shediac Lobster Shop. At Chapman Corner we made a right, heading north. When we reached Bae Vista, Jobin hung a left onto 134. It rolled past forests and Acadian farms of varying affluence.

"Almost there," he said. "Did your mother ever talk about Dr. Leroux?"

"I don't think so." I gave the answer almost in my sleep. It hadn't been a long flight, but there is always a huge rigmarole at Pearson International. Then, renting a car in Moncton, hooking up with Blanchette in Shediac....

Not to mention being whacked in the face with the reality of Parlee Beach. The flood of memories. Frankly, it had left me exhausted.

"Shit!" I said, snapping awake.

"What?"

"I just remembered something. It may not be relevant."

"Spit it out, while it's fresh in your mind."

"It's just something I overheard a long time ago. My Uncle John was in his cups. I think he was talking to my mother and Uncle George."

"What did he say?"

"Doctor Shediac. That's all. It was nothing. Just a phrase I remember."

***

Suddenly I was there, on the beach, skipping over the blistering sand with my sister, Moraine.

A pot of lobster was screaming over a fire, and the tables were set with butter, sugared lettuce, potato salad, Maritime baked yellow-eyed beans and coleslaw.

Doctor Fucking Shediac, my Uncle John said.

Settle down, John. My mother had a worried look.

Take it easy. Uncle George caught me in one arm and Moraine in the other, swinging us into a big bear hug. *You girls go for one last swim. We'll be eating soon.*

He dropped us onto the hot sand and we squealed, drowning out the sound of the boiling lobsters.

I hopped from one foot to the other, and was about to race Moraine to the water, when Uncle John staggered around the table, raised his beer in the general direction of a sandy ridge, and said, *Here's to Doctor Shediac, that miserable bastard. May he rest in peace.*

Johnny, knock it off, my mother said. *You've had enough to drink. Tillie, did you bring coffee? Better heat it up.* Mom grabbed the bottle from her brother's hand and emptied it onto the sand.

Moraine and I ran laughing into the ocean.

***

It didn't prove anything.

Regarded in the context of a childish mind, it carried no weight whatsoever.

Just the same, I rolled up my window and crossed my arms over my chest.

"You cold?" Jobin said, closing his window.

"A little." I took a deep breath. "What can you tell me about Leroux?"

"He had a house on the outskirts of Shediac."

"Oh."

"Yeah. In the early '80s he was the only doctor living in the area," he added.

I thought about that.

"He was a heart surgeon. He worked out of Moncton General. He left the hospital late one evening and never made it home."

"Anyone see him leave?"

"Hospital staff remembered saying good night to him. His car never left the lot."

"And that was in 1981?"

"Yes. Late summer."

I did some mental math. My mother, Naomee Tosh, had moved to Toronto in the Fall of '81. Moraine and I were born late in '82.

Thanks to my twin's sudden death earlier that summer, my DNA was on file with the Toronto Coroners' office. I quickly ruled out the possibility that Doctor Leroux might have been our father. My DNA had established that my younger sister, Grace, and I had the same father.

Leroux was already dead long before Grace was born.

Disappointed, I had to admit that Derek Moody was my biological father. Much as I might like to deny it, I carried the asshole's DNA.

"We're here." Jobin turned into the winding driveway, parking close to the old house. The new place was visible on the other side of the field, a comfortable distance away.

Aunt Zelda answered the door, looking a little heavier and a lot greyer, but otherwise exactly as I remembered her.

"Mallory, is that you?" she said. She glanced from me to Jobin, and back at me, suspicion clouding her eyes.

"Hi, Aunt Zelda," I said. "It's good to see you."

"What's happened?" she said.

"Don't worry, Aunt Zelda, everything's ok. This is Detective Jobin of the Fredericton RCMP. He just wants to ask a few questions, mostly about Mom. He asked me to come with him."

She recovered, pulling the door open and ushering us into the main parlor.

"When did you get home, dear? Did Gracie come with you? Have you seen your cousins yet? Your Uncles? Oh, it's been so long, you must have so much news."

That was an understatement.

Earlier that summer, my estranged twin, Moraine, who'd been missing for over fifteen years, had died. I learned she'd been living less than three miles from me, under the assumed name of Susan Baxter.

And, wonder of wonders, Moraine/Susan had a daughter! Carolyn Baxter, fifteen years old, was the spitting image of her mother, and by extension, my own mirror image.

My niece, Carolyn, was now living with me.

Yes, I had news.

But now was not the time to get into it.

"Aunt Zelda, Detective Jobin needs to ask some questions. Can I make tea while you and he have a chat?"

"No, thank you, dear. I think you'd better stay with us."

Her face darkened, and it was impossible to guess what she was thinking. She sat in her favorite straight-backed chair, leaving us to sink into the overstuffed armchairs near the fireplace.

"Mrs...." Jobin began.

"Miss. Miss Tosh. I never married, Detective. But you can call me Zelda. That's my name."

A defensive edge had crept into her voice, and my heart sank. Normally, Zelda was the most cheerful, unflappable person I knew.

Because I was raised by an unpredictable mother and a violent father, Zelda was my rock—my proof that there were good, strong minded adults, and that I could, by force of will, become like her.

"Zelda," he continued, "I have to ask you about things that happened a long time ago."

"My memory is exceptional."

"I'm glad to hear it. Back in 1981, when your younger sister, Naomee, was still living here, how old would she have been?"

My Aunt's eyes rolled upward, fixing on the ceiling for a moment. She was doing the math.

"I would have been twenty or twenty-one. Twenty, I think. So Naomee had just turned seventeen."

"Has your family always lived here?"

"We've been right here, on this farm, for generations."

"So you would have known everyone around here."

"Most everyone. If they went to the Anglican Church, or played Bingo, or had kids that went to school with my niece and nephew, or shopped at our supermarket. Of course, a lot of folks around here are Catholic. I'd still know most, at least to see them."

"Do you remember a doctor, a heart surgeon who lived here in the seventies? He had a place near the shore, near Shediac Harbour."

Zelda folded her hands in her lap, giving the question some thought.

"My doctor is in Moncton," she said. "What was this fellow's name? Maybe I'll recognize it."

"Leroux. Jean-Paul Leroux."

She kept her eyes on Jobin's face. "That's a common name around Shediac," she said.

"He would have been in his forties then. A good looking man. Tall." Jobin reached into an envelope and pulled out a photo. It was aged, but still clear. It showed a handsome, stern-looking man with neat dark hair and black eyes. He held it in front of Aunt Zelda.

She took the photo, mulling it over.

"I just don't know," she said. "I might have seen him around, but I don't think I knew him."

"What about your sister?" he said. "Did Naomee see the same doctor as you? Or did she ever mention a friend who was a doctor?"

"If you mean was she dating him, Detective Jobin, my sister was only a girl at the time. This Leroux was a grown man. My family would have put a stop to any funny business. No, I don't remember her ever mentioning a doctor friend."

The back door opened with the same screen-door-squeal that I remembered, and my Uncle George called out, "Zelda, is someone here? I saw a car out front."

"Yes, George, Mallory is here. She's with a detective from Fredericton." Zelda hopped up from her chair and headed for the kitchen, where George was washing up. My Uncle was always careful not to bring dirt from the field into the house with him.

Jobin followed Zelda to the kitchen, making sure she and George wouldn't have a chance to confer privately.

"Mr. Tosh," he said, holding out his hand, while George dried his, "I'm François Jobin. We'll need to speak with you, as well as with your brother, John. Is he here?"

"He's finishing up in the barn, then he'll head over to the new house. I'll try his cell phone. He usually carries it when he's working, in case Tillie needs him."

Uncle George made the call, and within five minutes my Uncle John was washing up in the same kitchen sink. I put on a pot of tea, notwithstanding Zelda's earlier rejection of the idea. I was embarrassed to note that Uncle John had been drinking. He wasn't far gone, but it was early in the day. I knew Aunt Tillie wouldn't approve, though with her good nature, she usually took most things in stride.

"Mallory, my dear," Zelda called in from her chair in the parlor, "would you make a pot of coffee as well? Your Uncle John doesn't care for tea."

"Of course," I said, forgetting my embarrassment as John winked at me. His sense of humor was contagious. I couldn't help but grin.

"Now that you're all here," Jobin said, "we've had an incident over at Parlee Beach. We've found the remains of a fellow who's been dead for some time. I'm wondering whether any of you might know this man." He held the picture out again, and this time Uncle George studied it before passing it to Uncle John.

"Don't know him," George said.

"Good looking fellow," John said, winking at me again. "But can't say I recognize him. Was he from around here?"

"Had a place in Shediac."

I watched their faces, as I'm sure Jobin did. Their placid brows didn't fool me for a moment. I couldn't guess what it was, but they sure as shit were hiding something.

"His name was Dr. Jean-Paul Leroux," Jobin repeated for the benefit of my uncles. "A surgeon out of Moncton General."

What occurred to me at that point was that none of them, not Zelda, George, nor John, had asked the obvious question: What had happened to Dr. Leroux?

Jobin must have caught the omission as well, because he studiously refrained from offering any details.

"There's a Leroux family I know in Riverview," Uncle John said. "They spend a lot of time over in Pointe Du Chêne."

"Haven't been to the Point in years," Jobin said. "I'll track them down. They might be related."

He lifted his teacup, letting a momentary silence build. We cops know how to do that. To let the silence do the asking for us.

With a suspect in hand, you never know how he or she will react to one line of questioning or another.

But they all respond pretty much the same way to silence.

First they twitch.

Then their eyes begin to dart.

This took place in a fraction of a second, my relatives glancing almost imperceptibly at each other, before Aunt Zelda coughed.

"We didn't know this man," she said.

More silence. I was sorely tempted to break it, just to make things easier on my aging relatives, but I knew better than to give in.

"Fellow must have had enemies," John said. He took a long swallow of his coffee. "Fellow gets himself whacked…" He caught himself, but too late to suck back his words.

Jobin looked at me, his eyes flashing.

"Whacked…" he let the word out slowly. "Yes. Fellow gets whacked, he might have enemies."

"We don't know this Dr. Leroux," my Aunt said, standing to let us know the visit was over. "My brothers have been working in the field all day. It's time I got George some dinner, and Johnny, you'd best be getting home to Tillie. You know how annoyed she gets if you're late."

Uncle George stood as well. He was a big man, taller even than Jobin.

"How long will you be in town, Mal?" he asked me. "Are you staying for dinner?"

"Can't tonight, Uncle George, but thank you. I left my rental car over at Parlee, and my niece, Caroline, Moraine's girl, is waiting for me at the hotel."

"Moraine had a daughter? What are you talking about?" my Aunt Zelda gasped.

"I just found out this summer. We all thought Moraine had died back in the '90s, but it turns out she'd run away. Must have been pregnant when she ran. Caroline is fifteen, so the timing is right."

"Caroline," Zelda said.

"I'll be damned!" John said.

"Bring her for dinner," George said.

"I will, I promise," I said. "Tomorrow for sure. We'll be here at four and help Aunt Zelda cook."

"I'll be damned!" John said again.

Jobin waited till we were back on the highway before saying what we both knew.

"They're hiding something. All three of them."

"Yup." I didn't know what else to say.

"I'll have to bring them in," he said.

"I know."

"And you have no idea? You don't know anything about this?"

"Nothing. I swear."

"I believe you," he said, but his eyes had a skeptical look.

Doctor Fucking Shediac. Here's to that miserable bastard. May he rest in peace.

"You'll be seeing them tomorrow?"

"Yes," I said. "I have to introduce them to my niece."

"Give it a shot," he said. "You never know. Maybe they're tired of keeping secrets."

That was something else we learned in Major Crimes. People tire of their secrets. They get weighed down, and eventually they just have to let go.

"I'll do my best."

***

The next day, full of Aunt Zelda's pork chops and rhubarb pie, we all sat in the parlor: Caroline, Tillie, George, John, Zelda and me.

"So," I said.

Caroline kept quiet. I'd filled her in on as much as I could guess.

John was sober. That in itself was indicative of how serious the situation was.

"It was a long time ago," Uncle George said.

"Doctor Fucking Shediac," Uncle John said.

"Now, John," Aunt Tillie said.

We all stared at the fire John had built against the evening chill.

Finally, George said, "Mallory, do you really want to know what happened?"

"Yes."

"It was a summer evening," George said. "Right about this time of year.

"Zelda was away somewhere, at one of those girls' camps she was always trotting off to.

"Your mother, Naomee, was too wild for camp. She'd rather scamper around the countryside with me and John."

"She was a great kid," John added.

"That she was," George agreed, "and so was our little brother, Harold. And Lord be praised, Naomee was so fond of him! The sun sang *Good Morning* and *Good Night* just for him, as far as she was concerned."

"They were closest in age of all of us," Zelda said. "They were inseparable."

I knew what it was like to be that close to a sibling. My heart broke for the thousandth time, in memory of Moraine.

George continued telling the story.

"John's buddy at the time, Guy Leblanc, told us about a delivery that was supposed to be made late that night, to the grocery store where he worked. He'd overheard the owner telling his son about it. *Cash,* he'd said, about forty thousand, lined up for a crooked contractor who wanted everything paid that way, and wouldn't take checks.

"Leblanc wanted to roll the safe, but was afraid they'd know for sure it was him, even though they'd never given him the combination. He was good at things like that—getting past locks and such. Also, the timing was bad. He had to take his father north to Bathurst to visit his dying grandfather. His father was half-blind and couldn't drive.

"Guy didn't know the combination, but he was sure the safe would be easy to lift. If the three of us, John, Harold and myself, big strapping fellows, could get it into the trunk of our car, we could hide it in our barn. When Guy got back to town, he could help us open it. Then we could bury it here at the farm. No one would ever find it.

"So off we go, merry as you please—but of course, Harold tells Naomee all about our plans, and she won't be left behind. *You'll need a lookout,* she says, and she's right. It would take the three of us to break in and cart the thing outta there. We'd need someone to watch for the cops."

"Let me just say, I knew nothing about this until after the fact," Zelda said.

"Thank God you came home when you did, Zelda," John said. "We had no idea what to do."

"Anyway, getting back to that night," George said, "we drove one of our old farm cars, with a fast engine and no plates. No one in town would be likely to recognize it. We got into the supermarket all right, without using Guy's key. That would have been too obvious.

"We found the safe, and even managed to get it outta there and into our trunk. Naomee was driving. John and I got into the car, but Harold thought he'd dropped his cigarette pack inside the store. *I've got lots of cigs,* I said.

"*My prints'll be all over the pack,* Harold said, then he scarpered back into the store.

"We saw him smiling at the glass doorway, waving the cigarette pack like a damn fool."

"That's when we heard the shout," John said. "It was a cop, doing his foot rounds."

"We froze," George said. "We couldn't drive off without Harold, but he was still standing at the doorway, trapped like a deer in headlights. Naomee honked the horn, and Harold came to his senses and ran for the car.

"I was in the front seat with Naomee, and John was in back. John left the door open for Harold. He damn nearly made it, too, but caught a bullet in the chest just before he reached the car. He didn't go down right away. John pulled him into the car, and we hauled ass outta there, burning rubber all the way.

"I got Naomee calmed down and reminded her to stay on the back roads, and to drive at a normal speed. We took Wynwood till we got to Highlandview, then were forced to scoot over to Shediac Road.

"We knew Harold was in serious trouble. We remembered there was a doctor who lived nearby, just outside of Shediac Proper, not far from Sandy Point.

"Well, we banged on that door for damn nearly five minutes, shouting and hollering, till the old bastard finally woke up and stuck his head out the window. We knew he'd more likely open the door for a girl, so Naomee did the talking, pleading for him to help her baby brother.

"We even hauled Harold out of the car, to show the Doctor we weren't making it up. The blood was all over the place. Any fool could see he was bleeding out.

"But the prick wouldn't come to the door. Sent us packing, back to Hub City, with orders to take Harold to Moncton General.

"We had no choice. We dragged our little brother back to the car. We weren't worried about speeding—if the cops caught us, at least they'd get Harold to the hospital lickety-split. But no one stopped us.

"We didn't say a word for miles. Then, somewhere near Miracle Road, John pipes up from the back seat."

"Harold was dead," John said. "He was down on the back seat with his head on my lap. He died in my arms, like an angel, without a whimper. There was no point trying to get to Moncton General."

"They brought him home," Zelda said. "Mom and Dad didn't know what to do. They called me at camp in the morning, and I came straight away and took charge.

"It has to look like an accident, is what I told them. We dug the bullet out of him and laid him out in the field. Dad couldn't do it to his own son, so it was left to me. I drove the little tractor, the one with the bailing fork, and made sure it speared him just enough that the doc wouldn't look too closely. We left the handbrake off, and made it seem as if the thing had rolled into Harold.

"They didn't question the lack of blood. After all, Harold had lain bleeding on that field for hours before we 'discovered' him and rushed him into Moncton.

"That so-called doctor in Shediac never made an appearance. At least, thank God, he never filed a report, either.

"It was put down to 'death by farming accident'. We watched the papers for any report of a cop firing at the store that night. There was a tiny write-up: Police are asking for any information regarding a break-and-enter and the theft of a safe." Aunt Zelda wiped her eyes. She might be stoic, but she did have feelings.

George picked up the thread where she left off.

"The safe," he said, "was empty. Either the owner had moved the money, or there never was any. Either way, we lost Harold for nothing. A few months later, your mother ran off to Toronto and took up with your father." His voice was thick with distaste for Derek Moody. "Naomee couldn't stay on our old farm without her baby brother."

"Naomee was never the same after Harold died," Zelda said.

"What happened to Doctor Shediac?" I asked.

"We tried to talk to him, but he wasn't at home," John said. "We figured he must work out of Moncton General. His name was Leroux—Doctor Jean-Paul Leroux. Turns out he was a top heart surgeon. Would've been able to save our boy easily, if he'd given a rat's ass."

I bit my lip. It was obvious to me that Leroux had done the only thing he could, under the circumstances. If caught treating a fugitive "off the record", he would almost certainly have risked losing his medical license.

But my uncles would never understand that.

"Did you talk to him?" I pressed.

There was a silence, but I let it build, knowing few people can resist the urge to fill a void.

It was Aunt Zelda who finally spoke.

"Naomee," she said, averting her eyes. In fact, I couldn't help noticing the entire family was avoiding my stare.

"She wouldn't let it go," John said.

"She was closest to Harold of all of us," George said. "She was crazy with grief. She said we had to talk to the doctor, to let him know our brother died because of him.

"We tracked Leroux down at the hospital. We caught him in the parking lot, at the end of his rounds."

"I'd had a few beers," John said.

"We both had," George said. "Anyway, we tried to talk to Leroux. He got pissy and told us to bugger off.

"Next thing we knew, Naomee had a tire iron in her hands. We didn't even know there was one in the car."

"She was out of her mind," John said. "It was over in minutes."

"Then we had to get rid of the body," George said.

"I told them to take it up to Parlee Beach at night," Aunt Zelda said. "There was a place where the kids don't play much, shrouded behind a ridge and some bushes. I told them to go as deep as they could."

My niece, Carolyn must have been shocked by the tale. To her credit, she didn't show it. She sipped her tea, tucking her feet under her.

I looked at my aging relatives, saw the pain, the obvious remorse...the grief that never goes away.

I could understand the rage they'd felt against the person they held responsible for their brother's death.

One day I hoped to find out what really happened to my twin, Moraine, and when I learned the truth, well...let's not draw that scene out to its conclusion.

I could understand what my mother had done. I could sympathize with her desire to avenge Harold. To cut herself a big slice of revenge, even though, deep down, she must have known it wasn't really the doctor's fault, what had happened to her brother.

I could understand it. But I couldn't cover it up.

Secrets, in my experience, are the very imps of evil.

It was time to nail this one to the gates of hell.

Donna Carrick is the author of *The First Excellence* (winner of the 2011 Indie Book Event Award), *Gold And Fishes* and *The Noon God*, available in both paperback and e-book. Her Crime Anthologies, *Sept-Îles and other places* and *Knowing Penelope*, are available for e-readers.

Her story "Watermelon Weekend", featured in *Thirteen* (Carrick Publishing), was shortlisted for the prestigious Arthur Ellis Award, 2014.

Donna's novels have reached over 100,000 readers worldwide.

Visit Donna at her Website
www.donnacarrick.com
or at her Amazon Author Page

DONNA AND ALEX CARRICK

The Case of the Carriageless Horse

Steven M. Moore

Editor's Note: With his characteristically gripping style, Steven Moore introduces us to those lovable, intelligent detectives Chen and Castilblanco, in this tale from their early case files....

Detective Rolando Castilblanco was no longer a patrolman; he'd graduated to the big leagues. The new detective sat on a bench in Central Park. He loved his city—its diversity, its character, and its green areas surrounded and protected by watchful and silent skyscrapers. He also loved its food and nightlife.

Late lunch was a hot dog with spicy mustard and relish, washed down with soda. He noted a drop of mustard on his tie. Knew enough to let it dry instead of smearing it with a napkin. Taking care of multiple uniforms had been bad enough, but new shoes, slacks, sport coats, and tie had set him back to the point that lunch from a street cart was the only option until next pay check.

What had Al Dempsey said about his promotion? "You'll be so rich, kid, you'll think you own the city."

Yeah, sure. At least, maybe his shoes would last longer because he didn't have to walk a beat. He smiled. Al was an institution. He hoped he'd learn a lot from him.

He was about to down the last two bites when he spotted the horse. He didn't know too much about horses, but he loved the ones in Central Park. Who wouldn't? Kids, tourists, and romantics loved them, in spite of that classic Seinfeld episode. Add fake gas lights and a bit more cop presence in the park to make nighttime rides safe, and you'd maybe need more horses and carriages to keep up with demand. The city had other charms, but its horse-drawn carriages provided something special, a quixotic clash between old and new.

He tossed the remains of his lunch into a trash barrel not far from the bench and sauntered over to match speed with the animal. He grabbed the bridle and halted the horse.

"Whoa, big fellow. Where did you come from?" The horse shook its head and whinnied. "I speak a few languages, my friend, but not yours." Pashtu was the most recent one he had struggled to learn, but he was sure the horse wasn't a rabid jihadist. "Let's backtrack a bit and see if we can find your carriage and driver."

He guided the horse through a U-turn and retraced its route along a straight section, and then around a bend skirting a pond to where he saw the carriage but no driver.

Correction: No live driver. The man's body was half-immersed under water from the waist up.

What was Al's first rule? Don't touch a damn thing. Second rule? Call CSU and let them come do their damn magic. Castilblanco's first rule, though, was to call Al.

He weighed down the horse's reins with a stone and dialed his new partner's phone. No answer. *Figures. Still out to lunch. OK, Al's rules for now.*

***

"Kid, I leave you alone to go do a chore and you find trouble," said Al Dempsey as he and Castilblanco watched CSIs do their magic.

Castilblanco knew Dempsey was jerking his chains, but he didn't like being called 'kid'. He might be inexperienced as a homicide detective, but he'd participated in some interesting cases as a patrolman, and overseas military duty must count for something.

"Is this now our case?" he said.

"Yes and no." Dempsey was always explaining how things worked as if Castilblanco knew nothing about police procedure. He anticipated what was coming. "If there are drugs involved, maybe Narcotics Division will take it. If there are sex crimes involved, maybe Vice. If there were tourists kidnapped here, we call the FBI."

"And maybe if there's cruelty to animals, we'll call PETA in to help us," said Castilblanco with a smile. He popped two Tums. *Damn spicy mustard!* "Who would kill this guy and set his horse loose?"

"There's no blood, and there weren't any gun shots. No witnesses either. My guess is the horse broke free and bolted. You wouldn't have heard the ruckus because the trees' leaves would filter out that wee bit of sound. We'll see what CSU says. We don't even have an ID yet."

"His name's Robert Jenkins," said Castilblanco. "The horse is Sam."

"How'd you know that?"

"Says so on his carriage license. Think Jenkins owns Sam?"

"Maybe he owned the horse, maybe not. It's a strange profession. Why don't you do something useful and have that uniform over there cordon off the area. We're starting to collect rubberneckers, although it's still damn cold."

"It's spring, Al. The sun's trying to warm us. Leaves are appearing on trees."

"When you're my age, anything below seventy feels cold."

***

"Detective?"

Castilblanco looked up from his terminal. A uniformed cop, a slender Asian woman, stood before him, notepad in hand. He had no idea who she was. *Should I?* The pad obscured his view of her name tag.

She wore the uniform well, as if a model had decided to put on a police uniform and step out on the fashion runway. Castilblanco remembered how disheveled he had looked in his ill-fitting uniform. He had a hard time making any clothes fit right, even in the Navy. That was one reason basic training had been hell. Training to be a SEAL had been worse, of course, both physically and mentally. Combat hadn't been a picnic either.

So recently out of uniform, he thought the chasm between detectives and uniformed cops wasn't appropriate. He stood and offered his hand. "Castilblanco. And you're...?"

"Officer Dao-Ming Chen, sir." She shifted the notepad to her left hand. Her grip was firm. "They told me to collect information about the vic's family."

He smiled and sat again. "I already know he was a 'Nam veteran. What else did you find?"

"He has a sister in Sacramento."

"California?"

"I'm not familiar with any other Sacramento."

There was no smile, but Castilblanco thought it was a good dig. *Yeah, where else? Iraq?* He smiled for Officer Chen.

"Anything else?"

"He lived in Brooklyn." She offered the address. "It's an old hotel converted into an apartment building."

Al Dempsey returned from the ME at that point. "Hiya, Chen." *OK, is there anyone in NYPD he doesn't know?* "You auditioned for Saturday Night Live yet?"

"Pardon, sir?"

"Don't 'sir' me, my Asian beauty who never smiles at my jokes. Are you flirting with my new partner?"

"No, sir!"

"Then get the hell out of here. Rollie and I need to take care of business." After she left, Dempsey handed Castilblanco a piece of paper with a string of numbers, some numbers with one digit, others with two. "What do you make of that?"

Castilblanco shrugged. "You first."

"I'll give you a hint. They're from a Chinese fortune cookie. Too bad Chen just left."

The rookie detective frowned. Dempsey was old school. Political correctness meant voting for the candidate anointed by the union. "If I had to guess, I'd say he used those numbers to play the lottery and kept the fortune to check them against results."

Dempsey thought a few beats. "That's as good an idea as any. I guess that wouldn't have anything to do with the murder."

"I wouldn't discount it. Suppose he played and won and someone else knew?"

"They'd be looking for the lottery ticket," said Dempsey. He thought some more. "Worth checking out." He looked at his watch. "You live in Brooklyn. Go visit the vic's apartment and then go home. Maybe you'll have some luck and find the ticket. Our fund could use an infusion of cash." Castilblanco frowned again. "Geez, Rollie, that was a joke. You're as bad as Chen."

Castilblanco smiled. *Dempsey's in rare form today.* "Do I need a search warrant?"

"The guy's dead, so he won't complain. If the landlord gives you crap, call me. My kid is in a talent show out in New Jersey. If I don't go, my ex might scratch my eyes out."

"You should want to be there for your kid."

Dempsey looked at Castilblanco as if he were from another planet. "Did you hear me say it's a kids' talent show?"

***

Castilblanco convinced the vic's landlord to let him in. The landlord entered first but stopped cold at the doorway. Castilblanco peered over his shoulder.

The old hotel room had been made into a studio apartment. It was trashed. Pictures that once hung on walls were broken and on the floor; wallpaper was peeled down to plaster board and studs in some cases; mattress, chair cushions, and pillows were ripped open, their stuffing scattered about; and even the stained and frayed carpeting had been sliced into sections and lifted off the floor.

"Someone was looking for something," said Castilblanco.

"Brilliant deduction, Detective. Who's going to pay for all this?"

"Not the vic's insurance, I'd bet. He probably doesn't have any."

"Well, I have a huge deductible. I'm going to have to raise rents to cover the repairs."

"How much does a room like this go for?"

The landlord told him. Castilblanco was surprised it was so exorbitant. No rent control here.

***

"I passed the intel on to the New York Lottery," said Castilblanco next morning while giving Dempsey an update. "They'll check to see if they've sold a ticket with those numbers and whether it's a winner. Right now I can't think of anything else to do. CSU says whoever ransacked the apartment must have used booties and rubber gloves. Real pros."

"I'm going to give the sister in California a toot as soon as it's a decent hour out there," said Dempsey. "Why don't you take a look at where that guy kept his horse and carriage? Those drivers tend to spend a lot of time with their steeds. Maybe you'll find something."

"Yeah, I can imagine," said Castilblanco, "and I have new shoes."

Dempsey smiled. *Just part of the initiation, kid.*

***

Castilblanco patted the horse—he seemed more at ease in his stable, hangin' with the fellows. "Well, Sam, I bet you know all old Bob Jenkins' secrets, right?" The horse snorted. "Yeah, I agree. It's pretty ripe in here." In front of the stable, there was a storage bin. The lock had been smashed, but he couldn't tell when. "Did this just happen, old boy?"

He could see how people were fond of horses. Sam seemed noble, although Castilblanco assumed he'd spent his whole life pulling carriages around with tourists in them. He'd probably made many people happy. *Maybe he's happy too because of that.*

"Wonder how many marriage proposals you've heard in your long life?" The horse looked at the detective with soulful eyes. "I bet you miss old Bob. Maybe you'll find another driver."

He rummaged around in the bin. It was filled with broken harnesses, tools to repair them, and spare parts for the carriage, but without any tools for that. There was also a thick, heavy book. He pulled it out and dusted it off.

"The Collected Works of William Shakespeare," he read. "Maybe there's more to old Jenkins than being a lonely old Vietnam Veteran. What do you think, Sam?" The horse eyed him.

He opened the book. The center had been removed, and the space was filled by an old pistol. It looked Russian. He knew veterans brought souvenirs back from overseas. He had done it, too. He also knew Russian and Chinese arms were used by the Viet Cong. But maybe there was more to the gun's story than just serving as a souvenir. He sniffed at the barrel and smiled. He dropped it in a plastic bag, removed his gloves, and tossed them in a nearby trash can.

He patted the horse again. "I'll see what I can do about getting you a new driver. I need to do forensics on this weapon. *Ciao*, old fellow."

***

"It's been fired recently," said the technician. "There weren't any bullets around?"

"Not one," said Castilblanco. "And the ME said Jenkins was beaten and strangled."

"Maybe the gun doesn't have anything to do with this case," said Dempsey. "I'm still betting on a lottery ticket." *What other motive can there be?* he thought.

"What's all this other stuff in the report?" said Castilblanco.

"GSR. Traces of mucous and saliva too. Maybe the horse's?"

"It's not human?" said Dempsey.

"No. Definitely not human."

"Can we test it to make sure it's the horse's?" said Castilblanco.

"Don't waste the man's time," said Dempsey with a growl. "The vic was around horses. Whatever he used the gun for—maybe to shoot a stable rat—the horse slobbered over it afterward. Right?"

"If you say so," said the technician with a smile for Dempsey followed by a raised eyebrow for Castilblanco. "We can confirm whether the traces belong to the old man's horse. If they don't, it's anyone's guess."

***

After the technician left, Castilblanco perched on the edge of his desk. He shared it with three other detectives on different shifts, but thought they wouldn't mind if he dusted a bit.

"Did you talk to the sister?"

"Pretty much estranged. She was against the war and they never talked after he went over. Their last conversation was a fight about that, in fact. She's filled with remorse now. That damn war almost tore this country apart. I guess it did the same to some families. She understood why he was close to horses. Said he always loved animals. Wanted to be a veterinarian."

Dempsey smoothed what hair he had left back over his balding head. "Any luck with the lottery?"

"Those numbers correspond to a minor winner, a million-dollar prize," said Castilblanco, "sold in Brooklyn at a convenience store near the vic's apartment. No one has come forward to claim the prize."

"Because they haven't found the ticket," said Dempsey. "If anyone does come forward, we'll have Jenkins' murderer. If not, ticket's still not found. We have to wait. Let's work on some other cases."

***

A week later, Castilblanco was sitting on the same bench, eating pastrami on rye with spicy mustard, this time with hot coffee—a cold breeze was blowing in from the Seaport. He had turned up the collar of his sports coat. Some preschool children went by, herded by parents, or maybe volunteers and teachers, because some of the adults looked young. He figured the ratio of grownups to kids was appropriate for the age of the kids. He could remember that excitement as a kid.

They're babbling about their trip to the zoo.

He jumped up, tossed the rest of his sandwich, and dashed off.

The zoo's administrative office was open. An office assistant, a gum-chewing young woman, seemed glad to have her lunchtime vigil interrupted.

"Any security problems here a week or so ago?" said Castilblanco.

"Sure. Someone took pot shots at our leopard. We reported it to you."

"You mean NYPD. I'm Homicide."

Smack. Smack.

"Whatever. The cops never discovered who did it."

"Is there any way I can inspect that cage?"

"I guess we can set that up, if you have a good reason."

He did.

"Now I know you're bonkers," Dempsey said to him two hours later.

The snow leopard was locked in his den. *Maybe pissed to hell*, thought Castilblanco. CSIs were in the outside pen used for public viewing, going over every square inch. A half hour later, one found the lottery ticket in a plastic sandwich baggie wedged into a crack in a mound of concrete playing the role of a boulder. Shortly thereafter, another found prints on a metal ladder providing a little-used alternate access to the pen for those who cleaned it.

"I'll be damned," said Dempsey. "You've found the lottery ticket and the murderer."

"Maybe, if the prints aren't those of a zookeeper. And assuming he's the same person who used Jenkins' gun to protect himself from the leopard while he searched the pen. He wouldn't have zookeepers helping him like we do."

"So, why didn't he find the ticket?"

Castilblanco smiled. "Maybe two reasons. He came in at night, but night was ending—snow leopards hunt at dusk and dawn. Second reason: Either he was a bad shot, or he didn't want to shoot the animal, only scare it. In either case, I'm guessing he ran out of bullets for that old gun he was using. Probably dropped it too—maybe out of fear—hence the animal slobbers. Somehow, he managed to grab it again and run."

***

The prints led to another carriage driver with a record who confessed and confirmed most of Castiblanco's theory. He'd beaten the information out of Jenkins before strangling him. He still had deep scratches on his left arm.

"He was lucky," Castilblanco said, "at least with the leopard."

Dempsey nodded. *Another case closed.* "The sister doesn't want the money," he said. "She wants to start a foundation for carriage horses and their friends in the zoo. Obviously, Jenkins loved both of them."

"He also loved the zoo enough to trust it as a bank for safeguarding a deposit of a million dollars," said Castilblanco. "Lord knows when he thought to cash it. Man didn't have a bank account as far as we know. Maybe he was going to talk to a lawyer first. The Lottery recommends that for big winners."

Dempsey eyed his partner, who was reclining in his chair, sipping from his mug filled with precinct coffee. A donut and plastic bottle of Tums would soon participate in his snack. "Not bad for a rookie's first case."

"Thanks, Al. That means a lot to me."

"Don't let it go to your head, kid," said Dempsey.

"I won't. And stop calling me 'kid'."

Dempsey only nodded again. *Kid's going to be a good one.*

Steve Moore writes sci-fi, mysteries, thrillers, short stories, and book reviews. At last count, he has written thirteen novels, including one novel for young adults. He also has two short story collections. His stories reflect his keen interest in the diversity of human nature that he has observed in his different abodes across the U.S. and in South America as well as in his European travels for work and pleasure.

His interests include physics, mathematics, forensics, genetics, robotics, and scientific ethics. He also has an active blog where he comments on current events and their meaning to the U.S. and the rest of the world, and posts opinions about writing and the publishing business from the perspective of an indie author.

Steve and his wife now live just outside of New York City. Visit him at his website:
http://stevenmmoore.com.

Cover Girl

Melodie Campbell

Editor's Note: With her customary wit, award-winning author Melodie Campbell brings us this hard-hitting, hysterical story of how looks can, indeed, be deceiving.

The door opened, and a big man who was all chest and no hair strode in, barking orders.

"I'm looking for Mel Ramone."

"You found her," I said. I find missing persons for a living. This one was easy. But I didn't think he'd pay me for it.

He looked me over thoroughly, and it wasn't with approval.

"You?"

I nodded, swinging both legs off the desk. "Mel, short for Melinda."

"Damned foolish name for someone in your line of work."

I jerked myself straight. "It's a foolish business."

Tony whined from the corner. The metallic squeal didn't help with the atmosphere. I ploughed ahead before the lecture started.

"Can I do something for you?" *Like maybe straighten your nose?*

The man with the attitude threw a look at my bodyguard. Tony was doing some assessment of his own. His android head swung to the left and addressed me with details.

"Regulation Beretta 9mm semi-auto, left side; boot knives, both sides. I don't detect anything else, Mellie."

I winced at the 'Mellie'. Tony is the premier development of RBMN Robotech's new sensitivity line: "Protection with Affection." That should read: "Overprotection." Unfortunately, they goofed on the sensitivity part. He sounds like my mother.

"My assistant," I stated bluntly. "He stays. For protection."

The big man nodded. This time he approved. I got the feeling he was familiar with the need for protection...like maybe people took regular aim at his face. It had that cross-me-and-I'll-break-both-your-legs appeal.

"I want you to find someone," he growled, throwing himself into the client chair. It squeaked in protest. "In confidence."

I nodded, and hit the RECORD button under the lip of my desk. No beep, no whirr...it's programmed mute.

"I've been away, off planet, for nearly a year. Security work; been incommunicado for the last month. Back on leave now."

He paused, frowning in my direction. The eyes, which were half closed, seemed to see a lot.

"Got back last night. Late. Got to the condo and it was empty. Not a sign. Not a single damned sign."

I leaned forward. "Of what?"

The eyes flashed open. "Of my wife. I want you to find my wife."

Tony clucked sympathetically from the corner. I pretended to jot down details.

Basically, it came down to this. Mr. Military had just returned from secret assignment, and it appears his wife was away on an assignment of her own. No forwarding address. No sign of foul play. A suitcase was gone, but as far as he could tell, hardly any clothes. Which could mean a lot of things. Or nothing. How much do men know about their wives' clothes?

"You checked at work?"

"Of course." He glared at me as if I were some sort of brainless thing that fed on flies. "First thing I did. They haven't seen her in a month. Say they don't know where she is. Won't release any information."

"She was expecting you?"

"I'm ten days early," he said dryly. The room felt instantly colder.

"What does she look like, Mr-"

"Gorgeous. She's gorgeous. Tall, slender, green eyes, long dark hair." He paused, glancing at my Cleopatra hair. "She looks a little like you." He reached into the breast pocket of his civilian jacket. A brown envelope–medium sized–landed on the desk.

I opened it and pulled out two photos; model proofs, full facial. I agreed with his assessment. She did look something like me; or rather, what I would look like if I were gorgeous. Which I'm not.

I'd seen the face before, too. And so had everybody else on the planet, if they had eyes in their heads. Not all of them do, of course.

Inez Orczy hit the front cover of Vogue about five years ago and had yet to come off it. She had a face you couldn't miss: all aristocratic bones. You could starve for light years and still not get that effect. Three months back, the cosmetic firms were vying for an exclusive contract, so the rumors went. The fashion piranhas tripped over their high priced heels in pursuit.

Funny. I hadn't heard anything about it since.

A throat rumbled clear.

"You'll want to check out the premises. Here's a passcard...the numbers at work...friends. Her mother's dead. I'll leave you to it. You can reach me at this number." He passed an envelope–this time white–and swung from the chair.

I spoke quickly. "About my fee-"

"I know what you charge. Just find her," he said, turning away.

"Look–there may be-"

"Just find her! I want her back. She'll come back, if she knows I'm home."

"I'll call you as soon as I know anything, Mr. Orczy."

"Beckwith!" came the roar from the doorway. "Colonel Beckwith! Orczy is my wife's name."

The door closed with a bang.

I looked over at Tony and grinned. Oops.

***

Two hours later, Tony was still whining.

"I don't like it, Mellie. I don't think we should take the case."

"Why not? And don't call me Mellie."

"I think he did it," Tony hissed.

"Did what?"

"Did her in. Knocked her over. Snuffed her out."

I sighed. "Have you been watching late night movies again?"

I was going through massive closets in the Orczy bedroom. Everything in the bedroom was huge, including the bed. Which was a thought.

"Boyfriend," I mused.

"Boyfriend?"

"Oh come on, Tony! It's got to be. Run off to be with a man, I'll bet my last credit. The husband thinks so, too. That's why he's so grumpy. But why she would leave these behind, I can't imagine."

It was hard not to want all the things in that closet. Row upon row of designer samples and runway castoffs, not a thing older than last season. A girl would sell her own mother for this bonanza. Maybe even her robot.

"How do I look in chartreuse?" I held up a pile of chiffon to my face.

"Avocado, not chartreuse," he corrected. "And you shouldn't be touching other people's clothes. You don't know where they've been."

I sighed. "These cost a fortune. Do you have any idea how big the fashion industry is?"

"230,472,898,720,000 credits."

"And that's only on this planet." I twirled chiffon. "Quite an empire. Really, the fashion mavens have us enslaved."

Tony's head tilted sideways.

"I mean it. One model slinks down the runway in fuchsia plastic, and the rest of us about kill ourselves trying to replace our whole wardrobes."

"Absurd." Tony shook his head.

"Big business," I said in response.

Tony squatted on the edge of a white flouncy divan. Hard to describe, how he squats like that. Imagine a seven-foot store mannequin folding into itself...like a kid hugging both legs to his chest.

"Can we go now?" he whined.

I touched a pressure sensor and the closet became a wall once more.

"Just a sec. Thought I'd do some calling from here, in case of a trace."

Tony moaned in moral agony. He really isn't cut out for this line of work.

"You stay here. I'll be back in a sec." I headed for the bathroom. It's the only way I can get rid of him. Otherwise, he clunks after me like a seven-foot shadow. Not that I'm complaining...it's his job. But whenever I want to be alone for a minute—which is often—I head for the nearest loo. All robots must have a ridiculous view of the capacity of human bladders.

The bathroom was surprisingly modest, compared to the rest of the condo. No bronze dolphins or tropical plants. Just marble. I sat on the throne, flipped open my cell, and punched a number. One not on Beckwith's list.

"Reynolds."

"Got time for a quickie?" I tried to sound sultry.

"Hiya Babe! Always time for that. Tonight still on?"

"Still on," I said to my favorite cop. "Look Pete—I've got a missing person, a special one. Think Cover Girl. Front page of every magazine in the country, if this gets out. Can you do me a check—female human, about 27, 5'10", ultra slim, shoulder length black hair, green eyes."

"Missing for how long?"

"A week at least. We don't know for sure. Husband just got back and found her gone."

"So why aren't you checking motels?"

I grinned. "Wanna help?"

He laughed and my heart did a flip.

"Didn't see that one coming, Beautiful. But you betcha. Tonight at seven. I'll check out the morgue on the way over."

"Pete, you're the greatest."

"You ain't seen nothin' yet."

I was still grinning as the phone went dead.

Dead. Well, she could be dead, but I doubted it. Chances are, Pete would draw a blank at the morgue. This case smelled of something else–high priced perfume and the rag trade.

I pulled the list from my pocket. Mr. Military had gone to some length...literally. Work numbers listed first, but I bypassed those. High priced agencies don't release info without six lawyers and a press conference.

Next came the relatives. Possibilities here, but not the first choice.

There are advantages to being a woman in this trade. Knowing how the female mind works, for one thing. If I were Inez Orczy, about to skip town, whom would I trust with the information? My mother-in-law? Not bloody likely.

According to the list, Inez's best friend was another model named Alison Davoe. Luckily, Alison hadn't skipped town with her boyfriend.

"Who are you?" Suspicion leaked from her voice.

"Mel Ramone. Colonel Beckwith has employed me to locate his wife. Apparently, he came into town yesterday and found her missing."

"Damn!" She exclaimed. "What is he doing back so soon?"

My nose started to twitch. "Soon?" I said. "I thought he'd been away for a year."

"But he wasn't due back until a week Friday!"

My pulse shot up. "Do you know where she is?"

Silence. I tried again. "He's really worried. Do you think you could get in touch with her?"

A pause.

"What did you say your name was again?"

I gave her that, and my number and sat back on the marble throne to think.

Like all nights spent with Pete, morning came too soon. Unfortunately, it wasn't Pete who woke me up.

"You didn't call. You said you'd call. I was worried." Tony's expressionless face loomed from the doorway.

I groaned. "What time is it?"

"Eight a.m. Nine-thirty in Newfoundland. You've already had three calls, but she wouldn't leave a message."

I sat up, suspicious. "How did you get in, Tony?"

"I over-rode the security codes. But don't worry. I reset everything."

Luckily, the phone rang. We both ran for receivers.

"Is this Mel Ramone?"

"Yup," I answered, before Tony could.

"This is Inez Orczy speaking."

"Hold it." I grabbed my bra and shirt from last night and tried to dress with one hand. "Hold it right there. Where are you?"

The contralto voice at the other end sighed. "Are you alone?"

I said, "Yes."

Tony said, "No."

I cursed out loud. "That was my robot."

She continued without missing a beat.

"Is Brian with you?"

"Brian?" I went blank.

"My husband."

"No."

She gave me an address and told me to ask for her at the desk.

***

It was a big desk. Not the sort of desk you find at a posh hotel, either. This one was staffed by a sergeant major of a woman, dressed in white. Easy chairs littered the foyer. There had been no sign on the building, and there was no sign over the desk. It was stark and unwelcoming.

I said Inez Orczy was expecting me. The desk-major picked up a phone and spoke quietly into it. Tony fidgeted at my side, visibly nervous. He hates hospitals, laboratories, or anything to do with people in lab coats....people who might be robotics technicians. I don't blame him. I had the same feeling about this place.

"Room 160, four doors to your left. That way."

She pointed and we obeyed. The corridor was quiet and vacant. I glanced at Tony as he plodded along, turning his head this way and that.

"What is it Tony? What is this place?"

"I don't know." He sounded nervous. "I can't conclude. A clinic of some sort. Perhaps a sanatorium? But no visible guards. No weaponry, no hidden surveillance. Some electronic activity, but not the level of-"

I shushed him at the door and knocked.

"Who is it?"

"Ms. Orczy? It's Mel Ramone."

"Come in," she said. "And shut the door behind you."

The room inside was equally stark, but bright. Light flooded in from the sliding glass doors. Inez Orczy stood framed in the sunshine, a dark silhouette. She looked like her photos...only more. The famous Aristocratic bones had some padding.

She smiled sweetly.

"So, you've discovered my secret," she said sadly. The lone figure walked away from the window and settled on a nearby tub chair. "Have a seat."

"Your husband is very worried about you," I stammered.

She sighed. "Poor Brian. He has no imagination. You've met him. You know what he's like. You'll understand why I had to do this in secret."

"I think so," I said slowly. Tony swung his head in my direction, questioning. I threw him a comfort-glance and waited.

She got up and started to pace. "The perfect model! Every measurement scientifically designed and crafted for the specific purpose of selling clothes. The perfect marketing combination–impossible to achieve with the human body. I'm a scientific masterpiece," she said bitterly. "The first of many to come."

Amazing. I looked her over, incredulous.

"I did the Paris and Milan shows my very first year. Shot a cover with Vogue, and kept going. Married Brian, and believe it or not, we've been happy. He doesn't want children, luckily. I checked that out before–it was only fair. Of course, he's off-planet a lot, and I have my career. Until now...but who would ever have guessed that skinny would go out, and the healthy buxom look would come in?" Her voice held a remarkably human wail.

"The bookings have suddenly dried up. My agent says I've got to gain weight or I'm finished. 'Eat more!' she says, as it if were that easy. No, they don't know I'm...manufactured. Neither does Brian. And I can't tell them. It was part of the contract."

"Contract?" My throat felt dry.

She nodded. "Top secret. I'm a test case. This is big business."

No kidding. Big business, big bucks. I could see the potential. Talk about scientific break-throughs...Tony looked like a kid's mechano project next to Inez.

"Why a model?"

Inez shrugged. "In the public eye. Not a lot of personality requirements, although I think I excel there. Ideal for a trial run and no damage if I slip up. Models come and go, so I can be removed at any time."

The room chilled. I caught a whiff of the future, and it wasn't pleasant. How many more Inezes were out there already?

I fingered the list of phone numbers in my purse. "Your friends?"

She shook her head. "They don't know. Alison thinks I'm in for cosmetic surgery. Which is sort of true."

Inez–a slightly filled out and even more beautiful Inez–reached out her hands and pleaded.

"Brian wasn't due back until next Friday. And I undergo breast implants tomorrow! You've got to help me. He can't know where I am. Not until Friday, at the earliest."

I frowned. "He's pretty frantic. We'll have to tell him something."

She threw up her hands and paced the floor. "Tell him anything, I don't care. Anything but this. I know–tell him I'm having an affair! That's it. That's perfect. I can manage a jealous husband," she said triumphantly. "I can handle that, no problem. I just can't deal with the truth."

She was still pacing the floor when we left.

***

"I don't understand it, Mellie. I don't understand it at all." Tony ambled along the corridor beside me.

"Why we tell Colonel Beckwith about his wife's affair? The one she isn't having?"

"We're confirming his worst nightmare, Mellie. And it isn't true."

I grimaced as we walked out of the oppressive foyer into direct sunlight.

"Sometimes, what you think is your worst nightmare, isn't. Which reminds me."

I took a deep breath and tried not to think of my mother.

"Tony."

"Yes?"

"Don't call me Mellie."

"Okay, dear. Watch the curb."

Billed as Canada's "Queen of Comedy" by the *Toronto Sun* (Jan. 5, 2014), Melodie Campbell has had a decidedly checkered past. Don't dig too deep. You might find cement shoes.

Her crime series, *The Goddaughter*, is about a wacky mob family in Hamilton aka The Hammer. This has no resemblance whatsoever to the wacky Sicilian family she grew up in. Okay, that's a lie. She had to wait for certain members of the family to die before writing *The Goddaughter*.

Her other series is racy rollicking time travel, totally scandalous, hardly mentionable in mixed company. But we'll mention it anyway. *Rowena Through the Wall*. Hold on to your knickers. Or don't, and have more fun.

The Goddaughter's Revenge won her a 2014 Derringer (US) and the 2014 Arthur Ellis Award in Canada. She has won seven more awards for stories which have appeared in *Alfred Hitchcock Mystery Magazine*, *Over My Dead Body*, *Flash Fiction Online*, and more. Publications total over 200 and include 7 novels. By day, she is the Executive Director of Crime Writers of Canada.

Visit Melodie at her Website
http://www.melodiecampbell.com/
or at http://www.funnygirlmelodie.blogspot.ca/

The Prime Suspect

Rosemary Aubert

Editor's Note: What happens when the "world of sound" threatens to drown our other senses? Diabolical, eerie, and downright frightening–award-winning author Rosemary Aubert brings us this tale of an unseen enemy.

***

This story is dedicated to Professor Eric Mendelsohn of Ryerson University, to whom I owe the premise.

It spread like a plague. How else to explain why it was everywhere?

She'd worked in a library all the years before her retirement, before she'd had time to take the math courses that were now her single pleasure. But in the end, even the library had been infected. Things had gotten a lot worse in the five years since she'd left.

As she walked up St. George Street at the heart of the university, she felt the deadly enemy invade the very pores of her skin. Same as every day. Noise. The unavoidable, intrusive foe, like a virus or a bacteria. Like a cancer cell that multiplied with exponential efficiency. Cancer was considered an epidemic now, wasn't it?

Noise. She had no husband to wake up to anymore. Which was a tragedy, because her Sam had been such a quiet man. She knew some women were cursed with husbands who snored. Thank heaven she had been spared that misery! When they had lived together in their beautiful house, she had awakened each day to the sound of exactly nothing. Not even the ticking of an annoying clock.

Well, that was all changed now. That morning, like every morning, she'd awakened to the racket of the old-people's residence where she was trapped. Except for her, everybody who lived there was half deaf, and everything had to be turned up to top volume in order for her fellow residents to hear what she could hear through the walls. Alarm clocks. The rush of water and the squeal of pressure in the pipes. The clink and clank of the heating system. The woman in the next room Skyping to her sister in Bangladesh.

As she neared the Bahen Building, she gave wide berth to the vendors with their long lines of students waiting to buy the sort of things the kids liked to eat: French fries, shrimp rolls, hot dogs. She didn't mind the smells, even at nine in the morning. What she hated was the sound of it all.

Their chatter seemed to comprise half the languages of the world, a sound like the buzz of a cloud of malaria-carrying mosquitoes. And the vendors themselves, calling out the orders for their foul-sounding wares: poutine, bratwurst, pho.

Worst of all was the music, if you could call it that. She'd heard a couple of math students had, as a semester project, figured out a trick to assign a musical tone to each hex numeral from zero to 15. This meant that, on their computers, their equations sounded like songs.

Thankfully, not everyone in the math department had figured out how to do this, or the racket would have been even more unbearable. Now: rap music; twanging squeaky female voices; young men engaging in an activity they called singing, but which, to her, was nothing more than arrhythmic yelling. And then there was that Beiber kid and the guy from Korea that hopped around with his wrists crossed. And all of this leaking out of the little plastic gadgets called ear bugs—or something like that.

Shaking her head in annoyance—not that anybody was paying any attention to her—she climbed the steps of the Science Building. The wide glass door groaned as she pulled it open. Didn't anybody lubricate anything anymore? She made her way quickly through the groups of students gathered around the entrances to the classrooms and clustering on the stairs. Of course, they couldn't hear her when she asked them to respect the safety regulations of the university by leaving stairwells clear of obstruction. The human voice, especially the voice of a small woman past the age of sixty, was as useless as the flu vaccine in July.

When she got to the fourth floor, she was relieved to realize no one had arrived there before her. No one was going to give her a hard time about using the "Little Room".

Theoretically, continuing-ed students such as herself were not supposed to use the room, but she had been granted a special dispensation from her con-ed math professor, an intense, handsome, silver-haired man with dark eyes that sparkled whenever anybody asked him a question. Probably because it was rumored no one had ever asked him a math question he couldn't answer. Anyway, the reason she was allowed to use the room was that, after taking a decryption course from him, she had—all on her own—figured out how to decrypt the security device that kept the room locked. She did that now, her fingers on the keys fast so that any unauthorized person seeing her, either in person or by means of the video camera mounted in the hall, wouldn't have a chance of copying what she was doing.

She had to be careful. Because she needed the computer in that room. Her own little laptop just wasn't powerful enough for the equations she liked to play with. And, more important—most important, she needed the quiet so she could concentrate.

Competition for the "Little Room" was so stiff that the story had gone around that a few years previously—before she'd entered the evening math program—a student had been found murdered there, lying bloody on the floor between the computer and the door.

Of course, that was probably an urban myth, though it was true that a student had died of some sort of heart failure somewhere in the building, and his body had been found months later. Well, that wasn't her problem. She set out her papers, signed in and got down to work.

It was fine. In fact, it was great. It was like going to the country when the racket in the city was starting to make you sick. There was simply nobody else around. For almost an hour, she worked away. It was a good day. The numbers she was playing with were co-operating beautifully. If she could keep on like this, she had a good chance of solving the set of linked equations that formed this year's math contest. The winner would receive a magnificent prize: A full year's expenses at the university, including tuition, room and board...It would be the opportunity to become a matriculated mathematics student.

Fine at first. But after an hour and a half, she thought she heard something. True, there was now the muffled buzz of students beginning to arrive for class, but that was one of the few sounds she didn't mind, because everybody respected the "no-talking-in-the-corridor" rule. Nobody wanted to be responsible for making a noise that might distract a fellow mathematician at the critical instant of insight, ruining his chance of solving a problem he had been working on during his entire time at the university.

No. This was some other sound. Vaguely rhythmical. Not as insistent as rap or rock. Not as entwined and intriguing as classical. Musical, yes. But not any music she'd heard before.

She was annoyed. Of course she was. But she would have been less the mathematician than she was if she had not been curious. Curious enough to leave her papers, the computer station, and eventually the room itself in order to investigate.

When she opened the door, she could hear the sound much more clearly, and now it had a dimensionality—that is, a direction.

She glanced down the hall. To the right was a single door which she knew led to a class that was always in session at this time of day. Basic Considerations of the Calculus. She didn't waste time going in that direction. There was no music there. At least not to her, though the professor of the course might disagree.

No, this was a real sound. This was noise and she set off in search of the source with the determination of an epidemiologist searching for the source of a virus.

Of course, the more she moved in the direction of the strange, tuneless, irregularly beating soundtrack, the louder it became.

Until she found herself in front of the door to the Number Theory Lab. She seldom bothered coming down here. She wasn't interested in number theory. In fact, it bored her, always looking at problems she found too basic for consideration.

The sound was throbbing now. It seemed to increase in intensity moment by moment. There was no window in the door, so she had no idea which of her fellow math students was responsible for this disgusting intrusion into the silence of the building.

She knocked, but knew it could do no good. The sound coming from the room drowned out any other.

She tried the door knob, but of course the room was locked and coded, just as the little room had been.

It didn't take her long to decrypt the lock, but the sound, the wavering, sometimes repetitive, sometimes wildly divergent tones kept growing in intensity. Somebody had to be in there, and somebody had to be told to stop that deadly, sickening noise...

After what seemed an eternity of seconds, the knob released and the door swung open.

Nobody. That's who she found in the room. Nobody.

And it was dark. The only light came from the screen of one of the computers ranged in a bank against the back wall, only eight feet away. A dazzling, dizzying light that seemed to change color and intensity with every note rising from the computer's speakers.

She wasn't entirely ignorant of number theory. She knew, for example, that there were classical searches. Infinite attempts to pin down some more decimal places in some number that would never end or repeat. The square root of two. The billionth decimal place of pi. The derangement number $1-(1/e)$. And she understood at a glance what this computer was looking for: the largest yet-unknown prime number. The primes, the numbers divisible only by one and themselves. The prime numbers that stretched to infinity but were becoming harder and harder to find.

Someone had set this computer to conduct that search and someone, some clever trickster, had set the search to music.

At first, she figured she could just turn it off. But the closer she got to the machine, the harder it became to move. Even a single step was difficult to manage. It was the number itself, as if it were some sort of animal defending itself against her. And its weapon was those dreadful sounds, those notes that rang in a deafening cascade. She was aware there were thousands of known primes, but so many had already been discovered that any new one might have thousands, even millions of digits. A million notes from a single numeral.

It was so loud she couldn't think. Couldn't hear anything but the sound of the number. She raised her hands to shield her ears. And she felt a liquid flowing out of them. When she looked at her hands, she saw blood.

Terrified, she moved away from the machine, as if it could stab her or even shoot her. As if it were a person, an enemy, with her demise as its only goal.

As she backed away, she tripped over a small stool someone had been using to sit at one of the screens in the room.

So afraid was she, at first, that she didn't notice the stool sliding across the concrete floor without a sound.

Nor did she hear anything when she grabbed the handle of the door and yanked it open, stumbling into the hall.

It was as she approached the room where she'd been working that she realized she heard nothing. Nothing at all.

It took her only a second to understand what this meant. Horrible as the thought should be, she smiled. She would never have to worry about noise again.

As this thought danced through her mind, she noticed it was growing dark in the library. Even the flashing lights on the computers were dimming. Was there a power failure? Or some other kind of malfunction?

She pondered the implications of that as she sank to the floor, its cool, smooth surface soothing her dying face.

Rosemary Aubert is the author of sixteen books, among them the acclaimed Ellis Portal mystery series and her latest romantic thriller *Terminal Grill*. Rosemary is a two-time winner of the Arthur Ellis Award for crime fiction, winning in both the novel and short-story categories. She appears in the acclaimed short story collection *Thirteen*. A popular teacher and speaker, Rosemary is a member of the Crime Writers of Canada and the Mystery Writers of America. She conducts a much-in-demand writers' retreat at Loyalist College in Belleville, Ontario, each summer, as well as mentoring writing students at the School of Continuing Studies at the University of Toronto.

As a hobby, Rosemary studies math and science and has recently completed her second stint attending lectures at the International Summer School at Cambridge University in England. She intends to use some of this math knowledge in future works. Rosemary is an active member of the Arts and Letters Club of Toronto, where she promotes Canadian writing and encourages other writers like herself.

Rosemary Aubert's latest book, *Terminal Grill*, is available at Quattro Books, Amazon.ca and at Chapters-Indigo.

Visit Rosemary at her Website for more information:
http://www.rosemaryaubert.com/

What Fresh Hell is This?

John Thompson

Editor's Note: Master storyteller John Thompson throws us headfirst into the nightmare of a long-forgotten century in this tumultuous tale of Timon Chiseldon.

Timon Dexter Chiseldon emerged from a riotous nightmare of angry faces to a waking nightmare of stench, uproar, and pain. His eyes opened first. Reports from his other senses queued up close behind to also demand immediate attention.

There was little light. Some came from a heavily barred window set high in a wall, and some dim light squeezed through the thick straps of iron in the door. Cut stone blocks, dark with old soot and clammy with fetid moisture, comprised the walls and ceiling.

What came through Timon's ears and nose were too much to quickly grasp: A tumult of voices: Sobbing, laughing, arguing, chattering, wailing, murmuring and babbling. Somewhere, there was the clink of iron and the thumping of heavy mallets. The smell was a gagging melange of sewage and vomit, of bodies that never washed; and uncut by any breath of fresh air or wholesome smells. The scent of the air was thick enough to taste.

Timon stirred, and that was enough to let in another cascade of reports: He was lying prone on a cold and clammy stone floor; there were rents in his clothing and iron shackles about his ankles; he had plenty of bruises; his head was beyond dizzy and his mouth was dry. He had a bellyful of something that disagreed with him and it was coming up...now.

He rolled over and spewed. After the first gush, as his stomach fought to bring up more, Timon learned he was not alone. "That's it...give the floor a good rinse. It needs it."

After a minute of dry-heaving and spitting; Timon was just able to stand. There were a half-dozen others sitting against the wall in the gloom, men and boys, but only one youth of Timon's own age bothered to speak.

"Where am I?" Timon's head was still reeling.

"You need to ask? You're in Newgate. I'm here because it's held that I am a thief—which I am to the shame of my grandfather—but they say you are a murderer."

There were growls from a couple of the other men, and one spat.

Timon sputtered: "But, but who? What did I do?"

One of the men growled again, "You 'ad your old man's serving girl, you did, then slashed 'er up and dumped 'er in the river when you was finished with 'er." The man who spat at Timon did so again. "H'it's a Tyburn dance for you, boy."

"Peggy is dead?" Timon's protest excited nothing but contempt from most of the inmates of the cell. It could not be true. Peggy was a wide-eyed and innocent 14-year-old country girl from Somerset. They were attracted to each other, but Timon had only recently worked up the courage to kiss her. This was all a nightmare, and at this very moment Peggy must be tending to the linens, or dusting in the ancient half-timbered House on the London Bridge.

Only the young prisoner seemed prepared to believe his innocence, although guilt or innocence didn't matter inside Newgate. What did matter was how much money one had.

Timon checked his waistcoat pocket; he had eleven pence there yesterday afternoon when he got home from his school. Now his pocket was inside out and quite empty. The gaolers expected to be paid to get you bread and water, or anything else you wanted. There was even a fee for "easement of chains", which meant they took off your shackles for a while.

After some hours of sitting against the wall, the Gaoler turned up with two of his mates. The Gaoler, in a long brown coat and no wig on his scabby, shaven head, held a lantern and a staff. His two mates were bare-handed, but grabbed Timon and pulled him out of the cell. The rough movement made him puke again.

There was a dimly-lit narrow corridor, busy with knots of people at the other strap-iron doors, but everyone eased to one side as the procession went by. The rumble of dozens of conversations died to a whispered susurration that surrounded Timon, and all eyes were on him until he had passed. That muted pocket travelled with Timon up a short stone spiral staircase, and into the old gatehouse itself.

They spiraled up another floor, passed through a stout wooden door and into a small stone chamber. Here, there was light and air, but it seemed to Timon that the stench from the cells had already woven into his clothing, if not deeper than that.

At one end of the desk, a clerk was perched on a stool with quill and ink-pot at the ready, and a sheaf of papers to hand. Behind the desk sat a rubicund man in late middle age, with a long wig that had probably been fashionable 30 years earlier; the tailoring on his coat and waistcoat were also neat, tidy, and of an old cut.

"This is him as what got delivered over that poor cut up Molly in the river last night," the Gaoler snarled and gave Timon a shove forward. Timon stumbled, thanks to his dizziness and the leg-irons, and so bumped the desk, which caused a small ink spill on the clerk's paper.

"My Lord..." Timon began, stopping as the magistrate glared at him. Then the magistrate's face relaxed.

"It is highly unusual for a prisoner to arrive in the hands of what seems to be a mob, simultaneously with the complaint itself." The magistrate looked to the clerk. "The complaint is of...?"

"Murder, your honour, of one Peggy Greendyke, come to the city last year from Glastonbury, 14 years of age or so, 'tis said."

"Ah me. Well, I see he has come through the Lodge and into the Condemned Hold so fast that the practice of chummage seems to have been bypassed; for which small mercies God be praised." The Magistrate shook his head, then addressed himself to Timon. "You are..?"

"Timon Chiseldon..." Before Timon could say anything else, another voice was heard.

The Magistrate beheld a man of the middling sort, a man whose coat, waistcoat and wig suggested he was a well-off tradesman or merchant. The new arrival was missing a leg and had come into the room with a crutch, and was wasting away with some ailment. The face had been handsome once, but was scarred by a blade, and the neat cut of the man's coat suggested he had also been a soldier.

"He is Timon Dexter Chiseldon, and has lived in my household since his mother died nine years ago in '46. I know him to be 15 years of age, and with no previous stains upon his character save that his parents were not married. He is a student at Whitmore's on Tower Hill, where he has been learning his grammar, French, some Latin and mathematics, plus some fencing instruction."

The Magistrate looked at the old soldier. "You run that shop specializing in curiosities and old books upon the bridge. I also remember, Master Reynolds, that you were once something of a swaggering rogue, but got the King's notice at Dettingen, and were struck at Fontenoy. I will take it as a given that I need not ask about this youth's father."

The Magistrate thought for a second or two. Then he studied Timon and beheld a scared looking youth, of about five feet and eight inches tall; neither skinny nor plump, and whose clothes—notwithstanding the ravages of his man-handling and a night in the worst cell the prison had to offer—seemed to have likewise been of good, though simple, quality. The boy wore no wig, but again had sandy hair that otherwise might have been neat. He had a broad forehead, betokening a ready mind and clear blue eyes.

"Not quite a gentleman, nor too much of one...and yet there is what you are accused of and the mob hopes to see you— or someone—swing for the crime. We shall wait upon the next Session of the Court." The Magistrate looked around once more.

"Gaoler, in the capacity of your office, I would be thankful indeed if someone were not too rapacious in this case. One must hope for charity in even the most unchristian of hearts, hmmm?"

This brief interview was all that passed between Timon and the Magistrate. Timon and Master Reynolds had a moment to themselves, but Reynolds was in even less of a talkative mood than usual. "Boy, staying alive in here will cost as much as your school does...and the trial will be worse. Say nothing about poor Peggy, I know you well enough to know that much about you." Before he limped away, he thrust a purse to Timon which, to the boy's surprise, contained a number of half-crowns.

Instead of the airless, dark, fetid Condemned Hold; the Gaoler's mates took Timon to a large room on the lower level with a window facing out to the court-yard. A couple of armloads of fresh straw were on the stone floor in an alcove by the window, but the ever-present smell of feces, urine, vomit and sewage from elsewhere in the prison never completely receded. Nor did the noise ever abate; the prison was never quiet.

Each half crown got Timon two exorbitantly over-priced daily meals of bread, cheese, and beer; and the privilege of visitors. Clean clothes and a blanket were sent by the Captain. The room he was in had a floating population of 20-30 men, women and children, ranging from syphilitics on the edge of madness, petty criminals, counterfeiters and thieves. Most kept their distance...the rumor had it that Timon was a dangerous killer.

There were women that offered themselves for a share of one of his meals, but Timon had an idea of what a beauty patch might be concealing, and at any rate the memory of Peggy and his own shyness added more inhibitions. A couple of preachers with a covey of the curious in tow visited and attempted to argue that the bestial nature of his crime would be evident on his face, and that his soul needed to be saved. Timon had enough self-presence to ignore them; although being the subject of public curiosity vexed him. This also held true when several schoolmates came to visit, largely for the dubious status of associating with him.

The first two weeks in prison also were occupied with his thoughts. Poor Peggy Greendyke had been only a housemaid, but Timon managed to convince himself that he loved her, and that she loved him in turn. (This was far from the truth, but the infatuations of the young do have a power of their own). Brooding over the loss of an unrequited love served another function...who might have done such a thing? His own memories of the evening were...well, they weren't there...he had none.

Search as he might, Timon could remember coming home, and there was a vague sense of an unwelcome but familiar presence, a brimming cup of rum, and nothing else.

After a couple of weeks, the monotony of his life was broken as he turned to his companions. He learned dance measures and card games, and lock-picking and how to "dip" a pocket. Freeing oneself from the shackles was child's play; but Timon also learned the ways to look for a locking mechanism (often concealed) and to pick the latch and slide the bolt inside a lock. London was always rich in lore, and the lore of the alleys and lanes was another dimension. Then Master Reynolds turned up.

"Timon, the Clerk of the Sessions has brought your case up and the Grand Jury will consider it in two weeks. It is possible that you will have your trial before All Souls Day. When it comes time for your plea, remember you are literate–claim benefit of clergy–it might help."

"But, father..." There was an awkward pause. Timon had never called him that before, and Reynolds had never acknowledged his paternity. "I didn't kill Peggy, I don't think I did, all I remember was coming home from school, and then I woke up here. That's it."

Captain Reynolds considered for a second, and Timon realized how old his guar...his father now looked. His face was shrinking closer to his bones, and his complexion was grayer. "Son, all I know is that she was naked, violated, and floating in the river downstream from London Bridge. Her throat had been slashed. So the Parish Constables came calling, I came with them and your brother William; and you were found in a stupor on the floor of her garret, her bed-clothes soaked in blood, with an empty bottle of rum beside you and a blood-smeared knife in your hand."

"But…" Timon tried to interject.

"But nothing; I know you two were casting glances at each other like two moon-struck puppies. I've never known you to be drunk. You stand up for yourself when threatened, yet I've never known you to bully anyone. All of that will mean nothing to the court. What's more I can't even hire affidavit-men to lie for you."

One thought occurred to Timon. "Was there no blood on me, I mean, if I killed her, wouldn't I have her blood on my face and hands, on my clothes? You've seen enough battle to know that. I had puke and slime all over me when I awoke here in Newgate, but no blood."

Reynolds looked thoughtful, pursed his lips and rubbed his chin. "Yes, that's true enough."

Another thought occurred to Timon, "And what was William doing here? I thought he was apprenticed to Dr. Mead since his return from Leyden."

"Ah, well, Dr. Mead required a…ah…more prosperous look to his apprentices. William is now attending a course of lectures and is engaged in the study of anatomy, here in the city. In fact, he is living at home once more. However, he was with me in the shop when the constables came."

Timon had no love for his half-brother William, who was some five years older than him; fleshy and petulant; and the bully of his first days under Reynolds' roof since Timon arrived after his mother, Anne Chiseldon, had died. It always outraged William that Timon had been born before Mrs. Reynolds had died. "And was he in the shop when Peggy went into the river?"

"Enough!" There was a flash of temper in his father's eyes. "William is no more capable of this crime than you are. Now, Timon, you should know your mother…helped later by me…had put enough aside in the Three Percents that you would be able to afford a Lieutenant's Commission. I still have my old Captain's commission from the 31st, and can sell it to get you enough to eke out your pay. However, it would seem I'm going to have to spend this to secure your future in...another way."

With that, Jack Reynolds left, having first replenished Timon's supply of half-crowns. It was also a luxury to lease a ewer and pitcher sometimes and to wash behind the screen of his blanket. Rats, lice and fleas were plentiful, but Timon was fastidious and loathed their touch.

The weeks went by and the Sessions in the Old Bailey resumed. However, what Timon had not realized was that the Old Bailey heard all manner of capital cases from all across England. Moreover, many prisoners who had missed Assizes were sent to Newgate in the autumn. The number of people in their cell grew with every passing week. The prison's legendary stench also grew apace. It became harder and harder to keep his nook and the quality of his benefits–thin as they were–grew worse. The Gaolers were now raking in money from so many other prisoners that the daily half-crown seemed less important.

In early October, a fever visited the ward. Those who had it were wracked with pains and a rash spread across their skin. The straw on the floor got foul, particularly as the ill started vomiting. Timon did what he could for the dying and fretted about his own health.

A couple of weeks after the contagion broke out, Timon got another purse–containing 20 golden Guineas–and a fresh set of clean clothing. This was a gift from his father, but there was a note: His trial would be in two days–the Grand Jury had decided the case would go forward.

The day of his trial, Timon had another meal of the same old bread, the same old cheese, and the same old small beer. As the nearby bells tolled for eight in the morning, the Gaolers came. Timon had secreted his own lock tools away in the lining of his breeches, and the shackles were in their proper place around his ankles when they came. A coffle of prisoners was already forming up in the courtyard, and they were arranged in line according to a list read by a clerk of the court. Timon was third.

There was a throng around the Old Bailey, and Timon soon found himself recognized and abused. The gaolers and some constables of the nearby parishes were around with staves, and Timon didn't get manhandled, but it was clear that many people still hoped to see him hang.

There was a waiting room, and it was alarming to see several people get lifted up outside so they could stare in at the prisoners. It also alarmed Timon that the first trial–a forger who had impersonated sailors to steal their wage tickets–only took twenty minutes, and from the baying of the crowd inside the Court they approved of the sentence. A gin-addled prostitute was next and took 15 minutes…whatever happened in there resulted in several gales of laughter. Then it was Timon's turn.

If it was empty, it would have been a large room, but the Court was cluttered with wooden enclosures, galleries, and noisy spectators. Timon was nudged to the prisoner's box in the room's centre. Now he knew how a stag felt when the hunters and dogs closed from all sides–naked, vulnerable, and alone.

A Clerk beside the seated judge asked Timon his name, and after Timon replied read out the charges of rape, indecency, and murder. Timon, aware that the bespectacled judge was staring at him quite closely, was then asked by the judge for his plea.

"I am not guilty, your honor." There was a susurration up in the gallery and the judge smacked his gavel to silence it.

"Anything else?" Timon got the sense he was still being closely inspected.

"I claim benefit of clergy, your honor."

The judge settled back in his chair. A black-clad lawyer stood and recited the Crown's case against Timon; it took about five minutes.

Then the judge asked the prosecutor, "Pray tell me, Mr. Morris, was the blood of this unfortunate girl also pooled on the floor?"

The lawyer paused and skimmed quickly through a couple of sheets of paper. "No, your honor, but that is of no account…"

"Really? Was there blood on young Master Chiseldon's clothing, or spattered upon him?"

"There must have been, your honor, and I can summon the Constables..."

"No need, Mr. Morris, no need. I just wonder if it were possible that some other party had done the deed, and then dragged an unconscious boy up, deposited him upon the floor, and stuck the blood-stained dirk in his hands. Of course, I wonder also why might a young man complete a rape and a murder, and then drink himself insensible after pitching the corpse of his late inamorata into the Thames? O tempora, o mores...Please go on, Mr. Morris, do."

"Your honor, I have presented the case." The lawyer was allowed to sit back down and Timor was asked if he had anything to say in his defense.

"No, your Honor, except that I remember returning home from school, and the next thing I knew I was in Newgate. I have a hazy recollection of a drink being put in my hand...but by whom or for what purpose, I do not know."

"Not much of a defense, boy, but the fact remains that you—insensible or not—were found at the murder scene. Accordingly..." The judge waved away a hastily proffered black cap from his clerk.. "...damn it, Archie, put that thing away."

There was a rising murmur from the crowd, which was gaveled into silence. "Transportation to Virginia, ten years indentured service, and count yourself lucky." There was a chorus of boos and hisses from the galleries, and the gavel cracked down on the table several times more. "Master Chiseldon, we also offer our sympathies on learning of the death of your father last night from his long illness. Next!"

Timon sank back down on the prisoner's stool and buried his face in his hands, but two strong guards seized him and dragged him out of the box. His thoughts and heart were in turmoil: Relief at being spared the noose, grief at his father's death; apprehension and disgrace at a conviction. His eyes filled with tears, and he only briefly looked up at the crowd, but could barely make out any faces...although just for a second he thought he saw that his half-brother William was up in the gallery.

Then it was back to the waiting room, and late that afternoon, when all 20 prisoners had been tried, it was back to Newgate. Three prisoners went down to the Condemned Hold to await the journey to Tyburn, and five had their chains struck off and were released. Timon found himself with four others, all consigned together to one of the cells on the ground floor.

"You're lucky", one of their Gaolers told them. "Normally transportation ain't until the spring, see, but we've got forty five of you now, so you're off to Blackfriars stairs first thing in the morning."

The cell was crowded and thickest around the door where many of the other prisoners bound for Transport had family and friends calling on them to say goodbye. Timon felt completely miserable and slumped against the wall. He had no visitors.

In the morning, the day of his father's funeral, the prisoners remained in their leg shackles and were marched down to the Blackfriars steps. Two lighters awaited them and their irons were removed. After that came two ordeals for Timon: The trip past so many familiar sights of his city, and the fearsome passage through the rushing water underneath London Bridge itself. Timon, however, had eyes only for his father's house on the bridge. Then the Lighters went past the Tower and down to the Isle of Dogs, where the Snow-Brig 'Gander' waited to carry them to Virginia.

The ship's carpenter and his mate were still busy in the hold, so the prisoners were settled up near what Timon was told was the "Foxhole". This latter turned out to be how sailors pronounced "Forecastle". Other sailors swayed up supplies for the voyage, crates of crockery and silverware for Virginia plantations, and baggage for a handful of passengers. Late in the afternoon, when the prisoners were being shepherded down into the hold, the first of the passengers boarded...and Timon was startled to see the stout figure and fleshy face of his half-brother. Whatever funeral observances had been held for their father, it was obvious they had been kept to a scant minimum.

The hold of the ship was not quite as bad as Newgate had been. It was damp and there was a thick fug of unwashed bodies, of sickness, and of sewage (the prisoners were not allowed out of the hold when they pleased and a "honey bucket" barrel awaited their "necessaries"). Rats, fleas and lice were common in Newgate; the hold had the added refinement of cockroaches. The timbers were damp, and the bilges below added their own flavor to the stench.

On the credit side of their affairs, the prisoners were no longer shackled, and the crew of the Gander let it be known it was in the Captain's interest to see to their welfare. "See, he gets £3 for each of you as what makes it alive to Norfolk and a small share of whatever price you fetches when you get there. It ain't as profitable as blackbirding, mind, but ain't as dangerous neither."

So Timon had a wooden shelf to sleep on, a blanket, and the reasonable prospect of two hot meals a day. They were five days out of London when the prisoners were finally allowed on deck. They had no choice, as the Captain believed a regular fumigation of the hold with tobacco and sulfur would prevent disease; but the middle of the English Channel is seldom pleasant in early November.

As the Snow-Brig tacked close-hauled down the Channel, cold spray periodically showered the deck and the prisoners shivered in the breeze. The ship's movement was easy, however, and Timon marveled at how steady it seemed. Then a sailor plucked the sleeve of his coat and conveyed him aft to the foot of the companionway leading up to the quarterdeck. There, huddled out of the wind, was William Reynolds. Timon was pleased to see his half-brother and hoped this meant his salvation.

"So, Timon, can you guess why I am here, you little foundling bastard?"

This was not what Timon needed to hear. He shook his head and started: "William, what's…"

A slap buffeted him. "Sir, you call me sir! Actually, the reason I am making this ungodly voyage is so that, for a time, you will call me 'Master'. Can you guess why?"

It all came clear. "Peggy, the rum, that was you…"

"Yes you little shyte."

Timon grabbed his half-brother's coat. "You ogre! You fiend…you…" and paused as he felt a sharp prick in his gut. He looked down to see a dagger in his brother's hand, and the tip was against Timon's skin.

"And you're a convicted murderer, while I am a physician. Let go of me."

Timon did as he was bidden and studied his half-brother's face. The mocking leer was everything he had hated when he was six and William was a bully of eleven…The only jarring element was the greenish tinge to William's cheeks, and he kept a hand on the companionway for balance. Timon had sea-legs; William did not.

Ill with a touch of mal de mer or not, the snarling and gloating tone of William's next words were undiminished. "My father loved your temptress whore of a mother more than his wife…and he loved his bastard foundling more than the son of his own body. I've waited for this a long time and once I understood how to use Sydenham's Laudanum effectively…well, it all just came together."

William smiled most cruelly. "You took so much from me; but having your little Mort and keeping you from ever sampling her quim was just the start. My father sold his commission to arrange your pardon already…did you knows that? I have it right here." William tapped his breast pocket. "It will never be delivered and I am going to buy your Indenture when we get to Norfolk. Then I'll see to making the rest of your life miserable."

Timon was shoved away, and when he regained his balance, two sailors were already taking him forward to join the other prisoners. William stood and smirked, and then retreated inside to his cabins.

For the next three days the prisoners remained in their hold and Timon brooded. He was powerless, but the desire for justice grew within him. Then came resolution; if William could long harbor a plan, then so could Timon—and exposure to the occupants of Newgate had taught him much. The cadence of the groaning of the ship's timbers and the roll changed. Obviously, the ship had left the English Channel and was out in the great deeps.

The next day, the motion of the ship became alarming, and air in the hold grew worse as the Honey Bucket was not removed. Many prisoners succumbed to sea-sickness. No hot food arrived, only ship's biscuit and water. There would be no cooking on a ship caught in a November gale.

This made it easy for Timon to volunteer. He secured an interview with one of the mates and reminded him that the prisoners had a stake in the survival of the ship, and there was no reason not to use the healthy ones as untrained Landsmen up on the deck. The offer was accepted.

On the fifth night of the gale, as the Gander beat its way on a close-hauled port tack, struggling to make enough westering to clear Cape Finisterre, Timon finally had his chance. He was left alone to tend the trysail mast when William staggered out of the passenger cabins, ready to spew his guts out once more. In the wet and pitching dark, he didn't see Timon as he went to the lee railing.

For Timon it was a simple matter. As William spewed helpless, one deft hand reached inside his coat pocket and plucked out the thin bundle of documents there. With the other hand, Timon levered his half-brother over the side and proved he was indeed one righteous bastard.

John Thompson was born into a Canadian Air Force family in 1959, served in the Canadian Army for 13 years, and was a researcher and commentator with the Canadian Institute of Strategic Studies and Mackenzie Institute from 1985 to 2014. He currently still sits on the officer's association of his old regiment and is a member of the Royal Canadian Military Institute.

Look for the 75th Anniversary Edition of his critically acclaimed *Spirit Over Steel, a chronology of the Second World War (MK II)*.

The Savages Among Us
Bianca Marais

Editor's Note: An ordinary day takes a harrowing turn in this brilliant and terrifying tale from emerging talent Bianca Marais.

I was prepared for it. It was expected.

If you've lived in Johannesburg long enough, if you grew up there during the horrific apartheid years that left South Africa's psyche pitted and scarred like a repulsive face whose eyes you cannot meet, you know what can happen. The stats are there; mostly airbrushed to make them look better, but you know the end result those columns of figures will reveal. Added up, subtracted or multiplied, the numbers provide the same answers. Like binary code, those digits tell a poetic numeric story you can follow through to their logical conclusion, though many choose not to.

If you are a woman living in Johannesburg, you are more likely to be raped, murdered or molested than you are to win a small-town beauty competition. Or get a degree. Or ever own a car. Your perpetrator, if not your husband or a lover you have spurned along the way, almost certainly will be black. And he will hate you because you are not.

The door did not, as I had expected, crash-in thunderously; it was not driven inwards with a deafening and immobilizing boom by the brute strength of a psychotic attacker intent on forcing his way into my home. It eased open, playfully and confidently, as it had a thousand times before. The gentle squeak was assuring. It said: *he who passes through me has been invited.*

I stopped copying out the Chicken Potjie recipe from the YOU magazine into my personal cook book and turned around. I didn't recognize the first man who slipped inside. Nor the second. They were both black, one lighter skinned than the other, both smaller than what you would expect. They smiled at me as though it was a social call, and eased aside in a choreographed dance within the confined space of my kitchen to make way for the larger man who was the last of the trio to slip inside. I recognized him immediately, and as he looked up at the wall clock where he knew it would be, he nodded in my direction, "Good evening, Madam."

"Themba," I breathed. He was our gardener. I knew his friendly face intimately; I'd seen him twice a week for over four years, and that's more than I've seen my own sister or mother in that time. How could he not feel familiar to me? As he looked around the kitchen, and headed for the panic button that lay mere inches from my right hand, it occurred to me as it never had before that he knew our property intimately. Not just the garden, garage and outside sheds, but also the inside layout of the house. My husband was a liberal man, one who felt strongly that the gardener and other help should use the toilet inside, and be served their lunch on the patio. His friends had warned him it would come to no good; how they would crow with self-satisfied righteousness now. *We told you Johan. They're all the same. Savages, the lot of them. Chop you to pieces with a panga just as soon as they'd look at you.*

Themba pulled the kitchen drawer open. I noticed he was wearing gloves, which the other two were not. He withdrew a steak knife and calmly held it out to me. He nodded at the panic button that was connected to the alarm system; his meaning was clear. My eyes shifted to his cohorts and confirmed what I'd previously noted—they both were brandishing guns, and the one whose eyes looked most vacant and alien had his index finger threaded through the trigger. I cut through the wiring and handed the knife back to Themba's outstretched hand. We girls are taught from childhood, and it is a lesson that is engrained: *Do not resist. Do not antagonize. Do what they say, and hope that they will take mercy on you. If you react unexpectedly and make them panic, they will kill you. If you scream, they will kill you.*

"It's almost time for the baas to be home. Sorry, 'Johan'," he corrected derisively, "It's almost time for *Johan* to be arriving home."

It's been said that your life flashes before your eyes in moments of extreme stress. Many people can't recall the order of events after a life-changing event, because shock fragments time and alters your perception of reality. A second can feel like an hour. Days can pass in a heartbeat. Many people are immobilized by fear—it's classic fight or flight. I do not react like ordinary people. I am calm and focused under pressure. My thoughts, emotions and reactions all crystallize, and it's almost as though I'm having an out-of-body experience. I am me. Watching me. I miss nothing.

I can see that they are all driven. Focused. They know what they need to do and have planned their actions. This is not a drug-fueled operation. I think of Johan's ironic T-Shirt that I'd put away just that morning: Keep Calm and Carry On. Apparently that is what it will take.

Themba turns to me and speaks in a neutral conversational tone, "Go to the safe. Take the jewelry and cash out. Put it in your Nike kitbag. I will send Mpho to watch you because you cannot be trusted." He does not sound angry. He is not antagonizing me, he is just being matter-of-fact. The other two look like they might have rape on their minds, but Themba is the clear leader, and he is not allowing any carnal distractions. I am relieved.

It is as I am crouched on our bedroom floor, in the walk-in wardrobe leading to the bathroom, that I hear a car in the driveway. I'd know the sound of that Lexus anywhere, I have lain awake many nights waiting for the crunch of its tires on the gravel. It is the sound of Johan returning to me.

I sit up in recognition and make to stand, but my armed chaperone taps his gun against my shoulder, and I sink back onto my haunches. All the jewelry is in the Nike kitbag; my diamond earrings, the diamond and sapphire engagement ring and numerous other tokens of love Johan has presented me with over the years. His mother's jewelry and the various pieces he inherited for the daughters we have not yet had have all been transferred across. I think briefly of those phantom daughters and wonder what is to happen to them. The last item remaining in the safe is a thick wedge of an envelope—its contours are crisp and uncreased. I tuck it into the bag and close the safe.

My mantra plays through my mind like a current top-forty song: *Let them do what they came to do so they can leave and it will all be over. Let them do what they came to do so they can leave and it will be over.*

Johan is not a stupid man. He is a thinker. He is also a bit of a coward. He will not confront them; he will not use violence. He will submit and give them what they want. It will soon be over.

I listen intently as the sounds of him closing his car door and setting its alarm filter across the yard to the quiet house. I wonder where Themba is. He is a known element; it's his thug companion that's a worrying factor.

Johan uses his key to try and open the backdoor, and struggles with the lock until he realizes that the door is already open. There is impatience in his gesture of opening the door with a bang. How many times has he told me to be more careful?

I hear him step inside, set down his travelling coffee mug and place his computer bag at the foot of the kitchen table, before he starts to make his way through the kitchen doorway into the passage.

"Marie? The front door was unlocked again, I really wish you'd be more..."

There is the dull sound of something solid connecting with something fleshy. This is followed by the unmistakable sound of a body dropping—it connects with the floor with no resistance.

I jump up and push my 'minder' aside.

As I reach the bedroom door, there it is. Finally. The thunderous noise I've been expecting the whole time. The solid and uncompromising sound of a bullet being fired from a gun, and finding its target at close range.

I scream and turn the corner into the passage.

Johan is lying sprawled across the parquet flooring; he is not as awkwardly splayed as you might expect. He is crumpled upon himself, lying on his side, his knee pulled up as it sometimes is in sleep.

I scream and scream as I hear the sound of Themba's accomplices being mobilized around me. The men are fleeing now that I've sounded the alarm. As I hear the kitchen door closing, I quiet and Themba holds out his hand forcefully. I hand across the Nike kitbag, my eyes not leaving my husband's corpse.

"Well done, you've done a good job," I say. "Make sure the other two are silenced so there are no witnesses, and there's another ten grand where that came from".

After all, I was prepared for it. It was expected.

Bianca Marais is a South African who moved to Toronto in 2012. She has aspirations of: writing great books, training her Golden Retriever to poop directly into the lemon-scented bags from PetSmart, and finding out once and for all what the plural of "moose" is. Also, she was once bitten by a giraffe. True story.

Visit Bianca at her Website:
http://biancamarais.com/

Antonia

Rosemary McCracken

Editor's Note: Award-winning author Rosemary McCracken explores the niceties of white-collar crime and conscience in this ingenious story of high finance.

I'd been managing Antonia Verdi's investments for almost a year before we realized we had a lot in common. We're about the same age, we have teenage daughters and we enjoy classical music. After a meeting in my office last September, Antonia presented me with a ticket to a performance of Mahler's *Ninth* at Roy Thomson Hall. She said the friend she'd planned to go with was away on business.

It was a delightful evening that began with dinner at Penelope's, the Greek restaurant on King Street. Antonia is funny and feisty, with a knack for turning her life into a great story. She had me in stitches with the saga of her impending divorce. "The prince of darkness wanted to split the cat." Her eyebrows lifted towards the ceiling. "Now what kind of bastard would want to split a cat?"

Maybe I shouldn't have laughed, because then she grew serious. She told me she was pleased with the settlement she and her soon-to-be ex had hammered out. She would get Marigold, the high-end spa they had opened ten years before, and the family home in Rosedale. The ex, who ran his family's construction business, would take the summer cottage on Lake Muskoka.

What I hadn't realized, with all Antonia's banter, was how shattering her marriage breakup had been. "Joe and I were in our teens when we met," she confided in a voice that was husky with emotion. "I thought we'd always be together."

I was surprised. I'd thought Antonia had everything. Looks, charm, style and a successful business.

"Another woman." She dabbed a corner of an eye with a tissue. "Younger."

I knew all about that. After my husband died, I discovered he'd had another woman in his life.

I shook my head. "Well, you seem to have landed on your feet."

She gave me a weak smile. "I've tried, Pat. I've most certainly tried."

After that, we started meeting for lunch every few weeks at Chez Félix. At a lunch in November, Antonia took two tickets out of her handbag. "*La Bohème*, my favorite opera." She kissed her fingertips. "When I visited my nonna as a child, we'd listen to her record of a performance conducted by Toscanini. Magnificent!"

She handed me a ticket. "Friday. It's my birthday present to myself."

***

On Friday evening, Antonia was uncharacteristically subdued. "It's good of you to come tonight," she said when we'd given the waiter at Alice Fazooli's our dinner orders.

I was taken aback. I love opera and the ticket she'd given me had cost several hundred dollars. "It's my pleasure," I told her. "I seldom get to an opera." I had ordered champagne cocktails, and I clinked my glass against hers. "To a lovely evening and the best year ahead of you ever."

She raised her glass. "To our friendship. Seriously, Pat, I'm happy you're here. This is my first birthday without Joe since I was eighteen."

My heart went out to her. I reached across the table and squeezed her hand.

During curtain calls after the opera, the audience roared its appreciation. Antonia turned to me with tears on her face. I gave her a big smile and nodded, knowing my words would be swallowed up by the noise around us. After a final round of applause for the orchestra and its conductor, we remained in our seats.

"Bravo!" I said.

"You liked it."

"Loved it!"

Then she reached into her handbag and pulled out an envelope. "Would you roll this into my portfolio, Pat? It's a little more than $3,000 from clients who paid with cash this month."

I was caught off guard, but her request hadn't come out of the blue. When Antonia first came to me as a client, I'd asked if she expected to make any cash deposits to her investment account. She told me that most of Marigold's customers paid with credit cards, although a few paid in cash. This was her first cash deposit, but I didn't blink an eye. Three thousand dollars in cash payments for the month seemed fine to me for a business that was a smash success.

I nodded and took the envelope.

"I've paid off most of the loans I took out when we started Marigold," she said, "so now I can put away more money."

I smiled in approval. Antonia not only had looks and personality, but she also knew the importance of making her money work for her.

***

I had a fabulous time at Antonia's Christmas party. I'd been itching to see the trendy Yorkville spa and I wasn't disappointed. Marigold was done up in grand style that night with lavish floral arrangements and a giant spruce tree beside the sweeping staircase. A string quartet played Christmas music, and waiters in white-tie-and-tails circulated with trays of champagne and hors d'oeuvres.

Antonia treated me like a celebrity. "This is Pat Tierney," she said, introducing me to her other guests. "She's my financial guru."

I spotted a few of my financial acquaintances among the well-dressed guests. "I'm looking to expand my client base," Antonia whispered. "But you're investing my money, not them."

I gestured with my champagne flute towards a handsome, dark-haired man with a touch of silver at his temples. He was talking to a dark-haired girl who was a younger version of Antonia. "Your ex and your daughter?"

"Yes, that's Joe and Bethany," she said. "Joe's here tonight for Beth. I think both her parents should be present on big occasions like this. Joe will be at my parents' dinner on Christmas Eve."

Joe gave his daughter a hug, then headed over to a cluster of men and women in formal wear.

"And them?" I asked.

Antonia shrugged. "Joe's clients or potential clients. Industry and government types. He asked me to invite them, said it would be good business for both of us."

Joe gestured for Antonia to join the group. "Time for introductions," she said. "Catch you later, Pat."

The rest of the evening flew by in a heady mix of champagne, music and laughter. I didn't see Antonia again until I was leaving.

She handed me an envelope. "A couple of grand from the past three weeks. I want to see it in your capable hands before we shut down for Christmas."

***

We had a brutal winter in Toronto. An ice storm in late December left much of the city without heat or electricity for five days. That was followed by three months of bitterly cold weather. Late one morning in February, Antonia blew into my office. "I'm taking your boss out of here," she told Rose Sisto, my administrative assistant. "She's working far too hard."

My next appointment was at two, so I let Antonia sweep me off to Chez Félix.

"I wasn't just talking about taking you out of the office," she said when we were seated at our favorite table. "We're going to the Bahamas next week. How does Nassau sound?"

A holiday in the sun was exactly what I needed, but I had client meetings scheduled back-to-back for the next three weeks.

"It won't cost you a penny," Antonia said when I expressed my regrets. "Consider it a favor to me. Otherwise, I'll be completely on my own down there."

I explained why I couldn't leave my practice just then. Antonia didn't look convinced, but then she ran a different kind of business. I moved on to another topic.

She had said she was in a position to put away more money, and I'd hoped she would funnel some of Marigold's credit-card revenues into her investments. Now that I knew she could afford a vacation for two that winter, I broached the subject.

"A week at a sun resort is an absolute necessity every few months," she said. "It's my way of recharging. And with all the stress I've been under this year, I'm in dire need of some serious pampering."

She had a point. But for me, sun vacations are strictly luxuries, and I seldom indulge in them.

"The cash Marigold brings in will go into my investment portfolio," she went on, "but I still have rent and salaries to pay."

Before we left the restaurant, she handed me an envelope. I took it, troubled by the pattern that had developed. While I was delighted that Antonia was putting more money into her investments, I knew that financial professionals like myself can be the targets of criminals who want to muddy the trail of the proceeds of their crimes. They see us as their tickets to turning dirty cash into stocks and bonds and insurance policies. That's why we're required by law to report cash transactions of $10,000 and more to the federal government's financial intelligence unit.

But Antonia's cash deposits were way under that amount. Besides, I knew this client well. She ran a business where some people paid in cash.

I gave her a smile and tucked the envelope into my briefcase.

***

In March, I found myself at Roy Thomson Hall again, this time with a friend from Montreal. Nancy was in Toronto for a conference, and I'd bought us tickets to a concert that featured the renowned cellist, Yo-Yo Ma.

We hadn't seen each other in two years, and we caught up over dinner. We were settling into our seats when I caught sight of someone who looked familiar across the concert hall. I adjusted my opera glasses and, sure enough, there was Antonia, stunning in a black dress with a plunging neckline, her dark, wavy hair swept back with combs. The man seated beside her was Joe.

When I pointed them out to Nancy, she peered through my opera glasses, sniffed and handed them back to me. "They're divorcing? Could've fooled me."

I took another look. Antonia and Joe were holding hands.

Antonia spotted me in the lobby on the way out. She gave me a jaunty wave. I waved back before the crowd swept us towards different exits.

***

The next day, she dropped by my office wanting to do lunch. I told her I had a client arriving in less than an hour.

She perched on the seat in front of my desk. Her face was pale and there were dark rings under her eyes. "Joe and I had dinner last night to thrash out the final details of the settlement. Then he surprised me with tickets to Yo-Yo Ma."

I waited for her to continue.

"He's hit a rough patch with the babe," she said.

"And he wants to come back."

"He's hedging his bets."

"You could trust him again?" I asked.

"They'll work it out." She shrugged. "He's too good a catch to walk away from."

She opened her handbag. But instead of taking out an envelope, she held out a pamphlet. "Interested in The Toronto Ballet's production of *Romeo and Juliet*? The guest star is Ludmilla Alexandrovich from the Bolshoi Ballet."

She placed the pamphlet on my desk. "The first performance is next week."

***

Antonia insisted on picking up the dinner tab before *Romeo and Juliet*. "It's the least I can do," she said. "You made me a lot of money in the last two quarters."

I was feeling mellow after an excellent meal. "I'd love to take the credit," I said, "but I can't. The markets performed well this year."

"Well, I'm happy and I want to celebrate." She placed her credit card on the tray on the table.

Then she took an envelope out of her handbag. "You'll do the honors, Pat?" she said with a smile.

I took the envelope, feeling uneasy.

***

Later that night, I called Antonia's home. "There's $12,000 in cash in the envelope you gave me," I said when she picked up the phone.

She told me the money had been paid by Carmen Ferraro, a Hollywood actress who had been in Toronto for a few weeks on a movie shoot. "I went to her hotel myself. Massages, hair, nails, the works. It came to $12,000, including a sizable tip. Carmen pays in cash."

Something scratched at the edge of my memory. "You have the invoice?" I asked.

"That's not how these people do things," she said. "They're rolling in money. I told Carmen what she owed me and her secretary gave me the envelope."

***

In my office the next morning, I called up Google, typed in Carmen Ferraro and found the newspaper column I'd remembered reading. "Hollywood North" is a weekly update on the film stars and directors who are in Toronto on movie shoots. Two weeks before, the columnist reported that Ms. Ferraro was in Toronto, and had brought her own masseuse and beautician with her.

Antonia had lied about Carmen Ferraro. And I could only speculate about her holiday in the sun. The Commonwealth of the Bahamas is renowned for its beach resorts. It's also known as a money-laundering haven. Had she set up an off-shore account?

And there was the Yo-Yo Ma concert. Her relationship with Joe was far from over.

I sent Rose off in a taxi to Marigold with the envelope that held the $12,000. As soon as she'd left, I punched Antonia's office number into the phone on my desk. When she didn't pick up at Marigold or answer her cell, I booted up my computer and hit the e-mail icon.

I told her that I was required to report cash transactions of more than $10,000, so I had decided to end our advisor-client relationship. I said I would transfer her assets as soon as she found another advisor.

If I had deposited that $12,000 into her account, I would have had to file a report or I could have been party to an offence. And, if convicted, I could have been fined up to $2 million and sent to jail for five years.

***

Construction Boss Faces Corruption Charge trumpeted the front-page headline of the next day's *Toronto World*. The accompanying article said that Joseph Verdi, president and CEO of Verdi Enterprises, faced charges related to the construction and maintenance of highways over the past five years. He allegedly used low-grade material that required subsequent repair or replacement, conspired with subcontractors to rig bids, inflated charge orders and paid kickbacks to win contracts. The Crown claimed Verdi had pocketed millions, and fraud investigators had been called in to determine where the missing funds had gone.

In a statement issued by his lawyer, Verdi protested his innocence and said he welcomed the opportunity to clear his name in court. The statement added that he was currently travelling in the Caribbean in search of business opportunities.

I folded the paper and shook my head. Antonia had played me for a fool, but I felt sorry for her. Her love for Joe had made her his partner in crime.

***

For the next few weeks, the newspapers had a field day with the Verdi case. The Builder And The Blonde, Nassau Love Nest and Secret Stash were some of the headlines that chronicled the missing money and Verdi's love life.

The reports culminated with accounts of Verdi being brought back to Toronto to face trial, amid speculation that there were other bank accounts yet to be found by authorities. Photos showed Verdi escorted by police and trailed by a blonde wearing dark glasses.

Antonia was not named in any of the accounts. One of the stories mentioned that Verdi had been divorced earlier in the year.

***

I'd received a letter from Antonia's lawyer, telling me where to transfer her assets. But apart from that, I heard nothing more about her. Until this morning.

"Mrs. Verdi made the *Toronto Sun*," Rose said when I arrived at the office.

Nailed! Verdi's Ex Tells All, the *Sun's* front-page headline screamed.

The article said Verdi had been found guilty of various fraud charges. His ex-wife, Antonia, had testified that she had put a little more than $500,000 of the missing funds into investment accounts at several brokerage houses in Toronto.

"Weren't you suspicious of cash packages?" the Crown attorney asked. Antonia replied that Verdi had told her the money was for their daughter's education and for their retirement.

The Crown didn't buy it. "But you continued to make deposits after you learned about his mistress and you filed for divorce. Why?"

"Joe can be a charmer, as I'm sure his blonde can tell you," Antonia replied. "He knew which buttons to push. But when the divorce went through, well, that broke the spell. I knew he wasn't coming back."

The money Antonia had placed with investment advisors was only a fraction of what Verdi had siphoned off, the Crown attorney noted. Where was the rest of the missing money?

"Better ask him." Antonia pointed to her ex-husband. "Or Blondie."

The article went on to say that because Antonia had co-operated with investigators, no charges had been laid against her. Verdi would be sentenced later in the month.

I put down the paper and punched a number into my cell phone.

"Marigold. Antonia speaking."

"You're in the news these days."

"Pat! I...I...I'm sorry about this whole business." She paused. "Can we still be friends?"

I hesitated. I was ready to welcome back my friend but I wouldn't be her investment advisor. "Sure," I said.

"Chez Félix at twelve-thirty?" she asked.

"Where else would we go?"

Rosemary McCracken is a Toronto-based journalist, specializing in personal finance and the financial service industry. So it's not surprising that Pat Tierney, the protagonist of Rosemary's mystery series, is a financial advisor with a knack for wading into criminal conspiracies.

Safe Harbor, the first novel in the series, was shortlisted for Britain's Debut Dagger Award in 2010. It was published by Imajin Books in 2012, followed by *Black Water* in 2013. "The Sweetheart Scamster," a Pat Tierney short story in the crime fiction anthology *Thirteen*, was a finalist for a 2014 Derringer Award.

Jack Batten, the *Toronto Star's* crime fiction reviewer, calls Pat "a hugely attractive sleuth figure."

Visit Rosemary's website
http://www.rosemarymccracken.com/
and her blog
http://rosemarymccracken.wordpress.com/

Delights in Novelty

Brad Ling

Editor's Note: A twisted tale of "crime against the senses", this riveting and original story by Brad Ling is sure to delight and disturb readers.

Some years ago I was diagnosed with hyperosmia, a heightened sense of smell, so none of Colin's attempts to mask the perfumes, like slathering on aftershave or chain-smoking, could disguise the underlying stench of infidelity. So I put my superhuman olfactory bulb to good use by categorizing all his girls by their scents. During our first few years, he was covered in floral-aldehydes like hyacinth and musk, most likely due to the popularity of Revlon's "Charlie" in the late nineties. The early millennium brought a bouquet of violet, blackberry, teased by patchouli.

Then came a stretch of sandalwood jasmine, Chanel No.19, and a sickening peachy odor that clung to him for days, even while we were away on vacation. The last few years have included cloves, cardamom, two more Chanel No.19s, a Black Pearls, ocean breeze, and a mild lilac stage. During particularly nauseating phases, I found an anti-seizure drug called topiramate suppressed the hyperosmia enough to let Colin succeed in his fragrance-cloaking attempts. It allowed me a break where I could lie to myself without conjecture, let alone proof, getting in the way. Unfortunately, topiramate gave me excruciating headaches. How fitting that the side effect of a clear mind was a headache.

The final straw occurred the night Colin came home and slipped into bed smelling of lavender and wearing a used condom. The condom was not the final straw, just years of guesswork finally giving way to proof. The final straw was what he said to me during our post-incident fallout: "I love you more than anything in the world."

And I believed him because I loved *him* more than anything in the world.

His assurance was followed by what I imagine to be the standard caught-in-the-act *mea culpa*, except without a shred of insincerity in his words. This coming from a high school teacher who can spot a lie quicker than a teenager can make one up. And maybe that's why I hadn't caught him lying over the years: he never thought he was doing anything wrong. After all, he loved me more than anything in the world. Believing him had been easier than not believing him, and now he had wrecked that. Now the guilt would eat me alive if I let it. No more clear mind for me.

A clear mind was the least of Colin's worries. Soon after our confrontation he was fast asleep, and I was in front of the computer browsing infidelity message boards. There were threads for people who just found out, those attempting reconciliation, those who tried unsuccessfully to reconcile, advice for those who survived and lived to tell, and even investigation tips.

Many spoke of suspected "emotional affairs" and debated if that was truly cheating. For a minute I wondered if his, too, had been one of these, an emotional affair that had ended with a hug long enough to pass off a breath of lavender. Then I remembered the proof that had just hopped into bed. Once again, I was looking for an excuse.

A topic at the bottom of the page, between "The dreaded 'D' word" and "New beginnings" caught my eye. It said "Monogamy Gene?" The poster was asking if anyone had used Dr. M's monogamy gene treatment. They included a link to a website. Out of the thirty or so replies, none had answers and all asked the same questions. Who had used it? And was it successful?

Monogamy gene? Seriously, who was that desperate?

The link took me to a page that said "Dr. M" at the top, and in smaller letters beside the "M" was "onogamy." There was a tagline at the top of the page in cheesy Comic Sans font: "We want monogamy, but man delights in novelty." This was a play on Dorothy Parker's "General Review of the Sex Situation," a poem I had just (coincidentally?) introduced to my tenth graders.

A big black box appeared, with white text reading, "Take your marriage back?" I clicked it and the black box swelled to full screen. More text appeared: "Would you like Dr. M to contact you in regards to taking your marriage back?" Below this were two boxes with space to input my name. I typed my name and hovered the cursor over the "Y" box, waiting for my mind to change. Before I knew it, the mouse had clicked and an excited yellow screen flew in front of me saying, "Please wait by your computer, *Mia!* Dr. M will be with you soon."

I eased back and bit my nails. Before I had time to rethink what I was doing, a man with a friendly smile appeared on the screen. I reached for the closest thing to a hat I could find, which, unfortunately, was an afghan. It draped over my shoulders like a Bedouin scarf. My image appeared in a small box beside a handsome man with dark hair, who spoke with an accent I took to be Argentinian. "Sorry for the wait, Mia. I'm sure you have questions."

I peeked over my shoulder to make sure I was still alone, and then whispered, "Is there really such a thing as a monogamy gene?"

"Absolutely. I've been studying arginine vasopressin or AVP for more than ten years. AVP is a neurohypophysial hormone that helps us retain water, but in our studies, we've found that with males, variations in the AVP receptor gene can lead to mate instability. This is what we call the monogamy gene."

"But instability isn't cheating," I said, my voice rising at the end of the sentence like I was asking a question.

"This variation affects pair-bonding behavior in men. Monogamy—or lack thereof—is obviously not only a male problem, but so far our cure is male-only. I would assume that is the nature of your visit today."

He smiled and it made me smile. Smiling when I wasn't happy had become second nature. Life was a put-on, so acting like others wanted me to act was not hard.

"So there is a cure?"

He nodded and opened a drawer that was hidden from my sight. When his hand emerged, there was a tiny pink pill in his palm. "One a day removes the genetic allele, or the 'bad' gene, and helps AVP to do what it's supposed to do: give your brain a high-five for staying faithful."

"How safe is it? What are the side effects?"

"That's the good news. Does your husband have large breasts?"

"No."

"Too bad. You could have gotten two for the price of one. Myspexin is also used to treat abnormally large breasts in men. Mother Nature can be a comedian."

I didn't laugh.

"It's safe. And it's fast."

"So that's it? A pill a day?"

"With any gene-altering medication there are always risks. Full committal is crucial in recovery. Your husband needs to want to heal and take the medication willingly."

"Of course."

We stared at each other for a few seconds before it became awkward.

"You have something else to ask?"

"Something I need to say. Am I crazier than my husband for wanting to change his nature?"

"Humans are monogamous by nature. Our genes prove it. We just need to fix your husband, not change his nature."

I had to type my initials at the bottom of a confidentiality agreement, and complete an online questionnaire, to be approved to receive the medication. But, at the price tag of $300 per bottle, I was quite sure the good Argentinian doctor would not deny one soul.

The questions were easy. "How many times has your husband been unfaithful?"

Proven: once. Assumed: hundreds.

"Do you want to work things out with your husband?"

Yes.

"Do you blame yourself for his infidelity?"

Of course not.

And with that one lie, I was accepted.

By the time the pills arrived, I had decided I was crazy, and Colin deserved a second chance. Who was I to try to change him? I had been smothering, over-bearing, unattractive. I had pushed him away. It was me that needed to change.

But two weeks later, after washing the sheets to get rid of a disgusting new citrus-with-a-hint-of-mothballs odor, I found myself standing in the kitchen holding one of those precious pink pills in the palm of my hand.

Colin was reading at the table, patiently waiting for me to serve his breakfast. We wanted the same thing, and he would agree to this treatment. But how I should bring it up? And how mad would he get? He loved me more than anything in the world, and he would understand this was the only way to be together, to be happy together.

I didn't want to leave him, but I would if the cheating didn't stop. I had to put my foot down, and if he got defensive then I was ready for a fight. And like Dr. M said, full committal was crucial to the recovery. He needed to want to get better.

Against my better intentions, the pill fell from my hand into his coffee and a pink slurry became a grey cloud. With a little stirring the cloud disappeared. He drank the coffee without batting an eye.

Colin came home that night and went to bed without dinner. The first two days, he complained of chills and a headache, but guilty as I felt, I kept quiet. By the end of the week, his symptoms subsided, and I began to see the perfume-free man I married emerge once again. One night, about a week into his treatment, I was awoken by a delicate and repeating *tsk! tsk!* sound. Colin was kissing my forehead. He stopped when he saw my eyes were open.

"I forgot how good you taste," he whispered.

"I need to sleep," I said, leaning up and kissing him.

"Sleeping is surrendering. I've been sleeping for a decade and I'm not tired anymore."

These nocturnal episodes continued to happen, though most nights I pretended to be sleeping. Most mornings Dr. M's magic pink pill worked deliciously in Colin's coffee, and on hangover days in his Caesar. But those hangover days soon dwindled. He began to complain about feeling ill after his first drink and mused that he might take a break from booze. Get back in shape. Start eating healthy. Spend more time at home. One evening I came home and found the living room full of flowers. I was in heaven.

One morning I was planting clover in our front yard when Colin's co-worker Vincent came up our path. "Hey, Mia. Colin around?"

"Out back. All okay?"

"For sure. Just haven't seen him for awhile."

After Vincent left, I asked Colin what Vincent had meant by that.

"He's been away," he said, then without taking a breath: "How long were you talking to him?"

I shrugged. He frowned at the road.

Colin began picking me up after school, even on days that I drove. "I just want to be near you," he'd say.

"And I love you for it, but I like my drive in. It gives me time to think."

"What do you need to think about?"

I laughed. "And aren't you going to be in trouble for missing so much work?"

"Why would they mind? I'm the top sales guy at the office." His face soured, and he held his stomach. "I was sick again today."

"What's wrong?"

"Playing squash again. Every time I start playing, I throw up. And it's getting worse with each new, uh, game."

I knew what "playing squash" meant, but I didn't care. Soon he would only play with me.

Summer vacation was closing in and school events were ramping up. The hallways were ablaze with hope and smiles and for once I was in on the joy and looking forward to the summer.

During most afternoon breaks, Ava and I would sit in the windowed teacher's lounge. She was my closest friend at the school, and someone in whom I could half-confide. To half-confide meant the luxury of offering half-truths. I could tell her that Colin had issues—like neglect and forgetfulness, instead of apathetic infidelity—and that Colin and I were receiving help for our issues, instead of me slipping him monogamy pills. In other words, she was a close friend.

"It's worth fighting for," she said, stirring her coffee and beating me down with tender eyes. No, they were condolatory. She hugged me like she always did when she didn't know what to say. It was more comforting than her platitudes. She squinted, distracted by something outside. I asked her what was wrong. "Thought I saw...Hey, there's Colin."

I looked out the window and saw Colin standing by a tree. He was staring at us. I waved and he didn't wave back. When I got outside, he was walking back to the parking lot. I called after him and he turned and smiled. I asked what he was doing and he gave me a hug.

"Had some time off for lunch. Thought we might get something."

"My lunch is over."

"Sorry, just needed to get out of the office."

As I watched him pull away, Mason, one of my students, wandered over from a group of students that had congregated to smoke on a nearby patch of grass, just off school property.

"Hey, Mrs. Pond, is that your husband?"

"Yes."

"He comes every day."

I tried to hide my surprise, but it didn't fool him.

"For at least the last couple weeks. He stares at you through the window. Someone said it was your husband so we didn't do anything about it." He grinned. "Except make fun of him." His smile disappeared and he became serious. "Are you okay?"

"We go to lunch sometimes if I'm not busy. Thanks for the concern, Mason." I yanked the cigarette from his lips and tossed it away, giving him my best stern look. He didn't buy it, but at that point I just wanted to get out of the conversation and hurried back to the school grounds.

The next morning, I asked Colin if he wanted to go for lunch, but he declined saying he had a meeting with Vincent. Instead, I invited Ava to lunch at a café across town, so I could half-confide in her again. When we arrived, I purposely grabbed the booth furthest from the window. Just as Ava was touching my arm, and giving me her usual sympathetic look, the waitress brought our food. When the waitress walked away, a looming figure was revealed. Ava and I looked up to see Colin staring down at us, red-faced. His chest was heaving.

"Mia, what's going on?"

"I don't know," I said, finally telling her the truth.

"Get your hands off my wife," he said through gritted teeth.

"Colin," I said, standing up in front of him as he charged towards Ava.

"I've seen you, your hands on her, she's not yours."

"You need to calm down," Ava said.

His face went the color of oatmeal and his bones seemed to liquefy, then harden again. He gazed down into Ava's eyes, trying with all his strength to speak.

"Colin," I said with a forced calm. "Think about where you are."

Ropes of anger twisted in his neck, tightening his vocal cords until he looked like he was choking. Though a large man, I never mistook Colin for intimidating, probably because I rarely saw him angry. But this was a new man.

I touched his arm and like a spark he came alive. "Touch her again…" he growled, brushing my arm aside and advancing menacingly toward Ava.

I jumped in before he finished his thought. "Stop it!" I led him outside, feeling the heated stares of the other patrons. "She is my friend and you need to calm down."

"I see her. She touches you whenever she can. I'm not stupid."

Tears began to well in his eyes. "I'm sorry, baby. I don't know, I'm so sorry. I'm just looking out for you. My head has been hurting."

He looked like a ten-year-old boy. I hugged him and began to cry. "Get some rest, you'll feel better soon."

"I haven't been well. Things I used to do make me sick now. I can't..." he considered his words. "When I talk to other people, I feel ill. I threw up all over somebody the other day."

"Go back to work. I'll see you at home."

"I can't leave you here."

"Why?"

"I don't know."

I walked him to his car and watched him drive away. It crushed me to see him so dazed, stung by an emotion he couldn't control or understand.

After school, I hurried home. My goal was to flush the rest of the pills and finally deal with this head on. As I pulled into our driveway, I noticed Vincent parked on the other side of the street. I pretended not to see him and bolted inside. He called my name and started to run across the street.

"Oh, hey," I said, fighting to get the key in the door. "Sorry, late getting home, need to jump on dinner."

"Just checking in on our man."

"Must have had a long day, too. I'll let him know you stopped by."

I turned my back to him, but his footsteps got louder.

"Funny thing, he wasn't at work today. He hasn't been to the office in weeks."

I held my breath and pushed the door open.

"Mia, can we talk?"

We sat at the kitchen table. The floor was filthy, but that's not why I stared at it; I couldn't bring myself to look at him.

"I'm the only one looking out for him. He's this close to getting canned. I need to know where he goes every day."

I drew figure eights on the table with my index finger and smirked. "Isn't that the question of the day?"

He worked his mouth like he was building words, but nothing came. I went to the sink and tossed a ceramic plate into it, chipping an edge off it. I picked it up and considered it a moment before smashing it into pieces. I heard him gasping, most likely trying to make more words, but he wasn't doing a good job of it. When I turned around, Vincent was up in the air. Colin's hands were clamped around Vincent's neck and he was throttling him.

I couldn't speak. Colin's teeth had pierced his bottom lip and blood streamed down his chin like a rabid dog. Vincent's arms were frantic fire hoses, flailing in vain against Colin's strength. I ran over and grabbed Colin by his tightened arm. "You're killing him!" His elbow thrust back and smashed my jaw. My legs buckled with the force of the impact and I fell against the stove.

He let Vincent drop to the ground and ran over to me. He cradled my head in his arms. "Are you okay, baby? You'll be okay. I'm so sorry."

Vincent grabbed at the table, pulling himself up, sending plates crashing to the floor. Colin kissed my head and released me. He walked over to the still-staggering Vincent and kicked his legs out from under him. As Vincent fell, he slashed at Colin with a knife he'd grabbed from the table. Colin flew back, looking down at a gash on his abdomen. He dropped to his knees. Vincent rose up and kicked him in the face and Colin crumpled to the ground. He leaped on top of Colin and began to punch him in the face. When Colin stopped moving, Vincent got up and reached for the phone on the counter. "You stupid…" he said, reeling for breath. "I was trying to help you!" He picked up the phone and hit three numbers.

I ran over to Colin and got on my knees beside him. His face was a bloody pulp. His lips were parted and labored breaths formed bloody bubbles, and all I could think about was the smell.

Before he became tainted with the stench of other women I had fallen in love with Colin's scent. Most men's fresh-sweat pheromone soon dissipates into a foul body odor, but Colin was different. He was able to maintain that pleasing essence, even when his sweat dried into a salty film. It may have been a trick my superhuman sense of smell was playing on me, but it worked. And it told me that he was the one. When he tried to impress me by wearing cologne I told him he didn't need it. His true scent was everything I had ever wanted.

Now, with one phone call, Vincent was about to take it all away. But wasn't it the right thing to do? After all, Colin was damaged. He was beyond saving. Born with a bad gene. Like a bandage, one painful rip and let the healing begin. Sure, life would hurt for a while. But hasn't it always? I would learn to live without him, and sad as it would be, I'd be better off. The real Colin had vanished, along with his true scent, more than a decade ago. Now, lying in a heap before me, Colin was giving off a new smell. And it wasn't the metallic odor of blood; that was just a mask. It was the smell of nothing. And it was worse than any perfume. Yes, Vincent was doing the right thing and I needed to accept that and let him make the call.

I don't remember how the knife got into my hands or how it got into Vincent's neck, but I remember his look of astonishment as he turned and tried to focus on my eyes. Next thing I knew, he was in a pile on the ground. I picked up the phone and told the operator that I may have just killed an intruder. "Please hurry," I said, and told her to save my husband, that he might be dead, but please, God, don't let him be dead.

A breeze blew in through the window and I breathed it in, flushing my lungs of the vacant smell of death. Colin exhaled and his eyes fluttered open. I brushed the hair away from his eyes, and kissed his forehead, allowing in his natural pheromone, the one I had long-feared extinct.

As weeks passed, and our life returned to normal (normal?), I thought about contacting Dr. M to break the news that genetics will always be a pushover for destiny.

I was in bed with a book in front of my face, but the words were too blurry to read. Of course, it didn't help that I was staring past the top of the book at the wall. To clear a mind, a blank wall is as good an option as any.

And it needed to be clear, because I knew what was about to happen. The downstairs door would open, the stairs would begin to creak, and a warm body would depress into the comfort beside me. The only question: what would he smell like? I tried unsuccessfully to recall all the words to that Dorothy Parker poem. The words I did remember became as blurred as the words in the book I was pretending to read. The blank wall held more wisdom; it held beginning, potential.

My eyes blinked and focus returned. I opened the bottle of topiramate and shook a pill into the palm of my hand. Instinct made me grit my teeth. Cue headache.

So, the question of smell...would it be patchouli, ocean breeze, lavender, sandalwood jasmine?

Did it matter?

Brad Ling is the author of two novels and over a dozen screenplays. As a scriptwriter he's represented by Integral Artists and his prize-winning scripts have been optioned as potential movies and television series.

His history as a storyteller began as a film director. His short film *Johnny in Limbo* was showcased at the Canadian International Annual Film Festival and he directed several episodes of the Global TV show *Going Green for Green*.

His latest novel *The Doll Nest* is a dark psychological tale about the extremes a mother will go to protect the most important person in her life.

Connect with Brad Ling on Facebook.

Runaway

Joan O'Callaghan

Editor's Note: Tense and action-packed, this un-put-down-able thriller comes to you from award-winning author Joan O'Callaghan.

***
Runner-up for the coveted Bony Pete Short Story Award, Bloody Words 2014

Queen station. Jed could hear the train. Bright lights bounced off the tunnel walls. He could see Finch in Day-Glo orange letters on the transom of the train. Someone jostled him. He spun round, fists clenched. Jostled meant pickpockets. But a young woman pushed past him. With an anguished cry, she threw herself onto the tracks in front of the speeding train.

The shrieking and grinding of brakes blended with the horrified shouts of the crowd. Jed shuddered and turned away. He stumbled over something. The woman's handbag. He looked around, reached for it, hesitated, then scooped it up, and hugging it to his chest, pushed his way out of the station.

He ran as fast as he could, dropping to a quick walk when he tired, until he got to his squat—a dirty brick building on Queen Street East, slated for demolition. He hunkered down on his ratty sleeping bag and spilled out the contents of the handbag.

"Watcha got?" Pit Bull flopped beside him. Jed didn't know his friend's real name and he didn't want to know it. Pit Bull was short and solid, with a shaved head. Jed thought he looked like a human tank, one of those transformer-type toys he played with when he was small.

"Stuff."

He snorted. "A purse? Watcha doin' with a goddam purse?"

"Found it. Maybe there's somethin' in it."

"Like what?"

Pit Bull had been good to Jed. When he was new to the streets, Pit Bull had helped him out of a couple of tight spots. Jed owed him. "Cash," he said. He counted the money in the wallet. Forty-two dollars and thirty-five cents. "Enough for burgers."

"What's this?" Pit Bull held up a book with strange writing on its wine-colored cover.

"Looks like a passport." Jed grabbed it and leafed through the pages. "Russian." There she was, the woman who jumped. Her hair was different than in the photo–longer–but it was her.

"How can you tell?"

Jed waved it at Pit Bull. "Because it says right on it, Russian Federation." Then he felt bad. Pit Bull couldn't read.

Pit Bull scratched his belly. "Let's get those burgers. Then you can tell me how you really got the purse."

Jed sighed. Pit Bull might not be able to read, but there was no fooling him. A small rectangular object at the bottom of the handbag caught his eye. He turned it around, examining it.

"What's that? Lipstick?" Pit Bull stood.

Jed shook his head. "USB key. For a computer. After we eat let's go to the internet café on Yonge and see what's on it." Maybe, he thought, there was something valuable on the USB key, something he could sell. He slipped the passport and the USB key into his pocket along with the cash.

On the street, Pit Bull stuffed the purse into a garbage bin. At Burger King, he chewed slowly, staring at Jed. Jed concentrated on his ginger-ale. Pit Bull opened a little package of vinegar and sprinkled it over his fries, watching and waiting.

Jed pushed his drink to one side. "You really wanna know where I got the purse?"

"Don't think too many people throw away a purse with a passport in't."

Jed took a big bite of his Double Whopper, and put it down. Then he told Pit Bull everything. How he'd jumped the turnstile into the subway when the fare collector wasn't looking. About the woman who leapt in front of the train, that he'd taken the purse she'd dropped.

"Woman don't need it where she's gone," Pit Bull said. "Whatcha gonna do with the passport?"

"Keep it for now."

They made their way through the crowds on Yonge Street to the internet café. Jed paid the clerk and booted up the computer, then inserted the USB key into the port and waited for it to download. Lists appeared in Russian.

"What the fuck is that?" Pit Bull asked.

"Dunno. Telephone numbers, names, addresses, looks like."

Pit Bull tugged on his ear, a sign he was thinking. "Names and addresses? Maybe you should take that passport and USB key to the Russian whatever-you-call it."

"Why?"

"Might be a reward for turnin' it in."

Not a bad idea. But they were sure to ask how he came to have the passport. "Lemme think about it." He turned off the computer and pocketed the USB key.

Beeb was waiting for them back at their sqaut, leaning against the wall near the door, an unlit spliff between his thumb and forefinger. He spat on the sidewalk.

"You had some visitors." He was called Beeb because he looked like Justin Bieber when he was cleaned up, which wasn't often. His greasy blond hair hung around his face in strings. The faded Blue Jays tee-shirt and jeans he wore were stained and torn, and there were holes in his sneakers.

Jed and Pit Bull exchanged looks and hurried inside, Beeb following.

"No kidding," Pit Bull said. Someone had taken a knife to Jed's sleeping bag and shredded it.

"Fuck, fuck, fuck! Who the hell did this! I'm gonna kill 'em." Furious, Jed kicked at the remains of the sleeping bag. Grey stuffing spilled onto the floor.

"See anyone?" Pit Bull asked,

Beeb shrugged. "There's this black car with tinted windows in front here. Two dudes get out. They don't look friendly. They duck into your squat, then come out a few minutes later. I found your bag all torn up like this. What's up?"

Jed shook his head. "Haven't a clue."

"Maybe you should give 'em what they want so's they don't come back."

"I just told you, I don't know who they are and I don't know what they want."

Beeb shrugged again and tucked the spliff into the pocket of his jeans. So he wouldn't have to share it with them, Jed thought, watching Beeb slink away.

"I don't like it," Pit Bull said. "You sure no one saw you lift that purse?"

Jed shook his head. "No one."

"Someone saw. How else they know where to look?" When Jed didn't answer, he continued. "They know you been stayin' here. They'll be back."

Jed shoved the mess to one side with his foot. "I'll sleep in the parkette for awhile."

That night, when he was sure he was alone, he picked up a rock and dug a shallow hole in a nearby flower bed. He wrapped the passport and USB key in a plastic bag he'd found and buried them, placing the rock over the spot to mark it.

Later, Pit Bull showed up with coffee and stale donuts.

"Maybe you should dump that USB thing and the passport."

"I put it where no one'll find it."

Pit Bull crumpled up the donut bag and tossed it into a nearby bin. "I don't wanna know," he said, standing up. "See you in the morning." He brushed the crumbs off his jeans, took his coffee and left.

Jed crawled under a bench, grateful it was a warm, dry night. His thoughts drifted back to the comfortable house where he'd lived before he hit the streets.

He was asleep when the two men dragged him out from under the bench. One of them pinned his arms back and covered his mouth while the second guy frisked him and turned his pockets inside out. They were big and dressed in black pants and hoodies.

"Where is it?" the one holding Jed growled. Russian accent. "I see you in subway station. You take purse when she jump. Where is it?"

The frisker nodded to his partner, who pulled a small gun from the pocket of his hoodie. "Give it to us," he said.

"I don't have it," Jed managed to say. His voice sounded like a squeak.

The man jerked Jed, sticking the gun into the small of his back.

"We find out what you know."

They marched him to a black Lexus, pushed him into the trunk, slammed it shut and drove off.

Forcing himself to remain calm, he groped for something, anything he could use to free himself, but they'd removed the spare tire and jack. He felt for the tail lights and connecting wires, but they'd been covered over with some kind of panel. There was no emergency trunk latch. He was fucked.

The car picked up speed. They were on a highway. Even if he did manage to get the trunk open, falling from a speeding car onto a highway in the middle of the night would be fatal. There was no escape. He huddled in his rolling prison, wondering if he was going to die. No one would miss him.

He remembered his home near Bancroft, before his father died of cancer. His mother had remarried and they moved to Trenton. She must have been lonely, he thought, or she wouldn't have fallen for Dickhead. His name was Dick, but Dickhead suited him better. He was in the Armed Forces, had done a couple of tours in Afghanistan. When he returned from his last tour, he was posted to the Search and Rescue Centre in Trenton. Dick worked with a research group that developed and tested clothing and equipment for the military.

He took Jed camping in the bush, and yelled at him if he didn't follow orders. Jed dreaded those trips. He just wanted to finish high school and figure out what to do with his life. He liked art. His teacher said he was good at it and he should apply to the Ontario College of Art and Design.

Then, six months ago, he'd talked back to Dick. In response, Dick slapped him hard across the face. His mother just stood there and watched. That's when Jed decided it was time to go. He hitched a ride to Toronto and disappeared into the streets. He was 15.

The car was slowing and turning, probably onto a dirt road because it sent him bouncing against the sides of the trunk. How long had they been travelling? At least three hours, he guessed. He braced himself on the floor, hoping to avoid being tossed about. And then the car stopped. Jed tensed, terrified, wondering what would happen next.

The trunk sprang open.

"Get out."

Jed scrambled into the darkness. His cramped legs couldn't support his weight and he dropped to the ground, tumbling against an exposed tree root.

Using the tree for support, he picked himself up. He stood there, hands against the bark until his legs felt strong enough to hold him. His eyes were used to the dark from being locked in the trunk for so long, and he was able to make out the silhouettes of the two Russians. One opened the back door of the car, removing grocery bags. Jed raised his head cautiously and sniffed the air. It was cooler here, with a bite to it. They must have come north. And something else. Decaying vegetation. He knew that smell from those hated camping trips. Muskeg.

The other Russian came around the tree and prodded Jed with the gun. "Where you put her purse?"

"I threw it away."

"You no throw purse away until you see what's inside. Maybe something valuable, eh? You kids live on streets. You do anything for money."

Beeb, Jed thought. They must have paid Beeb to rat him out. He felt the gun in his ribs again.

"What you take from purse?" The voice was guttural, threatening.

"Money. That's all." His mind raced. They wanted the passport and the USB key. Those lists of names and addresses. The men exchanged a few words in Russian and Jed caught their names: Boris and Igor. Igor, he decided, was the man holding the gun.

Reaching into the car, Boris withdrew a large flashlight and clicked it on, flooding the clearing with bright light. An animal in the brush uttered a sharp cry. Startled, Boris stumbled and swung the flashlight upwards, momentarily blinding his companion.

It was the break Jed needed. Throwing himself onto the ground to stay out of the light, he partly crawled, partly rolled into the dense bush behind the clearing. Moisture seeped through his jeans—the swamp had to be close by. He heard shots as Igor's gun fired wide. He sprang to his feet and ran, dodging in and out of the shadows to avoid the wide arc of Boris's flashlight.

There was shouting behind him, punctuated by gunfire. The ground was soft, wetter and the vegetation thicker. Now he could see moonlight reflected in a sheen of water. He didn't dare wade into the muskeg. Too dangerous. He couldn't see bottom. How much longer till first light? A large dead tree loomed in front of him. He crouched behind it, his chest heaving. He could still hear the Russians. He guessed they too wouldn't risk the muskeg in the dark. He glanced up. Saw the Big Dipper twinkling in the night sky.

A memory tugged at the edge of his mind. Think! Dickhead in the backyard, pointing to the Big Dipper. Dickhead's thick finger waving, telling him the Big Dipper was like a 24-hour clock at night if you knew how to read it. Look for the two pointer stars at the end of the bowl. And Polaris, the North Star. As the Earth turns, the pointer stars change their orientation to the North Star and you can get a rough idea of the time. About 3 am now. Still a few hours till daybreak. Then he could risk the muskeg. Shivering, he settled against the trunk to wait.

The blackness of the night faded to gray. Pale pink streaks washed the sky. Time to get moving. The Russians. Gritting his teeth against the cold, he waded to the water's edge. He hesitated, then decided to keep his running shoes on. Leeches, fish, water snakes—he shuddered. He arced his body forward in a shallow dive. Frigid water closed over his head.

Eyes open, Jed could see the bottom. Mud and weeds. Dickhead's gravelly voice in his head. Don't touch bottom—the mud'll suck you down. Float on the surface. Look for a corduroy road. It'll support your weight. He raised his head above the water and gasped for air. He could hear them now....low guttural murmurs. Careful not to make a splash that would give him away, he dived again and propelled himself forward. Lungs burning, he surfaced and gulped air. A vibration and the thrum of a motor. The Russians had a boat.

Closer now. The motor and the voices were louder. He had to move. A large blue heron snatched a fish out of the swamp just yards away. Startled he dropped below the surface with a splash. A shot rang out and a bullet ricocheted off the water a few feet ahead of him. Desperate now, he kicked and headed toward a thick clump of weeds and deadheads. A motor boat couldn't go in there without fouling the propeller.

Silence. They had cut the motor. He raised his head a few inches and listened. Gentle rhythmic plops. Paddles.

Jed turned his head to gauge their position. Mistake. The boat was closer than he thought. Igor stood and gestured towards the weeds with one hand, waving the gun in the other. Boris gave the craft a powerful shove with his paddle. It surged forward. Igor lost his balance and, with a hoarse cry, fell overboard. He surfaced, spluttering and shouting in Russian.

Sheltered behind the weeds, Jed pulled himself into the crotch of a thick dead tree, and watched, horrified. The water was up to the man's waist. He struggled against the suction, trying to lift his feet but the movement only worsened his predicament. Boris stuck out his hand. Panic-stricken, Igor grabbed it and pulled. The boat rocked violently, threatening to throw Boris overboard. He wrenched his hand free, fighting to keep his balance. Igor fell backwards. As Jed watched, he sank quickly beneath the water, his face twisted into a mask that would haunt Jed for years.

Boris waited for a moment, then fired up the boat's motor and turned in the direction from which they'd come.

Jed slowly scanned the landscape. There it was, barely visible. A channel through the dense vegetation. He took a deep breath and dived again, going as deeply as he dared without hitting the muck. The channel was too narrow for a boat. His shoulders touched the banks on either side as he pushed himself along.

Boris might not know where he was but Jed didn't know where the Russian was either, and he didn't think Boris would give up that easily. He could come up another wider channel and fire at him. Jed dived again, staying underwater, coming up for air only when he felt his lungs bursting. Exhausted, he grabbed a deadhead and dragged himself up, sucking in air. Shading his eyes with one hand, he studied his surroundings. Muskeg as far as he could see.

Wait. Further off among the weeds and deadheads, he could see logs resting against each other, stretching into the distance. Corduroy road.

Into the water again. He struck out in the direction of the logs. Finally he reached them and with his last ounce of strength, pulled himself up. He lay flat, gulping great breaths of air.

When his breathing slowed, he gingerly raised himself onto his hands and knees and looked around. Except for the drone of the insects, all was silent. The logs stretched into the distance as far as he could see.

Scrambling to his feet, he set out. He had no idea where he was going, only the certainty that going forward was his only option. The logs rolled and pushed against one another, making it hard for Jed to keep his balance. He fell, scraping his knees on the rough bark. He swished his tee-shirt around in the water, using it to wash off the blood.

He was hungry and he'd lost track of time. How long had he been on the corduroy road? Felt like hours. No way to tell for sure. He tried to remember what Dickhead had told him about survival in the wilderness—some insects and plants were edible, fish if you could catch one. The only fish he'd spotted were pike. Too bony for good eating, and raw. He wasn't hungry enough for that. If Jed ever saw Dickhead again, he'd ask him how to catch a fish. He trudged on, keeping a wary eye around him.

Shaking his head, he realized how often he'd thought of Dickhead in the past several hours. He might be an asshole—Jed wasn't ready to completely let him off the hook—but he had to admit his stepfather had taught him some important stuff. Stuff that had come in useful.

A hum. Jed stopped, crouched, and listened. Cars. There must be a road nearby. His heart leapt until he remembered Boris. If he'd been unable to find Jed in the muskeg, he might wait for him by the road. He slowed his pace, and inched forward. Now he could see the last of the logs. Solid ground ahead. A road with cars.

Warily he crept forward. He sensed the shot before he actually heard it and instinctively threw himself to the ground. The bullet whined over his head and buried itself in a nearby spruce. Boris had spotted him.

He ducked behind a large rock. On his right, the glint of metal - a culvert under the road. Another gun shot. The bullet hit a sapling sending splinters flying in all directions. No time to lose. Jed crawled on his belly into the culvert. He inched forward through the debris until, with a sob, he emerged on the other side of the road and into bush.

He edged forward keeping to shadows and trees. The sun was sinking and it was decidedly cooler. Another night in the open. Now he really was hungry. He forced himself to keep moving.

Just ahead—fruit clinging to a few straggly bushes. He scrambled towards them and filled his hands with wild raspberries, wolfing them down until he'd stripped the canes.

Not so hungry now, but thirsty. He trudged on. The sun sank lower. A clearing ahead with buildings. Keeping to the trees, he circled around. The clearing was overrun with weeds and the buildings were dilapidated. Shingles littered the ground. Broken glass. A faded sign, paint cracked and peeling. *Lucky Angler Lodge*. A deserted fishing camp. He listened. Nothing except the wind in the trees. There had to be a lake nearby. Steal a boat? Too risky. If Boris were looking for him, he'd be exposed.

He ran forward, thrust his hand inside the broken window at the side of the door and unlocked it. Inside, he leaned against the wall inhaling dust and musty air. A stone fireplace containing a few partly burned logs. Mice had nested in the sofas and chairs. Jed listened intently. The building was deserted. Quickly he explored the ground floor, grabbing a wool blanket and a sheet from a supply closet.

Kitchen. Nothing. Wait. In a dusty corner, an empty polybottle. He tried the taps. Water gurgled then splashed into the sink. He left the tap on until the water ran clear. Rinsed the bottle, filled it, gulped long draughts, wiped his mouth, then filled the bottle again. Rifled through drawers. He stuffed a knife into the pocket of his jeans. A prize find...a half-empty box of wooden matches. He struck one. A whiff of sulfur and it flared. Good. Stay in the lodge overnight? No. Safer in the bush. He stashed the matches with the knife and left the lodge, closing the door behind him, and disappeared into the woods.

The sun had nearly set. He had to work quickly. Ignore the mosquitoes. He found what he was looking for—two trees close together. He collected branches and pine boughs. With the knife, he ripped the sheet into ropes. Dickhead's voice reminding him how to build a lean-to. He wove the branches together, securing them with the strips of sheet, and then covered them with the pine boughs. Exhausted, Jed rolled himself in the blanket and slept in his rough shelter.

The first faint fingers of light creeping through the pine needles awakened him. He crouched, looking and listening, then quickly dismantled the lean-to, scattering the branches and boughs. He rolled up his blanket, stuffing the strips of sheet into it, and stashed it behind a rock.

He hadn't eaten anything since the raspberries and he was hungry. What had Dickhead said? Rabbit stick. Bring down a small animal. Primitive and crude, but effective if you knew how to throw it. And Jed knew how to throw one. Dickhead had made sure of that.

He searched until he found what he was looking for—a sturdy branch, slightly curved, a bit like a boomerang. He sat down on a rock and trimmed the branch with the kitchen knife. Slow and tedious—the knife wasn't made for this. At last it was ready. He found a clearing and made a few practice throws.

A murder of crows, cawing loudly and rising all together from the trees ahead, alerted him. A squirrel or rabbit wouldn't have spooked the birds. Had to be something bigger. Carrying the rabbit stick over his right shoulder the way he'd been taught, he crept towards his campsite. Boris. He'd found the blankets. Jed cursed himself for leaving them.

Jed watched from behind the trees. Boris's shoulder holster with his gun was clearly visible. Boris looked around, and satisfied that he was alone, pulled a water bottle from his utility belt. One hand to hold the bottle, one to twist the cap. No hand free to reach for the gun.

Now. NOW. Jed stepped forward. Hurled the rabbit stick so that it spun like a Frisbee. Swift and silent. Boris looked up at the last minute, dropped the bottle and reached for his gun. Too late. The rabbit stick struck him in the right arm. The bone shattered from the impact. The gun flew through the air, landing almost at Jed's feet. Boris fell to the ground, screaming. No time to waste. Jed grabbed the gun, stuck it into the waistband of his jeans, then emptied the Russian's pockets—money, car keys, and a cell phone.

Jed ran. He ran until he thought he'd vomit from sheer exhaustion, and found himself on the stony shore of the lake.

The shoreline led directly back to the camp. Something shiny that wasn't there last night. Jed crawled on his hands and knees and took cover behind the trees. The door to the lodge was open and in the clearing stood the black car. Boris's car. He jogged down to the water's edge and threw the keys as far as he could.

He worked his way back in the direction he'd come the night before. When he reached the road, he stood for a moment, breathing deeply and looking around him.

Then he took Boris's cell phone from his pocket. As soon as it registered a faint signal, he dialed a number from memory.

"Dad, I want to come home."

And heard Dickhead say, "Tell me where you are, son. I'll come and get you."

Joan O'Callaghan is an award-winning educator at the University of Toronto (OISE/UT).

She is the author of three educational books as well as two e-shorts: "George" and "For Elise" (Carrick Publishing).

Her short story "Stooping to Conquer" appeared in the 2012 Anthology *EFD1: Starship Goodwords* (Carrick Publishing) and "Sugar 'N' Spice" was published in *Thirteen* (Carrick Publishing, 2013). Her story "Runaway" won third prize in the 2014 Bony Pete contest.

Connect with Joan on Facebook
or at her Website Teaching Days and Dates
http://teachingdaysanddates.wordpress.com/

Live Free or Die

Judy Penz Sheluk

Editor's Note: In this gripping tale of green suits and green-eyed monsters, Judy Penz Sheluk shows us that freedom, like revenge, is sometimes best served cold.

The first time any of us met Jack, he was wearing a dark green suit. That seemed odd to me. It wasn't St. Patrick's Day, and the office attire was mostly business casual, with an emphasis on the casual. This was especially true in "cubicle hell," where an overworked staff of four plus supervisor made collection calls and routinely canceled insurance policies for non-payment.

Later, Jack would confide in me that it was his only suit. "Wear a green suit and everyone assumes you must own a black one, a brown one, and a blue one," he had said, and I had to admit it made sense. But the first time I met him, my only thought was, "Green suit, can't be from around here."

I should have known Jack was going to be trouble right from the beginning. In my defense I was twenty-one to his thirty-one, and until a few months earlier, when I'd been dumped for a girl with the improbable name of Ankh, I'd had the same boyfriend throughout high school.

Anyway, my inexperience with men aside, there was something riveting about Jack. It was more than his stature—six-foot-two with the build of an athlete; you could imagine six-pack abs and muscled thighs—more than the penetrating stare of eyes a bluish shade of tanzanite verging on violet. It was as if he wore his charisma like a suit of armor and polished it up every morning.

Jack came to the company as an efficiency expert, imported from the U.S. Head Office in Portsmouth, New Hampshire, to the Canadian head office in Toronto. The suburb of Don Mills, to be exact.

Apparently, we were inefficient at collecting monies owed. I could have told them it was because we tended to empathize with the insured, if only because we were all stone broke ourselves. Thanks to our minimum wage jobs and age-rated auto insurance, most of us couldn't afford to pay the premiums, let alone own a car. Extending payment terms for a week or two, where was the harm in that?

My first mistake was agreeing to have lunch with Jack, though to be fair, he asked all five of us in the Credit Department, each on a separate day. My day of the week was Friday. Jack made me feel as though he'd saved the best for last.

He drove a midnight blue Chevy pick-up with a front bench seat and extended cab. The license plate included the message, "LIVE FREE OR DIE," which Jack informed me was the State motto of New Hampshire. I preferred Ontario's more mundane "YOURS TO DISCOVER," but I'll admit to being somewhat biased.

I suppose I was expecting a sandwich at the local deli, or maybe fish and chips from Captain Sam's, given it was Friday. Both were just south of the office, and regular hangouts for the many white-collar workers in the area. But Jack drove west on Eglinton. Clearly we were going to take more than my allotted hour for lunch.

"Molly tells me you like authentic Mexican," Jack said, not taking his eyes off the road. "I was in Toronto a few years back. I remember a decent place on Yonge Street. Viva something-or-other."

Molly was my supervisor. I wondered how the subject of my food preferences had come up. "Molly told you I like Mexican food?"

Jack grinned, his teeth flashing in the sunlight. "Let's just say I was curious about you."

The Mexican restaurant was no longer in business, but that didn't stop Jack. He navigated the truck into a tight parking spot along the street, hopped out, put change in the meter, opened my door, and led me to a British-style pub a couple of blocks down.

"It's not Mexican, but I was here a couple of nights ago," he said. "Typical pub food, but a good atmosphere, and a nice selection of draft beer."

I don't like beer, but the idea of dining out in a pub on a workday lunch hour had a certain charm. "I could go for an order of bangers and mash," I said, trying to demonstrate my worldly knowledge of tavern fare.

"So could I," Jack said, and chuckled softly. I got the distinct impression we weren't talking about the same thing, and found that I didn't necessarily mind. It had been a long time since Norbert had dumped me.

Lunch lasted a couple of hours, during which time I found myself telling Jack my life story, or at least the *Reader's Digest* version. I even told him my real name was Emerald, although everyone called me Emmy. It was only after we were headed back to the office that I realized he hadn't shared anything about himself.

"How long are you going to be in Toronto?" I asked.

"For a while. I'm starting with the Credit Department, but there are inefficiencies in all areas of the company that need to be identified and resolved."

"So you're moving here?"

Jack nodded. "I have a one-year contract. The company found me a rental apartment near Fairview Mall. But I'll be doing surprise audits in other cities now and again. I'll also be going home to New Hampshire for a few days every three weeks or so. To be honest, I'm already homesick. It's lonely, not knowing anyone."

"You've met people in the office, though, haven't you? I mean, besides those of us in Credit?"

"Oh sure, but it's not like anyone's really opened up to me. Not the way you did, Emerald."

"Emmy," I said, embarrassed. "And you're just being kind. I probably bored you to tears."

"Not at all. As a matter of fact, I'd like to get to know you quite a bit better."

And that's the way it started. We spent every moment of the weekend together, walking downtown for hours, taking in the CN Tower, the Eaton's Centre, Yorkville, Yonge Street, City Hall, both the old and the new. We made plans to visit the Royal Ontario Museum, the Art Gallery of Ontario—even the Bata Shoe Museum. Jack's thirst to see and experience everything was contagious, and I found myself being a tourist in my own hometown, and loving every minute of it.

We were driving back to his place late Saturday night when he mentioned it might be best if we kept our friendship a secret.

"Not that we have anything to hide," he said, "but why fan the flames?"

I thought about my co-workers, gossips each and every one of them, and my supervisor, Molly, who didn't appear to care much for Jack—likely because she felt her job was in jeopardy—and decided he was probably right.

"Okay." I edged myself closer to the passenger door, not quite sure what else to say.

"Why don't you slide over here, Emmy," Jack said, patting the seat beside him. "Otherwise, folks might think we're married."

***

It was about six weeks later when Molly came to my desk, carrying a card and a large brown envelope. Jack was back home in New Hampshire for a few days, returning midweek. I missed him.

"I'm collecting for the Jack-and-Jill shower on Wednesday," she said, handing me the card and envelope. "Whatever you can afford."

I looked at the card, which had an image of a man and woman holding hands and standing under a white umbrella, a glittery rainbow behind them. It was the first I'd heard about a Jack-and-Jill shower, but then again, I'd kept pretty much to myself since getting involved with Jack. It was safer that way.

"Who's getting married?"

Molly gave me an odd look. "Well, Jack, of course, and what's totally ironic is that his fiancée's name is actually Jill. I thought he would have told you, that day you and he went to lunch. You were gone long enough. Say, you weren't…"

"Of course not," I said, fighting the urge to throw up.

"It's just that Jack developed a bit of a reputation as a womanizer the last time he was here. Of course, that was five years ago. He might have changed."

It was the way she said it, more than what she said, that made me realize why Molly didn't care for Jack. And it had nothing whatsoever to do with job security.

Five years ago, Molly had been me.

***

"He slept with you, didn't he?" Jill spoke so quietly I almost convinced myself she didn't say it. I took a deviled egg from the paper plate on my lap and popped half of it into my mouth, trying to look nonchalant.

"Didn't he?" Jill said, again. Her otherwise pale cheeks had bright red splotches on them, as if someone had painted a clown's face on her.

Jack was standing at the other side of the room, his back to us. He was laughing at something one of the sales guys had said. He hadn't said one word to me since he'd been back. Hadn't given me so much as a passing glance.

"I didn't know about you, Jill. You have to believe me. I'm not the kind…I know what it feels like…"

Jill looked over at Jack, who was still kibitzing with the sales team, then back at me. "We need to talk. Somewhere private. Tonight, when Jack's out drinking with his buddies."

I agreed to meet her for dinner at a local Italian restaurant known for its great food, good wine, and generously proportioned booths—an entirely sensible combination of public and private. After all, I had no idea what Jill wanted to discuss with me, but I was pretty sure she wasn't going to ask me to be in the wedding party.

***

"Let me start by saying that I believe you, Emmy," Jill said.

We were sitting near the back of the Italian restaurant—our choice given it was a Wednesday night and there was plenty of available seating. We'd ordered a liter of house red and a basket of bruschetta to split as an appetizer. The whole thing felt a bit surreal.

"I appreciate that you're taking my word for it," I said, fingering a piece of bruschetta. I didn't have the appetite to bite into it.

"It's not like you were the first. And you're unlikely to be the last." Jill studied the diamond ring on her left hand. "I suppose I thought once we were engaged Jack would stop misbehaving."

"How long have you been engaged?"

"Three months. About a month longer than you've been sleeping with him, if my math is correct."

It was. "You're still willing to marry him?"

"I suppose you think that's pathetic."

I thought about my initial reaction when I found out about Norbert and Ankh. Devastation, certainly, but also a sense of determination, an irrational desire to win Norbert back, if only to be the "dumper" versus the "dumpee". "I understand what it's like to invest years in a person. You don't want to think it was all a big waste of time."

Jill nodded. "That's exactly how I felt before we got engaged. But now I'm done. Finished. You were the last straw. No offense."

"None taken."

"Good. Now, the way I figure it, Jack owes both of us, and more than just an apology. What I'm wondering is, how would you like to get even?"

"Get even with Jack?"

Jill nodded again. "You see I have a plan, and I need your help to pull it off."

***

There are times when you have to commit a crime to prevent an even bigger one. At least, that's what I tell myself when I can't sleep at night.

I'm not going to go into a lot of detail here. Suffice it to say that if we had implemented Jill's original plan, we both could have done twenty-five to life. What did either of us know about guns?

As much as I hated Jack in the moment, and as much as I commiserated with Jill, I wasn't willing to go to prison for either of them.

Which is exactly why I came up with my own plan.

I never said it was perfect.

***

"Live free or die." Jill and I spoke the rehearsed lines in perfect unison when Jack walked through the door. We were standing in Jack's apartment, and judging by the shocked look on his face, he wasn't expecting to find his fiancée and mistress waiting for him.

"What are you two talking about?"

"Live free," I began.

"Or die," Jill finished.

"Free of the cushy job that allows you to travel across North America and pick up unsuspecting women," I said. "Women who don't know that you're already spoken for."

"Free of all your money—well, actually, free of anything you own of value," Jill said. "I just wish the pick-up truck was black. I've never been a fan of midnight blue."

"You can always trade it in, Jill, maybe get a nice little sports car," I said. "A black one."

"I'm not sure I'm following," Jack said, but it was clear from the hint of perspiration forming on his forehead and upper lip that he was getting the gist of it.

"It's actually very simple," I said. "Tomorrow morning, you're going to hand in your resignation, citing personal reasons. Then you're returning to New Hampshire on your own dime."

"Except you won't have a dime—or a vehicle, come to that," Jill added. "Because you're going to transfer all of your money into my personal bank account. And your vehicle ownership into my name. Don't worry, we'll come with you so you don't screw it up."

"What you're asking is preposterous," Jack said, his face flushed. "Why would I do any of that?"

"Because if you don't, I'll have to tell upper management how you took advantage of your position of authority and how you coerced me into bed." I leaned back into the wall. "Perhaps I'll even hire a lawyer, file a sexual harassment suit. The company would love that."

"Maybe I wasn't completely upfront with you," Jack said, "but there was no coercion." He turned to face Jill. "As for the money and the truck, you're delusional if you think I'm just going to hand it over."

"It's called payback time, Jack, for being a liar and a cheat." Jill folded her arms in front of her. "Consider it a pre-nup, without the nuptials."

"Of course, you're perfectly free to ignore the 'live free' part of this plan," I said.

That got Jack's interest. "What happens if I decide to do that? Ignore the 'live free' part?"

"Ah," Jill said. "That's where the 'or die' part comes in."

Jack had the nerve to laugh, the smug S.O.B. "You two? You're threatening to kill me? How do you propose to do that?"

"Let's just say you'd never see it coming," Jill said.

I nodded and tried to look menacing.

I'm not sure Jack believed us, but in the end he chose to live free. Who wouldn't, given the option? After all, living free had its benefits—at least you were living without the threat of death hovering like a dark shadow.

There were some negotiations, of course. I like to think we were reasonable in our demands, and the reality is that, despite his philandering ways, Jill still wanted to marry Jack. Especially since she'd found out she was pregnant. I didn't pretend to understand—surely she and the baby would be better off without him—but it wasn't my place to judge.

We eventually agreed Jack could keep his job. Jill would move into his apartment. They'd get married earlier than planned, given Jill was now with child. And that way we could both keep an eye on him, me at work, her at home. Ultimately, it would mean more money for Jill and the baby, since his paycheck was going to be directly deposited into her personal bank account. All Jack had to do was stay on the straight and narrow.

Some men never learn.

***

"Seriously," Molly said. "A green suit? At a funeral?"

I didn't tell her it was Jack's only suit. Maybe when they'd dated five years earlier, he'd had other suits. Suits no longer in style, or maybe too big or too small. Maybe he'd lied to me and had a closetful, ready to pull out for a special occasion. It hardly mattered.

"I don't mind the green," I said, more for something to say than anything else.

We both stared at the open casket, at Jack's hands clasped loosely together in front of his stomach. The mortician had done a good job of disguising the damage from the accident. I could have said Jack looked at peace, but I didn't believe it.

"A true tragedy," Molly said. "Jack falling into the subway tracks like that." She gave me an odd look, eyebrows raised, lips pursed. "Do you...do you think he'd been drinking?"

"I don't know." And I didn't. All I knew was that the ruling of accidental death would haunt me forever.

Jill was sitting in a pew at the side of the chapel, a black lace shawl draped loosely around her shoulders, her face bent down in prayer. For a moment, I thought she glanced my way, but I couldn't be certain.

The next time I looked, her eyes were averted, a solitary teardrop finding its way down her face.

As a full-time freelance writer for more than a decade, Judy Penz Sheluk's articles have appeared regularly in U.S. and Canadian publications. She is also the Editor of *Home BUILDER Magazine*, and the Senior Editor for *New England Antiques Journal*.

Judy's first mystery novel, *The Hanged man's Noose*, is coming out in Summer 2015 from Barking Rain Press. Her short story, "Plan D", is included in the Toronto Chapter of Sisters in Crime anthology, *The Whole She-Bang 2* (November 2014).

Find Judy at
http://www.judypenzsheluk.com/
and on Facebook.

Writer's Block
Kevin P. Thornton

Editor's Note: Kevin Thornton is sure to tickle your funny bone in this inventive and ingenious tale of an author's worst nightmare.

***

"The problem with blood is that it sticks to your skin," said Jonathan, in between the screams of the electric saw.

Leila glanced down at her naked body, and then across the room to where their clothes lay, piled on a small table, away from the red spray.

"It's all very well washing it off in the first ten seconds," he continued, "but if you let it set you'll have the very devil of a time getting it off. Once we're finished we'll have to help each other; make sure we get rid of it all."

This was not a normal day.

It had started with the coffee machine dripping all over the counter. Then there was the perfectly hideous accident that wasn't really her fault. And now, she thought? Now she had progressed to taking off her clothes in front of her neighbor and helping him cut his wife into little pieces.

No, it was definitely not a normal day.

"I'll be able to clean myself, I'm sure," she said. She was starting to dislike Jonathan.

He put the saw down and picked up a bucket. "Shouldn't be long now," he said. "We'll take her through to the carnivores, and with any luck Jessica will be tiger poop in about eight hours. He started to slop the remains into the container and then, when he noticed he wasn't getting any help, turned to look.

"Jessica?" said Leila. "You told me your wife's name was Mandy."

***

"I'm stuck," said Enoch.

"Yes dear," said his wife. Enoch and Portia had been together for 15 years and he loved her profoundly, even if she rarely listened when he needed her to.

"I put a shotgun shell through my foot and I'm bleeding to death."

"That's nice dear," said Portia. Enoch began to count the seconds silently. One mzuri sana, two mzuri sana, three...At eleven Portia frowned and said, "You did what? Why didn't you say something? We need to call an ambulance. We need to..." She was stopped by her husband's giggling.

"Enoch, that's not funny."

"It was pretty funny, actually, darling. I do wish you'd listen to me when I need you to."

"All right, I'm listening now."

"Do you remember two years ago CBC ran a page-turner challenge with the Crime Writers of Canada?"

"Crime Writers, hmm. Aren't those your friends you meet every year in Toronto to dress up and party?"

Enoch could feel the steam rising. "Portia, please try not to demean my vocation so. Bloody Words is one of the finest Crime Writing Conventions in the world and the networking I do is very important for my career."

"Yes dear."

Enoch stopped himself from saying *don't 'yes dear' me*. He breathed gently, slowly.

"If you remember, I came fifth in the competition. Anyway I met one of the judges at this last conference and she said she'd love to see the finished story."

"So why are you stuck? You entered it two years ago. Send it to her," said Portia.

"The competition was about writing the first 250 words of a page-turner story. I did that. Here, read this." He turned his laptop across the kitchen table. Portia read it. It didn't take long.

"It's very macabre."

"It's supposed to be," said Enoch. "There's also no way out. For the sake of an amusing 250 words I have painted myself into a corner and I can't extricate myself. How did they end up in a big cat feeding room? What is the nature of their relationship, in that they are both naked and covered in blood? Is the coffee pot significant? Why can't Jonathan remember the name of the woman he is dismembering? They are all impossible questions. It won't do, you know. I am such an idiot."

"Well," said Portia. "Why don't you write something else?"

"Because," said Enoch, slowly, infuriatingly, "Juanita Greatrock is one of the most important publishers of short stories in North America. She has never shown the slightest interest in my work until now. If I can write this story, it'll open up a whole new market to me. Short stories are in, you know; especially after Alice got her Nobel. Nobody's ever received one for short stories before."

Portia bit her lip. She loved to jerk Enoch's strings when he displayed his tenuous grasp of literary knowledge, but she sensed now was not the time.

"Well, you have that appointment with your agent today. Maybe he can talk you through this block, dear. Now I must dash. Don't forget to take Misri for a walk."

"I don't have time now. It'll have to wait until later. That bloody Misri. If she tries to run away again, I'm going to let her. She is a bloody misery. I wish we'd named her after someone else. Is there a writer called Stupidassmutt in the Canadian canon?"

"Now dear, beagles are excitable dogs. They always follow their noses. A brisk walk will calm both of you down." As she turned to leave, she couldn't resist showing off. "Ernest Hemingway, Rudyard Kipling, Nadine Gordimer, Rabindranath Tragore."

"What are you talking about?" said Enoch.

"Munro wasn't the first. All four of them were awarded the Nobel, in part because of their short story writing."

She was halfway down the driveway when she heard his retort; valiant, but as always, misinformed. "Hemingway doesn't count. He didn't write short stories, just stories that were short."

***

The Hunterman watched the woman leave. He was hiding on the trail in the trees behind the house, and he had with him four different ways to kill. He wished he could have bought a gun, even a rifle, but that was impossible. Apart from the general difficulty of getting a license in Canada, the terms of his release had been quite clear. He had to stay away from all shotted weapons, all arms dealers, all gun ranges. And he had to stay on his medication.

One out of two wasn't bad.

He watched the actions below. The bastard had large, uncovered back windows on his wide-lot home and it was easy to see him walking around the living area. Presently, he went through into the bedroom and bathroom. The Hunterman knew from previous scouting sessions that was a preamble to going out. He relocated to position two, which offered an open line of sight to the door.

***

Enoch paused to pick up the car keys on the shelf. He drove an Audi, top of the range back when he was at the top of his game. It was ten years old. He opened the door and felt it push back against him, accompanied, or it must have been preceded by, a rushing sound through the air. *What the hell was that,* he thought. Then he saw the arrow sticking two inches through the solid wood door, outside to in, and his legs jellified below him as he sank to the ground, scrabbling back into the sanctuary of his home, unable to think of a word to describe what he felt.

***

The Hunterman cursed under his breath. How unlucky was that? Planning dammit, planning. The six Ps. He hiked his pack up onto his shoulders and headed out on evac route 4. As he ran-shuffled, he chanted the Marines' mantra in his head, imagining he was Clint Eastwood circa *Heartbreak Ridge*: 'Proper Planning Prevents Piss Poor Performance, Proper Planning

Prevents Piss Poor Performance, Proper Planning Prevents Piss Poor Performance...'

***

"No sir, I don't think you were the victim of an assassination attempt," said the Mountie, Sergeant Ramsbottom. "I think it was a hunting accident, and when we find the shooter he will likely be a city boy with a fondness for Robin Hood and beer."

The Sergeant wasn't sure of the level of importance one should have, to jump from an attempted murder to a putative assassination, but he felt fairly safe concluding that Enoch Powlle, aged thirty-five, occupation writer, did not qualify. Also, he thought to himself, any half-decent attempting-murderer would have looked at which way the door was hinged before firing.

Enoch reassured himself with Sergeant Ramsbottom's words. He was right. Of course he was. Nobody wanted to kill him, surely? They walked out together and he phoned his agent to let him know he was on his way.

***

"Can't you use it in a story? With the newspaper article, it could get you back into the public eye."

"The news will be in tomorrow's *Fort Clearwater Gleaner*. I can't possibly have anything written by then."

Saul Coldman sighed. He had been Enoch's agent through thick and thin. Lately thin was winning. That was fine, if you were a ramp model. Less so an agent with ex-wives to feed.

"Enoch, there were times when I could phone you at seven at night saying I had a market for three thousand words, and you'd have it done by eight the next morning. What's happened to my young and hungry anarchist who was going to turn crime writing on its head? Do you remember the reviews? 'The most interesting voice since Elmore Leonard'. 'Powlle plots like Ed Hoch, scares like Stephen King...'"

"'And is as elegiac as Dennis Lehane'. Yes Saul, I remember the taglines. There haven't been too many of those lately."

Saul shrugged. He possessed many shrugs, as if he had memorized *Fiddler on the Roof*. This one said, '*What can I do? I can only work with what you give me.*'

As if tossing a lifeline, Enoch said, "I'm working on something."

"The series? Is Nick Coil coming back?"

Enoch gave a shake of his head.

"A new character? A new series?"

Again the shake.

"That idea you had about the detective with the cat that solved crimes? Er, the one that ate canned meat? I'll even take that. What was the name again?"

"Spam Spayed? No that idea was too silly."

Saul breathed a sigh of relief.

"I'm going to finish my page-turner entry."

Saul, who had been buoyed by the possibility of having something to sell, sagged back into his chair.

"That's the one you've been stuck on for two years?"

"Mmm-hmm. I'm still stuck, as a matter of fact."

"So how will you unstick yourself?"

"I'm waiting for a brilliant idea from my agent."

"You never listen to my ideas, never take my advice. Why now?"

"Portia said so. She's usually right."

Saul had always liked Portia. He saw her as an ally in the quest to keep Enoch earning money. He leaned further back in feigned contemplation, then slowly came forward, hoping he looked inspired.

"I still think the arrow in your door this morning is the place to start. Go home and write how you felt. Treat it as if it was an assassination attempt. It failed, so find out other ways people are assassinated and incorporate them."

"What about Juanita Greatrock? She wants the story I started at the page-turner competition."

"You let me worry about Juanita. Go home and write. Now. Go."

"What happened to all the boozy lunches you used to buy me?" said Enoch. "The hotel does a decent prime rib buffet and has an excellent wine-list."

"Those lunches were paid from your commission, back when I was still actually earning a commission from you. Now, I have to see my other writer in town, the historian, and I'm on the last flight out of Fort Clearwater tonight as I have to be in Calgary in the morning. I'll stop by this evening on the way to the airport, and I want to see the beginnings of a masterpiece."

***

The Hunterman was a much better killer in his mind's eye than in reality. He knew all the theory, and he had even read several of Andy MacNab's books, stopping only when he heard they had been ghostwritten. He had planned every stop, had backup plans and multiple ways to exit every killing spot. The truth was, he hadn't expected anything to go wrong. By all rights, the bastard should be dead now.

Except for the damned door. He drove back to his basecamp, also known as room 104 of the Northern Lights Motel and strip bar. In theory, packing all the gear in his faux US Marines backpack up into the tree line had seemed bold and dashing. In his mind he was a lean mean killing machine. In reality he was a 350 pound stroke waiting to happen, and the walk into the forest and back had turned his soft, flabby body into a sticky, sweaty mess. If he were to get to killing-site-two in ready mode, he would have to shower and change so he didn't stick out like a painful opposable digit.

***

Enoch left the hotel and walked along the outside to the free parking lot two blocks away. Ten years ago he would have paid the valet. He glanced at his reflection in the shop windows. He looked seedy and tweedy, like a Duke who'd fallen on hard times, running out of Atkinson Grimshaws to peddle. His Harris jacket had been bought on his first Scottish book tour, and his walking shoes were by a distinguished Savile Row cobbler who had his size on file so he could, at a whim, order up an evening slipper or an elegant tennis shoe.

"Something else I haven't done in a while." He saw that one of his shoelaces was coming undone. "Better tie it," he thought, bending down. "I'll bet they cost a fortune to replace, hand-made shoelaces. Hmmmph. Probably rolled in ewe urine on the thighs of an Orkney lass until they're…"

The glass window of the shop window exploded and shards of glass bounced off the ground and into Enoch's hair, beard and favorite tweed jacket.

***

The shuriken is, in the right hands, a deadly killing weapon. Typically a star-shaped, keenly-sharpened throwing device, it reached the pinnacle of its popularity in the Hong Kong martial arts B movies popular in the last part of the twentieth century. Bruce Lee or Chuck Norris would calmly propel one of them across a warehouse and it would slice an inch into someone's throat where it would sever the carotid artery and cause a dramatic, blood-spouting death.

The Hunterman hadn't really practiced with them, so he wasn't as skilled as Bruce Lee. Not by a long way. His first attempt, from a distance of about forty yards, didn't even reach the target, bouncing instead off the middle of the road and landing in the gutter.

Typically, the Hunterman blamed his tools. "Shit shuriken", he whispered to himself, taking it up as a perversely pleasing chant. "Shit shuriken shit shuriken shit shuriken." All the while he was getting closer to his oblivious bastard target. He threw another one, this time an underhanded flick. He felt it slice open the pad on his index finger, and through the pain he saw it miss the target by ten feet and embed itself into a plastic plant-pot hanging outside the cannabis accessory store.

The Hunterman wanted to scream at the injustice of his luck. He pulled out the last two, ignored the pain of his bleeding finger, and hurled them both with all his might, more or less on target.

And the bastard ducked.

The Hunterman allowed the momentum of his throw to take him down the alley next to the shop while the glass was still shattering. As he ran, he scared the bejeezus out of two Rastafarians who stood at the back of the store testing their new bongs.

***

This was one of the strangest days Sergeant Ramsbottom had ever experienced, during the two years he had been posted in Fort Clearwater.

Taken in isolation, the incident with the arrow and then the window at the smoke shop might have been considered unusual, but not shocking. There were certain God-fearing people in town who objected to the shop's existence, and this wasn't the first time it had come under attack.

Ramsbottom, though, was a good investigator. After the arrow had penetrated Powlle's front door he had backtracked the shot to a clearing that had shown evidence of a large, heavy man (size twelve boot marks, deeply imprinted).

He had also just finished speaking to the two Rastafarians, who were less mellow than they should have been, given what they had inhaled. Ramsbottom knew them both. The older, Tommyjohn Tosh, rarely had anything coherent to say, but he had nodded fiercely when his bong buddy, Dreadlock Davey, had told him, "We nearly been knocked over by fuckin' Humpty Dumpty, and he was already cracked, mon."

"What do you mean cracked?"

"He was leakin' mon."

"Leaking? What was leaking? Egg? Yolk?"

"Nah mon. Blood. From his hand."

Which was when Sergeant Ramsbottom began to suspect maybe somebody was trying to kill Enoch Powlle, aged thirty-five, occupation writer. The technician had already found blood on the road, and he had found the four shuriken, three of them coated with blood. In his mind, Sergeant Ramsbottom drew a line between the largest patch of blood and the spot where the two shuriken had been found.

They would have hit Enoch, if he hadn't bent down to tie his shoelaces.

Ramsbottom dialed the number for the detachment. "Send someone inconspicuous and out of uniform to the crime scene."

He hung up. He didn't have enough evidence to be sure, but it was worth having someone follow Enoch Powlle for a while.

Ramsbottom found Enoch and went to talk to him.

"Sergeant," Enoch said, "I had nothing to do with this, I promise. I was just walking by."

"I know. You're free to leave, but before you do can you tell me where you're headed now?"

"Well, my lunch plans fell through, so I was going to meet my wife at her work and take her to the Sandwich Shop."

***

"So that's what happened," said Enoch, as Portia delicately nibbled on her lobster aioli, sprouts and gherkin on rye. His wife had the strangest taste in food combinations. As if she were pregnant, something that sadly had never occurred.

"It sounds as if you have something to go home and write about."

"Go home and write? Did Saul Coldman phone you? Are you two conspiring against me?"

"Don't be silly dear. There's no conspiracy. We both just want what's best for you."

Enoch studied his wife with a keener eye than usual. While it was rare for a writer not to be besieged by conspiracy theories, Enoch had foolishly never believed himself to be so inclined.

And yet, he had just told his wife about two most extraordinary events, and she had seemed to be almost unconcerned.

Enoch started to panic inside, where it bubbled like indigestion. No. Not Portia. Surely she wasn't behind this?

And, as all conspiracy theorists do, Enoch put two and two together and made twenty-two. They were unable to have babies, he was not making money as a writer, they had moved to the backwoods of Northern Alberta so he could regain his muses.

She must be unhappy, he thought. *Was she unhappy enough to hire a killer?*

"Portia," he said, standing rapidly, "I have to go."

"All right, dear," said Portia, who was pretending to listen, but was already thinking about how best to rearrange the shelves of wool at the back of her arts-and-crafts store.

She always tried to listen to Enoch, she really did, but sometimes his whining exasperated her and she found her mind wandering. It was only when she saw he had left the second half of his bacon and sausage ciabatta that she grew concerned. In all their time together, she had never seen him walk away from a sandwich.

***

The Hunterman was speechless with rage and pain, a powerful combination that served to drive him forward even harder than before. He had wrapped his hand in a handkerchief and circled back to his rental car. He wanted to return to the hotel and clean himself up, but he had no idea where his quarry would go next. Holding his hand tightly closed, he screamed when he had to put the car in Drive.

Five minutes later, he was in a layby on the edge of town, using a first aid kit he'd bought in Cabela's on his way up. The Hunterman loved outdoor stores. They didn't judge you by the way you looked, as long as you had a credit card.

He nearly fainted when he opened his hand and the blood started to flow again. He didn't know what to do, as he hadn't read any of the instruction manuals, so he settled for closing his fist and wrapping a large absorbent bandage around everything, leaving only his thumb free. It meant he wouldn't be able to use the compound bow, but he still had two other means of killing. This time he was going to get close to his target, make it personal.

As he drove back, trying to channel the attitude of John Rambo, he thought about his next move. "Stakeout her shop", he thought. It was, it turned out, a good thought. Which was lucky for the Hunterman, as it was the only one he had.

He arrived there just in time to see his quarry go into the store. Three minutes later he left with the woman. The Hunterman followed them to the sandwich shop, then calculated his next move. If the bastard left here and went to his car in the public parking lot, he would walk past the Derry Dive Bar. Nearby was the spot the Hunterman needed. Despite the pain in his hand, the Hunterman went to that good place in his head, the one where he always agreed with himself. The plan was back on, the execution would be executed.

***

Enoch left the sandwich shop at almost a full run. 'No' he thought, 'It's impossible. Portia loves me.'

By the time he turned the corner, he'd remembered the large insurance policy over his head, the look of pain on her face when she found out why she wasn't getting pregnant, her reaction to his reaction when she had suggested a sperm donor. "Over my dead body," he'd said at the time.

Maybe she'd taken him at his word.

He crossed the road to pass in front of the Derry and take the pathway to the parking lot.

***

Ceramic knives have a lot of advantages. Chief among them is they won't set off a metal detector. The Hunterman hadn't bought it for this reason, as he had not encountered any metal detectors during the drive up from Edmonton. Instead, he'd bought it because it was cool.

Ceramic knives also have one big flaw. They break easily. The early ones used to shatter when dropped and, although they are better made today, they are still susceptible to damage if you are unlucky.

The Hunterman was unlucky.

His plan was simple. About halfway to the car park, the path opened out so there was room for a bench. The Hunterman, having given up all efforts at subterfuge, planned to wait there for the bastard and shove the knife between his ribs, reaching the heart and causing instant death.

He saw his target turn onto the path, about 20 yards away. The Hunterman reached for the knife, then realized the sheath was strapped to his belt for a right-hander, the hand he had swathed in bandages.

A lesser man would have cried, but the Hunterman believed himself made of sterner stuff. He reached 'round frantically with his left hand, desperately trying to grab the knife, to unclip it.

***

Enoch was so busy analyzing his conspiracy thoughts that he was barely five yards away when he noticed an astonishing sight. There was an extraordinarily fat man trying to contort himself into some maniacal, impossible position. He was flailing away with his left arm, trying to reach something behind his back. He reminded Enoch of a fat corgi chasing his tail.

Enoch thought to offer to help him, but one look at the man's face made him keep moving. He looked apoplectic and his ears appeared as if they would detach and ignite, they were so red. Enoch hurried by as quickly as was decently possible.

I wonder what's got him so upset, he thought, followed by, *Where do I know that man from?*

***

The Hunterman couldn't believe it. Three times in one day the bastard had walked away from his destiny. Then, as his quarry hurried by, the knife came free and the Hunterman had a tenuous grip on the blade. He tried to swing it out from under his jacket, intent on grabbing it by the handle and rushing after his target.

The hilt caught on the edge of his jacket and, as he kept pulling, the spring-like effect shot it out of his hand and into a high arc above his head, back towards the road and the Derry Dive Bar. The Hunterman started running after it, but he hadn't a hope in hell. It fell to the ground on the hard concrete, shattering into slivers. The Hunterman, still running, didn't notice the young woman in his path trying to stop him. He crashed into her, pausing to see if she was all right, but the sickening thud of her head against the wall persuaded him to keep going.

***

Constable Alison Campbell had come to the RCMP detachment straight from training, and she'd been in Fort Clearwater for six months. She wasn't the first choice of Duty Sergeant Mel Bruce for Ramsbottom's undercover assignment, but she had been the only police officer who had a realistic chance of getting downtown in time to follow Enoch Powlle. What would she do if Ramsbottom was right, and someone attacked Powlle? Well, Sergeant Bruce didn't rightly know. Campbell stood about five-two in her dress boots and weighed about one twenty, tops.

Oh well, should just be a surveillance job. What could go wrong?

***

Ramsbottom heard about the injured police officer on his car radio. He headed over to Derry's in time to see Constable Campbell being loaded into an ambulance. She was conscious, but sounded delirious to the attending paramedics. Not to Sergeant Ramsbottom.

"He was big, oh Geez he was big. He ran through me like I wasn't there."

"Can you describe him, Constable?"

She hesitated.

"If he was a nursery rhyme character," said the Sergeant, "Who would he be?"

"Humpty Dumpty," she said before she could stop herself, and Ramsbottom had his confirmation. Someone, a very large someone, really was trying to kill Enoch Powlle.

***

The Hunterman was unravelling. "Three times three fucking times three times three fucking times." The chant unrolled in his head as he made it back to his car. How could he fail three times three fucking times?

"No," he shouted at himself. "I. did. not. fail. I prepared for this. I still have one more chance. He headed back to the bastard's suburb, this time taking the high road to position himself above the tree line.

***

Enoch made it home, feeling better about things. The drive had allowed him to think rationally. That, and the sight of the mad giant on the pathway trying to do, well, God knows what, had cheered him up and put to rest his anxiety about his wife.

"Of course she loves me," he said, and this time he meant it. Instead of heading for his study, Enoch celebrated his good mood by taking two beers from the fridge and going outside to sit on the lounger.

The combination of the beers and his earlier anxiety soon put him to sleep. When Portia came home, he was still out there, warbling gentle snores through slightly open lips.

"Oh, Enoch," she said, "You haven't written a word, have you? Saul Coldman will be coming by after dinner and he'll be ever so disappointed that you have nothing for him."

"Aha, but that's where you're wrong. I have the kernel of an idea that I must just nibble at for a while, to see where it goes."

"Well, while you're nibbling away, take Misri for a walk. Don't give me that look; you know she sleeps better at night after you've walked her. Take her the long way around this time, up the escarpment to the lookout point. I don't expect to see you for at least forty-five minutes."

Enoch knew better than to argue with Portia when she was in her motherly mood. Besides, he always took Misri off the leash up there, half-hoping she'd head for the horizon. Enoch started to think of the breed of dog they could buy if the beagle ran away: a proper dog, like a Great Dane maybe, or an Irish wolfhound. Something with dignity. And brains.

***

The Hunterman had taken almost an hour to walk the half mile along the path to the top of the escarpment. When he got there, he thought his heart was going to pound out of his chest. From the top, amid the boulders at the edge of the cliff, he had a 360 degree view of his surroundings. If the bastard came out the back door, he had a downward shot of about a hundred and fifty yards. He sat there, heart heaving, hands shaking. He suspected that if he'd ever read the instructions for the crossbow, he'd have discovered it didn't have anywhere near that range, and even if it did, he was in no shape to make the shot. He wanted to wail at the injustice of it all. He had spent every last cent he owned on this trip, and now, to have come so far and not succeeded, well that was a short, sharp description of his life. Mister Not Quite. Mister Didn't Make It. Mister Nearly.

He happened to be looking down at the bastard's back door when he saw him come out with his dog on a leash. The Hunterman had been up here every day during the past week, scouting around, trying to find the best way to kill him. He didn't know much, but he did know that whenever they set off on the northern path, they were on their longer walk, the one up the escarpment.

Straight towards him.

He unpacked the crossbow.

***

Halfway up the hill, Enoch let the beagle off its leash and said to her, "Go, run away, head for the horizon." Misri galloped off, following her nose, making her own path, no doubt tracking the faintest hint of food in the next province.

Enoch kept walking up the path, trying to turn his idea into something he could tack on to his impossible start to a short story. He wrestled with it as he continued up the slope, and he had just about reached the final turn before the last part of the path, across the clearing to the rocky outcrop, when he stopped, defeated. He just couldn't get 'round that impossible beginning.

"Nobody could finish a story with that start," he said. Nobody answered.

***

The Hunterman was poised to let fly. He had the crossbow leaning on his jacket on a rock, aimed at the last turn on the path. His breathing had slowed to the point where it sounded like a bloodhound, as opposed to a steam train, and he was as ready as he'd ever be. He heard the bastard's footsteps, then nothing. Where was he? Why wasn't he coming?

It was at that moment that Misri, tracking a long lost French fry through the trees, came up behind the Hunterman looking for food. She climbed on the rock next to him, leaned over for a taste, and licked the Hunterman on his ear and cheek.

The Hunterman, wound up to a nervous pile of tics and twitches, seemed to jolt six inches into the air. It was the final shock to his overloaded, over-jaded system, and his heart had already stopped before he toppled over the edge of the cliff face.

***

Enoch, having worked out all the flaws in his kernel of an idea, turned the corner in despair to see Misri, looking very pleased with herself, sitting on top of a rock like a lion on its throne.

"Come on then," he said. "Maybe I'll be luckier tomorrow."

Four hours later, after Enoch had endured the disapproval of Portia and the disavowal of Saul Coldman, the doorbell rang. It was Sergeant Ramsbottom.

"Honey," said Enoch, "someone fell off the trail and the Police want us to look at his picture." He peered at it. "You know, I saw him on the car park path today. He was behaving very strangely, and I actually thought I knew him from somewhere. I'm sorry I can't remember."

Portia didn't know either, and the Sergeant was about to leave when Saul Coldman came back from the bathroom. In for a penny, he thought.

"Mister Coldman is a visitor, he can't possibly help you," said Portia.

"I'm trying to find out if he was seen anywhere today," said the Sergeant. He showed the picture.

"My word," said Coldman. "That's Adagio Hunter."

"Who?" asked the Sergeant and Enoch in chorus.

"Adagio Hunter, wannabe writer, talent in inverse proportion to his size."

"He is a big lad, isn't he? I've remembered now where I know him from," said Enoch. "He was at the page-turner awards."

"You beat him into sixth place," said Coldman. "That was the closest he ever got to an award. Didn't he end up in a loony bin somewhere?"

Portia started to giggle. "I'm sorry, but I've just remembered what he did at the awards banquet. He was announced as sixth place, and then you won fifth. Well, as you headed toward the stage, he shouted that he was going to get you someday. Then he called you a bastard."

"Charming", said Enoch. "I wonder what he was doing in Fort Clearwater."

"Well," said Sergeant Ramsbottom, "if you have some time, I think I have a story for you."

Kevin Thornton is a five-time Arthur Ellis Award finalist, a short story writer and a published poet of work that actually rhymes. Born in Kenya, he counts North America as the fourth continent where he has lived and worked. He now resides in the frozen north of Canada. It is well named.

His ramblings and strange sense of humor
may be found at
http://theoldfortamusingfromtheoilsands.blogspot.ca/
and on Facebook

Belief

Jane Petersen Burfield

Editor's Note: When is it a "crime" to harbor secrets? In this magical and uniquely sincere tale, Jane Petersen Burfield leaves us wondering: Mob boss? Master smuggler? Or beloved hero of those who believe?

Light strobed outside the dark window, and rain tap-danced on the wing. Nothing like a winter storm over the North Atlantic to bring added terror to a nervous flyer.

I sat back, squooshed into my seat, and closed my eyes, trying to ignore a wave of nausea. I wished I were back at home and not en route to my childhood house for Christmas for the first time in ten years.

This trip would give me a chance to decide what I should do.

Memories of holidays past swirled through my mind. Christmas time was magical when I was a small child. It held suspense, excitement, and mystery. Glass ornaments, gently scratched by the years, foil icicles saved in tissue, and bubble lights for our tree were ingredients for a perfect Christmas. Most important was a snow globe of Santa on his sleigh, surrounded by elves, which sat on our mantel.

It was much later when I understood this holiday of choreographed chaos was the perfect showcase for my Mother's remarkable organizational skills and my Dad's wizardry with outside lights. When I was a child, we had one of the best Christmas celebrations in North Toronto. I didn't realize the planning or the work it required. Back then, there was no question about 'belief' in the magic of Christmas.

But, that was back then.

When I was little, my sisters and I got excited a few days before the Eaton's Santa Claus parade. I didn't mind being muffled into my snowsuit, a process I usually hated. I knew we were going downtown to see the clowns walk upside down. We waited on the curb and watched police on horses, huge floats and marching bands go by. Dad would buy us caramel apples as a treat, or even a whistling bird on a stick. More floats would pass, until Santa cracked his whip and called out, "Ho, Ho, Ho", on the last float. His reindeer seemed huge. They lunged forward high above us. I thought that, if they were just freed from the float, they really would fly.

Santa sat atop the sleigh, his beard contrasting with his red coat and black belt. The black whip he carried in his right hand seemed a little sinister, but it gave him a certain power. He was wonderful. He was magical.

He was real.

After a few weeks of lively anticipation, we would put the tree up in the living room. We had to wait until a week before Christmas so, as my Mother would say, it wouldn't dry out too much and cause a fire. I would help unwrap all the old ornaments, the soft metal icicles, the colored glass balls and the strings of beads from crumpled tissue paper. My hands would smell of old pine and mildew.

Mother was as particular in her decorating agenda as she was about everything else in our lives. The lights had to be strung first, a process that seemed to take forever when I was impatient to put on the tinsel. Bubble lights, ones that had narrow cylinders atop round, water filled globes, were the most magical. Next we put the ornaments on. It's hard to remember what they were like—mostly thin glass balls. Some were formed like Santa, or misshapen pine cones.

I dropped one once, and it shattered into a flying star shape. I was careful after that. Some ornaments were plastic, a modern type that wouldn't break as easily, but they weren't nearly as wonderful as the old glass ones.

Strands of gold and silver beads went on next. I wrapped them around the lower branches that I could reach. My older sisters looped them over the top branches so they dangled down artistically, the way mother instructed. Finally the tinsel went on, never thrown in clumps, but carefully untwined, a few strands at a time, and placed on individual branches to look like angels' tears. I often seemed to end up with more static charged tinsel on me than on the tree.

Finally, the silver wire Angel was put on the top, so high above me.

When we had finished, Dad turned off the room lights, plugged in the tree, and we gloried in the enchantment. As the branches were warmed by the lights, a rich pine scent filled the room. Mother tidied away paper and packing boxes and then made hot chocolate, and we would sit and look at the tree.

I adored it! I loved the sense of disorder that came from having a tree grown in the country put up with great ceremony inside our overly tidy city house at this special time of the year. This tree developed the aura of another person living in the house. I would talk to it, quietly, when I walked by, and I always half expected to hear it whisper back. It knew the secrets of Santa.

Just like my snow globe.

I opened my eyes when a particularly vivid flash lit the cabin. I was too frightened to close my window blind. I needed to see outside, as the storm blew. I tried to get more comfortable in my window seat.

As a complacent North Toronto child, I'd gone to school with neighborhood friends. We went to Brownies together, to camp and confirmation class. Most of us attended Havergal College together in grade seven, and celebrated each others' Sweet Sixteen birthdays. We moved, en masse, to St. Hilda's College at U of T, and along with taking the same programs, we joined the same sororities.

By third-year University, when I had finally started to think for myself, I needed to separate from the North Toronto gestalt. I got interested in Greenpeace, stopped going to class and started wearing sweat shirts instead of sweater sets.

My Dad thought I was building character at last; my mother was horrified. But it was when I refused to join the Junior League that she pretty much stopped talking to me.

When I graduated the following year, I took a summer secretarial course, and applied for a job at an overseas company. Its location in the north of Finland was far enough away for me to live without the burden of my mother's heavy disapproval. I believed I would find out who I was. I thought I would only be away for a few years, but I had been overseas now for more than ten.

Initially, I'd worked as a secretary to one of the corporate managers. During the cold, dark winters I met a number of people at work and at home parties, made many friends, and ended up marrying the older son of the boss. He was working hard then, and so we married in a stave church in Finland to take as little time from his work schedule as possible. No one from my family came. I'd always intended for us to go home soon after, but Nick never managed to get away. My Dad never met him, and I somehow doubted my Mother ever would.

Ironically, they had both known his father when they were children. But I wasn't anyone that.

***

After my escape overseas, I had gradually lost touch with North Toronto life. And I began to lose the magic of Christmas. The holiday now seemed to be just hard work. Our company had so much to do before year-end that I barely saw my husband, or anyone else, unless I went down to the warehouse. I felt lonely. I saw Nick so rarely that I had to use notes on his dresser to communicate.

There was something I hadn't found a chance to let him know before I left. Something I couldn't tell him in a note.

It is good to have your own secrets at times.

In Finland, I missed the sense of wonder my mother and dad had managed to give to Christmas when I was a child. After being away for so many years, I was going home for Christmas. I regretted not having made the trip before Dad had died, four years earlier. Mother was getting to that early forgetful stage of vulnerability. I needed the reassurance of one of her Christmases while we could still have it. I needed to relive my memories of my childhood with my sisters.

Especially now.

***

Towards the end of November, Nick was busy checking inventory, meeting deadlines, doing everything he could to hasten product delivery. I asked if he would mind me going home to Toronto; he barely took the time to look up before saying, 'No, of course not'. When I asked if there was any chance for him to come with me, he glanced at me briefly, and said perhaps sometime in the next few years, but he didn't know when.

He did ask me to be discreet when talking about his company. The Board always worried about industrial espionage.

That night, I went on the internet and booked my travel arrangements. Nick's company jet would get me to Copenhagen, and I would take a good old Air Canada flight home from there.

I arrived at Pearson International in a snow squall, but it was nothing compared to the storms I was used to overseas. I expected to catch a taxi home, but my sisters were waiting for me as I exited customs. I almost cried when I saw them. My emotions were brittle.

"Carol! Over here!" Brenda called to me across the heads of other travelers in the terminal. I pushed my luggage cart over and gave her a hug. Lynne, my quieter sister, gave me a huge hug next.

"Have you been waiting long? Where's Mother?" I asked.

"We just got here, and Mother's at home. She's not as strong as she used to be. This snow storm would be difficult for her to walk through."

I didn't want to hear this. I had come home to experience a Christmas like we used to have. I began to doubt I would find any magic, after all.

We drove across the 401 in heavy traffic, traffic that overwhelmed me after the quiet roads of North Finland. At least the colors were different here. I was tired of the unceasing monochromatic landscape, and the ever present red worn in North Finland to combat the whiteness of the winter.

When we got to the house, the front bushes were outlined in multi-colored lights, and a wreath had a jaunty tartan bow. Brenda opened the door and called to Mother. As we took off slushy boots, and put my suitcase in the hall, she came down the stairs, slowly, leaning on the bannister. She looked at least six inches shorter and twenty years older. When she said hello and reached up to embrace me, I felt her bones, sticklike, beneath wrinkled skin. I hugged her as tightly as I dared.

Lynne brought us some tea as we chatted by the fireplace. She said they had delayed putting up the tree, an artificial one now, until I got there. We would do it tomorrow.

We talked for several hours, before jet lag forced me to head for my old bedroom. I was grateful to have some quiet time. It was very peculiar, but rather comforting, to go to sleep surrounded by the pictures and stuffed animals that had been important to me so many years ago.

From the night table beside me, I picked up the glass snow globe, the one with Santa on his sleigh that my parents had given me for my tenth birthday. I shook it gently, and watched as shimmering flakes obliterated the little figures inside. Its music, Silent Night, soothed me. I thought of Nick, and my life in Finland. And then I slept deeply, for the first time in weeks.

I awoke very early, and went downstairs to make morning tea. Sitting by a sunny window, I studied the kitchen and found it much the same as I remembered. Mother came down around 8:00 am. I had worried about talking with her alone, but we seemed to skirt around any uncomfortable subjects, like daddy's death, my not coming home, and my not having children.

I heard about her friends, the ones still alive and mentally competent. She told me about my friends, the staunch little Junior Leaguers with husbands and multiple children. "Children" was said in a slightly louder tone.

"I've arranged a tea for you and your old friends, dear", she said, striking terror into my heart. What could I tell them about me? I wasn't allowed to reveal much about Nick or his company. All I ever said was that he was the boss of a large import/export business, one affiliated with Nokia. I wouldn't share my own secret with anyone until I had told Nick.

My sisters came down for breakfast and we made plans for the day. We decided to do some Christmas shopping at Yorkdale, and then come home and put up the tree, before having Mother's Chili and homemade bread.

The crowds at Yorkdale were startling. I had forgotten how many people can fit into a mall at Christmas time. Santa's Workshop was set up in a central location, and the Claus wore an authentic looking suit. Did the kids believe as strongly as I had? I bought a few things for Brenda and Lynne, and found a lovely scarf for Mother, one with a signature that would please both her and her bridge playing friends. We went home gratefully midafternoon, sat with a cuppa, and talked about our current lives.

Brenda and Lynne sensed that I was guarded in what I could say. I muttered something about corporate espionage, patents, and the need for total discretion. We decided to have a rest before excavating the tree and ornaments from the basement.

Despite suffering from jet lag, I couldn't sleep—too much stimulation, and too many memories.

Late that afternoon, Lynne carried the artificial tree up from the cellar, and Brenda and I fetched dusty boxes of ornaments. They were beautifully packed in tissue—but when I unwrapped them, they looked small and a little shabby. All but one of the bubble lights had long ago broken, so we put mini lights on the tree, and then began to hang the ornaments. Most were now unbreakable plastic, but a few of the old ones were still intact.

I found a woven gold thread to replace the colored beads of long ago. Finally, we unwrapped the tinsel from its nest of tissue. I'm sure some of it was the original tinsel from twenty years earlier. When I was careless and put too much on one branch, Mother ordered me to do it properly, strand by strand. Finally, we put the worn-out Angel on top. It was now more tarnish than silver, but it still looked both magical and very high.

Maybe there was a little enchantment left. I half-expected the tree to whisper to me.

Over the next few days, I met with old friends. I looked at pictures of their families, and thought it might have been pictures of us when we were small. When they asked to see pictures of Nick and my family overseas, I pulled out one of Nick by himself. He was sitting on the seashore in summer, not wearing the inevitable red of winter, but in jeans and a sweater.

To my newly reborn North Toronto eyes, he looked a little strange, sort of like the scraggily-bearded owner of a Swedish furniture franchise in the ads on television. I could sense they thought Nick looked old. How could I explain that he was both perpetually old and perpetually young at the same time? I couldn't tell them much of anything about him. But looking at him, I realized how much I missed him, and our life so far away. I knew I didn't really belong in North Toronto anymore, at least not now.

***

The next two weeks passed quickly. We went to a carol service at our old school. We Christmas-shopped whenever we thought the mall would be quiet enough to navigate. Newly released holiday movies were a luxury I rarely enjoyed overseas. I refurbished my wardrobe—buying blue and green and brown, anything but red. I bought sweaters for Nick's brothers, and pretty bags and scarves for their wives. I found some lingerie I thought Nick might enjoy seeing me in—a present for both of us. If he ever had the time.

We listened to Christmas music, watched television specials, and baked. I helped out at the Daily Bread Food Bank with Brenda and her kids. When Lynne and her husband wanted to go out one night, I babysat her two boys, and enjoyed a chance to know them better. I took them to see Santa at the mall, a rather bizarre experience. The hired elves were much too big. I hoped the boys would like the toys I'd chosen.

On Christmas Eve, I sat quietly in the living room near the fire, my water globe at my side. The tree lights shone softly, and carols played on the stereo. I was gazing at the fire when I swear I heard a whisper.

I looked up quickly, but no one was there. I pulled out the packages I had put aside—glass ornaments wrapped in red paper for Brenda, Lynne and Mom. I thought perhaps I could start a new tradition.

My sisters came in and sat with me until Mother was ready. She took time to get down the stairs, and I knew her arthritis must be painful. When she stepped into the living room, she had packages ready for us—Christmas pajamas, just like when we were little. I hugged her, gently, and thanked her for Christmas, not just for this one, but for all the years when she had created so much magic. And I thought ahead to next year when our own baby would be enjoying Christmas for the first time.

As I said goodnight to Mother, she whispered in my ear," Do you know why we named you Carol?" When I said no, she explained, "Both your Dad and I loved Christmas so much we wanted you to carry a name that would remind you and us of it all year 'round. You are our Christmas Carol. We thought the Santa globe would remind you of the magic, but you left it here."

"I know, Mom. I'll try to come home again next year. I've missed all of you. And Daddy. I miss him so much."

As Mom climbed up the stairs, I lifted the globe from the table and swirled the snow. There was magic in it. There was magic in this night, Christmas Eve. I just had to believe.

That night, in my bed, I thought of Nick. This was his busiest night of the year. I realized how much I missed him, and I looked forward to going home in a week.

He might not be the perfect husband, one able to take the time to be with me as often as I would like, but he sure brought magic to a world of people. I picked up my Santa snow globe, shook it gently, and whispered to him, "Fly carefully, Nick. May your Christmas Eve go well. I'll be back soon".

I swear I heard a whisper say, "I love you, Carol. Merry Christmas".

Jane Petersen Burfield was a co-winner of the Bony Pete Short Story Award in 2001 for her first story, "Slow Death and Taxes". After several years of success with the Bloody Words story contest, she decided writing was a misery-making but delightful challenge. She has had short stories published in *Blood on the Holly* and *Bloody Words, the Anthology*, as well as in *Thirteen, an anthology of Crime Stories*. (Carrick Publishing, 2013)

Jane is honored to be a member of Mesdames of Mayhem, and looks forward to the creative buzz that comes from an association of women writers.

Connect with Jane Burfield at her Website:
http://www.janeburfield.com/
Or on Facebook

Ghost Protocol

Angie Capozello

> *Editor's Note: Sparkling with originality, this espionage caper by Angie Capozello will grab your imagination and leave you checking your watch....for ghosts!*

Purgatory, thought Virgil, *is a designated smoking area outside an office building.*

All of the unclean souls gathered, reeking of nicotine, huddled together in a feeble attempt to ward off the elements. They stood there every day, unable to pass through the steel and glass gates until their penance, in the form of a tiny white stick, was paid out in a cloud of smoke.

Virgil, in his disguise as "Algernon P. Stoblenski", was an outcast amongst the damned. He slouched up to the entrance, took a spot to the left of the doors and tapped a cigarette out of its pack. The real Algernon was sleeping off the mickey Virgil had paid a hooker to drop into the man's beer the night before. With any luck, he wouldn't make an appearance till long after Virgil was gone.

A few of the other smokers cast wary glances in his direction. Virgil used his Telepathy to broadcast a mild suggestion that they were seeing Algie sucking down his first cigarette of the day. A slight touch of his Empathic Talent enhanced their natural dislike of the man, (he was a bit of a toad), which made sure no-one would get close enough to see through his disguise.

He hung around outside just long enough to make sure he had plenty of eye witnesses to say that Algie had shown up for work. Then he ground out his cigarette and shoved through the doors into the lobby of the Stoblenski Arms Corporation.

It was obvious the Stoblenski's didn't spend their money on their employees. The lobby was clad in a dingy faux marble that showed every scratch and chip, and every one of the potted plants was plastic. Even the guards' uniforms looked cheap. The only things that didn't look like they'd been made in some foreign sweatshop were the guns the guards wore on their hips. The owners might be skinflints, but their business was designing weapons, and they didn't stint on the armaments the guards carried.

The guards looked like they knew how to use them, too. No rent-a-cops here.

Despite the risk, Virgil took his time crossing the lobby. Algernon never went anywhere in a hurry—he moved with the inexorable pace of a rash, the sort that could only be endured until it went away.

A group of women in off-the-rack business suits scattered as they caught sight of him, but one, distracted by reading something on her phone, did not see him coming. Virgil sensed a bit of anticipation from the guards— they were taking bets on how long it would take for 'Al' to get slapped. Virgil could not afford to do anything that might break character, so he moved to stand right behind the woman. "Did you think about my offer?" he whispered, running a hand slowly down her back.

She jerked away from him, dropping her purse. "Back off! Unless you want your family to get hit with another lawsuit!" She snatched her purse from the floor and stormed toward the elevators.

He gave her retreating back an oily smile. "Oh yes, and that worked out so well for the last lady. What was her name?"

Her shoulders stiffened as she entered the elevator. She jabbed at a button and turned a molten glare on him. "Sandra. Her name was Sandra."

Virgil smirked at the closing elevator doors, taking a quick read on the thoughts of everyone watching. His careful study of Al's speech patterns and mannerisms had paid off, aided in part by the human mind's tendency to fill in the blanks. People see what they expect to see. The woman was so busy fuming she never noticed that Al was a bit taller today, and the guards were still arguing over their bet. Apparently a put-down was worth less money than a slap. Virgil breathed a sigh of relief and hit the 'up' button for the elevator

His next move was the riskiest of the entire mission. There had been no way to hack into their network and take over the surveillance systems from the outside. Algernon might not look like much, but the sleazy systems administrator knew his business. He'd set up what was known as an 'air gap,' completely cutting off the company's network from the rest of the world.

And that was why Virgil was here. Agents from the Army's Tactical Paranormal Unit got loaned out like this, on occasion, when a normal FBI or CIA agent couldn't do the job. Virgil more often than most, since he had a knack for infiltration. Still, even with all his Talents, it was no easy task.

He got on the elevator and made a point of keeping his head down, as if reading something on his phone. He didn't allow the cameras a clear view of his face. A bald cap, some makeup, stolen clothes and a bit of Telepathic mojo was enough to convince the casual observer. Security cameras, however, did not possess minds that could be fooled. He'd have to leave fixing that problem to his partner.

He looked at his watch, and a small indicator light on its face blinked twice. The paranormal half of this little team was ready to go. He could already feel the chill on his wrist as the ghost pulled in a bit more energy from the air around her.

The elevator pinged as they arrived, but he held the door for a moment and scanned the hall with his Talents, searching for the presence of other minds. He sensed at least five people on this floor, but none were in the immediate vicinity. He stepped out and made a left, heading down the hall to the office at the far end.

Even though there was no one to see him, Virgil continued to walk at Algie's agonizingly slow pace. An agent never knew when someone was going to pop a head out of a door or turn a corner. It was nerve wracking, but it did give him time to take a good look at the surroundings. Here was where all the money went. Alabaster light fixtures cast a soft glow over hardwood paneling, and the carpet in the hall was so deep it completely muffled his footsteps.

Under other circumstances, he might have appreciated the quality of the setting, but all it meant to him now was that he would not be able to hear anyone coming up behind him. He kept scanning the area with his Talents, and by the time he finally got to Algie's office his heart was racing. He quickly pulled out the ID card he'd stolen from the thoroughly drugged Al that morning, and waved it past the security panel to the right of the door. The light shifted from red to green, and the door swung open. He didn't let out the breath he'd been holding till the door shut safely behind him.

The lights came up automatically, revealing a large, posh leather swivel chair behind a mahogany desk, and rows of top-shelf liquor lined a bar set into the wall on one side. The rest of the walls were taken up by paintings. Virgil compared it to Algernon's apartment. Obviously someone with good taste had decorated Algie's office for him.

He sat down at the desk, took off his watch and turned a dial that wrapped around the edge of the clock face. "Evie, activate."

The digital clock was replaced by a grey screen, and the words E.V.I. (Ectoplasmic Voice Interface, Mark Seven) appeared in tiny white letters. The metal of the watch body went ice cold as the ghost stored inside became fully active, and drew in enough energy to interact with the electronics. The voice that came out of the watch was decidedly feminine. ::Hello, Agent. What is our status?::

"We're in. Are you ready to hack this security system from the inside out? Remember, we need a total data dump without triggering any alarms. I acquired some of the passcodes, but I can't be sure I got all of them."

::Understood. Preparing to transfer.::

A vague, shadowy figure emerged from the watch and expanded, hovering near the laptop. For a brief moment, Virgil's senses picked up on the memory of a classy looking brunette, before the ghost disappeared into the screen.

::Enter the passcodes, please.::

The voice still came out of the watch. On the screen, a small alert box announced the new Bluetooth connection was set up. "You work fast, Evie."

He typed in the passwords he'd lifted from Al's mind. Then all he could do was wait, his fingers drumming impatiently on the desk, while a dozen scripts ran.

The email software came up on screen. Algie's inbox was filled with flagged alerts, each one color-coded depending on the type of request moving through the office system. Al had his fingers in everything—orders for office supplies, customer complaints, accounting invoices and yes, HR requests. He also had a folder that held a copy of each employee's e-mail box, including those of his relatives.

"Spying on your own family," Virgil said, shaking his head in mock disapproval. "You really are a douche-bag, Algernon. Lucky for me."

A message popped up to let him know the file transfers were in progress. All of the data would get stored in the watch along with the ghost, doing away with the need for a more obvious portable drive. If he got caught, it was unlikely anyone would think to check his watch.

"How are we doing, Evie?"

::Processing.::

He grumbled at that, blowing out his cheeks in frustration. There wasn't much he could do to help. He was no hacker. His only job was to walk the ghost in and get her back out again, since she couldn't hold cohesion without a power source. Knowing that didn't make the waiting any easier. To kill some time, he started rifling through the rest of the office, although he didn't expect to find much. Algernon was a digital-or-nothing kind of guy.

He was inspecting the selection of liquors when a knock at the door stopped him in his tracks.

A woman's voice, hesitant and nervous, came through the door. "Mr. Stoblenski? Algernon? I've been thinking about your offer to…get together."

Virgil's eyebrows rose up so high they nearly disappeared beneath the bald cap. It was the woman he'd groped in the lobby. *What the hell does she want?* He frowned in concentration, and stretched his senses out to take a quick read of her surface thoughts.

Rage/fear/disgust/nerves/oh god what if this doesn't work/...

He muttered a curse. 'Catherine' had worked herself up into doing something drastic, and he was pretty sure she wouldn't take 'go away' for an answer. *Guess I'm going to find out how good my full sensory illusions are.*

He triggered the screensaver on the laptop and whispered, "Evie, run silent." One slow, deep breath later he had calmed his thoughts and focused them on making Catherine see what he wanted her to see. Then he raised his voice in Algernon's oily tones. "I told you, honey-britches, all roads lead to my office eventually."

Catherine walked in, a little unsteady as her heels sunk into the thick rug. Her shoulders were hunched, and she clutched a large purse to her chest. "You wanted to see me, Mr. Stoblenski?" She shut the door behind her, triggered the lock, and then the whole meek act disappeared. Before Virgil could reply, she reached into her purse, pulling out a gun that looked like it was straight off the set of Buck Rogers, and aimed it at his head. "Well, here I am, and we're going to have a nice long talk."

Virgil took a quick, desperate look around the room for some way out of this mess. He'd thought up plans for dealing with security guards, but a disgruntled employee? The only thing he could think of was to stay in character and stall for time.

"Whoa, take it easy honey." He gave her a weak laugh and held up his hands. "I was only joking with you, right? Why don't you put that down and we'll discuss it over a drink?" He started to reach for one of the liquor bottles, but stopped as the gun made a threatening whine, like a jet turbine spooling up.

"You know what this gun can do." Her brows knit together in a scowl. "So shut up and listen, you little weasel. I know you're going to fire me as soon as you finish sucking what's left of my company dry. I've got nothing left to lose." The sound from the gun went up in pitch, and little indicator lights on the barrel glowed blue. "Got the picture? Give me what I want, and you won't have to witness a live fire test up close."

Virgil had no idea what she wanted, and he sure as hell didn't want to see what the space gun would do to him. He sank back into his seat and acted terrified, quivering in the vain hope that she'd take pity on him. "L-l-look, you'll have to help me out here, I'd give you want you w-w-want, but I don't know what that is."

"Liar," she snarled, taking another step closer. "I want the acquisition documents from when you bought my uncle's company. The real ones, with all the bribes you paid to get the 'merger' approved. And I want to know every senator you've bought, every judge you've paid off. I'm going to expose the whole dirty underbelly of Stoblenski Arms."

What is it about guns that bring out the bad movie cliché's? he wondered. The gun was less than a foot from his face now. Not the best time to be critiquing her line delivery, but at least she was close enough for him to do something about the gun. He wasn't part of a Tactical unit for nothing.

He exploded into action, pushing her hand to one side and twisting the gun around, disarming her in one smooth motion. A step to the side and a pivot later, he was behind her, with one arm pinning her against him and a hand pressed over her mouth. He dropped Algie's speech patterns and growled, "Quiet. Not a word. I'm not here to hurt you, but you picked a bad time—owww!"

She was biting his hand. He strangled back another yelp. "Would you stop it, lady? I'm on your side!"

The watch on the desk bleeped, and the ghost's voice came out. ::We have a problem, Agent.::

"No kidding. You're supposed to run silent!"

Catherine mumbled through his fingers, "Agent? You wif da FBI?"

"Yes, now would you quit biting me?" As soon as her jaws unclenched, he let her go and sat on the edge of the desk. He kept the gun, just in case.

And it was a good thing he did, because as soon as she stepped away she pulled another small pistol out of her purse and pointed it at him. "Prove it."

"What the...oh, for crying out loud, how many do you have in there?" he said, pointing the space gun back at her. "Prove what?"

"That you're from the FBI, and not just from some other company, out to steal a few secrets." She backed out of his reach and took up a shooter's stance. "I know how the Feds work. They would have come in with warrants and cleaned the place out."

"Only if they had 'probable cause', and someone has to get that for them."

Her eyes narrowed. "And you expect me to believe that?"

He could think of only one way to convince her. Virgil glanced over his shoulder at the computer screen. "Evie, respond. Have you found anything yet?"

::Oh my, yes. The Stoblenski's have been very naughty boys.::

"Anything to connect them with the shipment that ended up in those militants' hands?"

::Possibly. The data will require further analysis, but there are several crates full of prototypes from Devon Armaments that appear to have gone missing.::

Catherine's face went pale. "That was my company - Devon Arms! They sold our guns to insurgents?"

"Killed 29 soldiers in Iraq," Virgil said. "The Stoblenski's claim the 'merchandise' was stolen from a warehouse. We have reason to believe otherwise, but no proof yet."

Her expression turned hard. "And they'll bury the evidence just like everything else, with bribes and threats." She lowered the pistol and put it back in her purse. "Is there anything I can do to help? Because if you're about to put their balls in a bear trap, I want in on it."

Virgil let out an amused snort. "Hell hath no wrath..."

"You don't know what all they've done." She walked over and showed him how to shut off the space gun. "That lady I mentioned in the lobby? Sandra? Algernon harassed her every day. But by the time she filed a lawsuit, the Stoblenski's had already paid off the lawyers. And the judge. And then they found 'evidence' that she was embezzling from the company. They ruined her, made her serve time and then found ways to ruin all her close family members over the next few months. No one has had the guts to stand up to them since then, for any reason."

"Except for you," Virgil said, giving the gun a wry look. "What is that thing, anyway?"

"Portable Sonic Immobilizer. Like a hand-held version of one of those sonic cannons they use on ships to repel pirates. Non-lethal, but effective. Designed it myself."

Evie's voice cut in. ::Agent, I'm sorry to interrupt, but we still have a problem.::

"How big a problem?"

::277.6 pounds of problem. The real Algernon Stoblenski emailed his father a few minutes ago to tell him that he would be in to work shortly. Perhaps you should have doubled the dose of the sedative, considering his size.::

"Son of bitch," Virgil said pushing off from the desk. "He'll be here any minute. Catherine, do you still want to help?"

"Absolutely."

"Good, find me a way out that isn't the front door."

She nodded. "That's easy. The Stoblenski's have a private elevator just down the hall. Takes you straight to their personal motor pool. Or to the helipad on the roof."

"That'll do," he said. "Do I need a key?"

"Just his ID card, which I see you have. Can I do anything else?"

"Yeah, check to see if the hall is clear." He waited until Catherine's back was turned to say, "Evie, eject."

::Yes, Agent.::

The ghost floated out of the screen as a glowing orb of light, and settled into his watch. He slipped it back on his wrist and shut down the laptop. "All clear?"

Catherine gave him the thumbs up. "This is the most fun I've had in months!"

"Trigger happy and an adrenaline junkie. You are in the wrong line of work, lady."

She flashed him a grin and headed out in into the hall.

Virgil followed close on her heels, his senses stretched out to pick up on any other minds in the area. They seemed to all be clustered behind one set of double doors, and a low murmur of voices came through it. One voice raised up above the others. "Where the Hell is Al? Well, tell him to get off his lazy ass and get in here…that boy can't be one of mine. I swear, if his mother was still alive I'd slap her."

Virgil raised an eyebrow and whispered, "Apple doesn't fall far from the tree, does it?"

Catherine grimaced. "Mr. Stoblenski makes his son look like a true gentleman."

They hurried past the doors, and turned a corner that ended in a small alcove with a fancy, old fashioned glass and brass paneled elevator gate. They both stopped at the same time, and Virgil held out his hand. Thankfully, she shook it instead of biting.

"Thanks for your help, Catherine. Keep your head down, and don't do anything crazy while I'm gone. Leave the heroics to the professionals."

The corner of her mouth quirked up in a half-smile. "I'll try to stay out of trouble. No promises though."

Virgil laughed and waved the stolen ID badge at a small screen set into the wall. The doors chimed as they opened.

The real Algernon was inside the elevator, flanked by two guards.

There wasn't time to warn Catherine. He grabbed her in a similar one-armed hold as before, fired up the sonic gun and pointed it at Al's nose.

"Out of the elevator. NOW!"

Al shuffled sidelong past them, his eyes wide in disbelief at the sight of his double. "What the Hell is going on here!"

"No questions," Virgil growled. "Move!"

The guards followed Algie out, their eyes glued on Virgil and their hands near their weapons. Virgil backed toward the elevator, holding Catherine in front of him.

Algie's dad rounded the corner, his expression black as a thundercloud. "If you ever make me wait like this again, boy, I'll take strips out of your hide…" He looked at Virgil, and back to Al. Then he barked at the guards. "What are you waiting for? Shoot through her."

Virgil shot first. The sonic pistol made a sound like God's own revolver, a blast that sent the Stoblenski's reeling and set Virgil's ears to ringing. He shoved Catherine away from him and hit the button to close the doors– there was no point in letting them think she was involved.

He'd tried to push her out of the line of fire, but Catherine, bless her vindictive little soul, had other ideas. She not only managed to knock over both guards with an exaggerated stumble, but also kneed papa Stoblenski in the groin as they all fell. The last thing Virgil saw as the doors shut was her stepping on Al's hand as they all struggled to get back to their feet.

He laughed and shook his head, trying in vain to stop his ears from ringing. "Evie, can you run ahead and start up a car for me?"

::I can do better than that.::

An orb shot out of his watch and disappeared into the control panel of the elevator. The lights dimmed as she drew in energy, then came back up once she was gone.

As Virgil got off the elevator, a grey sedan slewed to a screeching halt a few feet in front of him. It was one of the new 'steer by wire' luxury cars. Almost everything in it was run by computer. Evie's voice came from the radio. ::Get in, Agent.::

He opened the passenger door and dove in, just as another pair of guards pelted out of a nearby stairwell. The car sped off before he was all the way in, bullets smacking into the trunk with a loud *PTANG! PTANG! PTANG!*

Evie slalomed between pillars and parked cars, and it was all Virgil could do to keep from being thrown out. Somehow he managed to drag himself the rest of the way inside and get the door shut.

He twisted around in his seat to see where the pursuit was. "Two cars coming up on us fast, Evie."

::Hang on.::

The engine growled as she upped the throttle, and a little light that said "Sport Mode" turned on in the dashboard display. They caught air as they hit the speed bump at the exit to the garage, and landed with a bang and squeal of tires as Evie threw the car into a left-hand slide. Two brown sedans followed close behind, although they didn't make the turn as easily. More bullets shattered the rear windshield as they darted out into traffic.

::Please keep your head down, Agent.::

"I need to see behind us."

::If you bleed on my upholstery, I will never forgive you.::

"Very funny."

He stretched out his senses, picking up on all the minds around him. It wasn't easy, with Evie juking left and right through traffic and bullets whistling past him, but he managed it. He clenched his jaws with the effort, sweat beading up on his brow. Then he reached out with his Telepathy, and for one brief moment, everyone driving behind them got confused about which way was left, and which was right.

Cars turned into each other with a resounding crash. The two sedans following them were lost in the tangle of crumpled bumpers, jackknifed trailers and angry drivers.

Evie sped away and dove onto a side street. After a few miles of random turns to make sure they weren't being followed, she pulled into an empty alley and parked. The engine shut off and made ticking noises as it cooled, and the two of them, man and ghost, took a long moment to pull themselves together.

Evie tentatively broke the silence.

::That was not one of our better exits.::

Virgil broke into helpless laughter, and started peeling off his disguise. "I don't know, any mission you can walk away from is a good one."

::Do you think Catherine will be okay?::

He tore off the bald cap and shook out his sun-streaked hair. Algernon's clothes came off next, revealing his own shirt and jeans beneath the air bladders he'd used to make himself look heavier. "I'd be more worried about the Stoblenski's. She's a holy terror!"

:: I liked her.::

"Yeah, I did too." He let the air out of the bladders and rolled them, along with Al's clothes, into a small bundle. "The best thing we can do for her is make sure this data gets into the right hands, along with our report. Speaking of which, you are going to take responsibility for that wreck back there, right?"

::I was busy driving.::

"Without a license."

::I'm a better driver than you.::

The ghost floated out of the dash and settled back into his watch.

"Don't worry about Catherine," he said. "We'll make sure the Stoblenski's go down."

Virgil strolled out of the alley and joined in the flow of pedestrians. All it took was a touch of Tel-empathy, and no one paid them any special attention. In a way, it was almost like they were two ghosts, moving through the world unseen. He shoved his hands into his pockets, and made his way back to the safe house to report to HQ.

Angie Capozello has been fascinated by ghosts ever since she was a child, having spent weekends at her grandparents' haunted hunting lodge. She's been researching the myths and science around ghosts ever since, and will write about them in any genre she can get away with. She also has a green thumb, likes blacksmithing, archery, and firmly believes one can never have too many books. She currently lives in Pennsylvania, in a very old house.

Visit Angie at her Website:
http://www.pennydreadfulpress.com

The Angels Wait

Ed Piwowarczyk

Editor's Note: The best debut fiction this reader has encountered in years. Ed Piwowarczyk's prose flows perfectly to its inevitable conclusion.

Ella Fitzgerald's "Let It Snow! Let It Snow! Let It Snow!" drifted through Paddy's as Blake Malloy stared at falling snow through the pub window. He cursed silently, fearing the late afternoon snowfall would escalate into a blizzard on his drive north, and turned back to face the stranger in the tinsel-trimmed bar mirror.

Blake barely recognized his own reflection. Gone were his pinstriped stockbroker's suits and the Armanis he favored for his nightlife prowls. Today, they'd been replaced by a ski jacket, denim shirt and jeans—all designer quality, nothing but the best.

Except for the black watch cap, Blake mused. Nothing designer about that, he thought as he took a sip of his Jameson whisky. The knitted cap was standard army surplus issue.

This trip had better be worth it. He took another swallow of his Jameson. *Gabrielle had better be worth it. It's Christmas Eve, after all.* Not that he gave a damn about the season.

"Too cold in here for ya, then?"

Blake snapped out of his reverie. The bartender, Mike O'Shea, as much a fixture at Paddy's as the dark oak bar, was pulling a pint of Guinness for a businessman perched on a stool in front of him.

Mike finished serving the beer and turned his attention back to Blake. "I said, is it too cold—" The bartender leaned back, squinted and ran pudgy fingers over his closely cropped white hair. "Blake? Blake Malloy, is it?"

Blake nodded, smiling. At least, he hoped it was a smile, not a grimace of pain.

"Sorry I didn't recognize—"

Blake held up his hand. "It's okay. I got here before you came on shift. Jason was pouring."

"Still, is it too cold in here? I mean, the cap. Surely you're not needin' it in here. And it's only hiding that handsome head o' black hair o' yours. C'mon, let's get it off ya."

Mike reached over, but Blake raised his arm to block him.

"The cap stays."

"All right, all right." Mike threw up his hands, then picked up a rag and began wiping the bar. "Even if I'd've been on when ya come in, I don't think I'd've recognized ya. And it's not jus' the clothes, you understand."

Blake nodded.

"What's wrong, boyo?"

Where to start? He'd been feeling miserable for about a week and a half—headaches, aching joints, nausea, abdominal pains, vomiting. He felt too weak for his regular workouts, and he'd called in sick at his investment firm.

Then there was...this. Blake gingerly patted the back of his cap.

It couldn't have come at a worse time. *Gabrielle is waiting for me.*

"It's that nasty flu bug, is it?" Mike asked.

Blake nodded, then glanced up at the TV that played silently above the bar mirror. Probably a sentimental Christmas movie. *No! It's...her!* "Mike, switch the channel!"

"Sure, boyo," the bartender said. "Don't think anyone's watchin' this."

Mike tuned in a sports channel. "Jeez, boyo, you're lookin' worse now than before. You seen a ghost or somethin'?"

"You might say that." Blake gulped down the rest of his whisky and motioned for a refill.

The ghost of Christmas past. The ghost of Christmas one year ago.

Mike poured Blake another whisky. "Well, maybe the spirit of Jameson will chase that ghost of yours away."

The bartender turned to serve customers at the other end of the bar, and Blake took a swig of his drink. *No, the whisky won't chase away the memory of the late Holly Thorne.*

Holly was the star of *Sing, Angels, Sing!*, the made-for-TV movie that had first been broadcast shortly before her death a year earlier and was likely to become a holiday season staple.

Sing, Angels, Sing! was a *Bells of St. Mary's* wannabe—spunky music teacher tutors unruly kids in an underprivileged neighborhood and creates a top-flight choir, all the while concealing a life-threatening illness, collapses at the climax of a benefit Christmas concert that helps save farmland from greedy developers, then dies in hospital, a smile on her lips as her teary-eyed charges serenade her into the hereafter with "Angels We Have Heard On High."

Her ticket to the big time, Holly had told him.

Sentimental claptrap. Blake swallowed more whisky.

From that one performance, he couldn't judge how good an actress Holly might have been. But he'd enjoyed the talents she brought to the bedroom. The willowy blonde with the pageboy cut and hazel eyes had been a great lover.

But after the sexual sizzle of summer, she started talking about their future together. Best to make a clean break, he'd decided. He was a love-'em-and-leave-'em guy, not someone who wanted Holly—or any woman—clinging to him. Sobs, tears and pleas followed, but soon Holly, like others before her, was out of his life.

Or so he'd believed.

Then a month before last Christmas, she'd tried to get back into his life.

There were her phone calls, which he promptly hung up on before she could get a word in.

There were her emails, proclaiming her love for him and that it was important that they meet. He'd deleted all of them.

He found her waiting for him, outside his office building or outside the waterfront condo complex he called home. He made surreptitious exits to avoid her, and instructed the security people at both facilities that she was not to be admitted.

Three days before Christmas, Holly donned a dark wig, glasses and a posh accent, and bluffed her way past the condo's concierge. She pounded on his door, insisting he leave with her to have dinner with her family. Security officers were called, and a sobbing Holly was marched out of the building.

Blake remembered looking down to the street to make sure Holly wouldn't remain lurking nearby. She stood stock-still for a few moments at the crosswalk, then dashed into oncoming traffic. To her death.

In the days that followed, there was a minor media splash about Holly's death because *Sing, Angels, Sing!* had aired recently. But Blake refused to read the newspaper accounts, and promptly shut off the TV and radio the moment he heard her name. He booked a last-minute vacation to Aruba to put Holly out of sight and out of mind. Holly was part of a past he didn't intend to revisit.

Pain shot through his abdomen. He started to reach into his jacket pocket for the bottle of Tylenol he'd bought, but hesitated. He'd had a couple of drinks, and he needed to stay alert for the drive ahead of him. Pain would be his companion on the road, he decided, and he reached again for his drink. *If only I didn't feel so weak.*

As Brenda Lee's "Rockin' Around the Christmas Tree" was piped through the pub's sound system, Blake's thoughts turned to Gabrielle.

He'd first seen her about six weeks earlier at the seventies retro club, The Soul Depot. She was a brunette, her hair styled in a layered shag, wearing a devil-red cocktail dress that hugged her lithe figure as she gyrated beneath a mirror ball to "Disco Inferno."

That first night, she was aloof to his advances. She danced to "The Hustle" with him, then left the club.

The next time he saw her at The Soul Depot, she agreed to a couple of drinks and a few dances before calling it a night. But she'd given him a name—Gabrielle.

There were a few more drinks-and-dances nights with Ms. Hard-To-Get, then a breakthrough. He suggested few drinks at a quiet hotel piano lounge the following night, and she agreed.

Her warm smile, gentle laugh and the sparkle in her chocolate-brown eyes told him that the wine and his charm had gone down easily. She didn't tell him anything about herself, but he was confident he'd soon find a way to get her to open up.

He was about to suggest they share a nightcap at his place when she reached into her shoulder bag and pulled out a card.

"Merry Christmas." She leaned over, letting her lips graze his cheek. "I made it myself."

Her lips formed a mischievous smile as she watched him tear open the envelope. "You'll find everything you want in there."

The front of the card featured a silhouette of an angel blowing a trumpet. Inside, the greeting read, "Celebrate the season." Gabrielle's signature was followed by a set of driving instructions to someplace north of the city.

"You won't disappoint me, will you...*lover?*" She leaned toward him and gripped his hand. "I promise you it will be very special." She gazed at him intently. "No other commitments this Christmas?"

"I'm an only child. My parents are dead."

"So you'll be there?"

Blake couldn't believe his luck. "You can count on it."

"Can I?" She grinned, released his hand and stood to leave.

"Wait! Have another glass of wine."

"Sorry, lover, not tonight."

"How about a phone number where I can reach you in case—"

"You get lost? Don't worry. Just bring the card. You'll have no problem finding the place. If the weather's decent, the roads will be fine. Figure on a few hours' drive. Be there on Christmas Eve. Early evening."

"And if the weather's bad?"

"Lover," Gabrielle said coolly, "you just said you wouldn't disappoint me. You're not going to let a little snow come between us, are you?"

Blake shook his head.

"Good." Her tone became seductive again. "I'll be waiting. See you then."

That had been ten days ago, Blake thought as he nursed his whisky. His anticipation of intimate delights with Gabrielle had soon given way to the misery of a host of pains, aching joints and fatigue. He'd never felt so weak, and he didn't believe it was simply the flu. Surely *this*, he mused as he touched his cap, wasn't the flu.

Anne Murray crooned "Winter Wonderland" as Blake took another look out the pub window at the snow that continued to fall. He wondered if he could make it to Gabrielle's. He'd barely been able to get out of his condo and down to the car rental agency to pick up an SUV. Stopping at Paddy's probably hadn't been a good idea—there were police spot checks to watch for—but he needed to stiffen his resolve, take his mind off his aches. He figured the whisky would help.

He glanced at his watch. *Better be on my way.*

Hoisting his six-foot frame from the bar stool, Blake winced in pain. Simple tasks had become like something out of *Mission: Impossible*.

"I'd better settle up with you, Mike. Merry Christmas," he added when he removed his card from the debit machine.

Mike smiled at him. "And a Merry Christmas to you, too, boyo. Now you best be gettin' home and takin' care of yourself."

As Blake tucked his card and wallet away, he wondered if he shouldn't take that advice.

You won't disappoint me, will you, lover?

He'd come this far, Blake told himself. Making it up there the way he was feeling should earn him brownie points.

And who better to nurse me than Gabrielle? He smiled. When he got back some strength, he'd enjoy playing doctor with her.

"One thing before you go." Mike motioned Blake to lean forward. The bartender pointed to the cap on Blake's head. "I know you're not wanting to talk about it, but the cap? Why leave it on?"

"Mike, I really don't want—"

"No, listen. It's a shame to hide that hair. I wish I had it." Mike ran his hand over his cropped white hair. "Might make me a hit with the ladies, like you."

The bartender chuckled. "It brings out the Black Irish in ya. Reminds me o' the way that lad who used to play James Bond wore his, you know, what's his name now? The one before Daniel Craig. Ah! Pierce Brosnan. That's it. The ladies ever tell you that?"

Blake nodded, feeling glum.

"Well, then, will ya…"

Blake sighed in resignation. The cap would have to come off when he got up north. Better get it over with.

He peeled off his cap.

Mike stared at him and inhaled sharply.

Blake couldn't help but turn to his reflection in the bar mirror.

His scalp glowed dully in the pub's dim light.

***

Hunched over the steering wheel of the silver Nissan Pathfinder, Blake heard the snow crunch under the tires as he cautiously steered the vehicle along the private road on the last leg of his journey to Gabrielle.

He glanced down at the card beside him to double-check that he'd turned off the highway at the right place.

The drive had been both better and worse than he'd expected. Better, because the roads were clear and traffic sparse. Worse, because the symptoms of whatever he had were growing more acute. His feet felt as if they were burning. He was nauseous. The abdominal pains were sharper. His strength was waning.

Blake inched the SUV forward between the snow-covered birches that lined the sides of the road, following a gentle bend that led to a clearing. He sighed in relief as the headlights picked out a two-storey log house.

He pulled to a stop, put the vehicle in Park and leaned his head against the steering wheel. He'd arrived.

He peered through the windshield, taking a moment to gather the strength and the confidence the trip had sapped from him. To his right was a garage and a tool or garden shed. A red Honda Accord was parked to his left.

Mustering what little energy he had, he stepped gingerly from the SUV. He braced himself against the door before taking halting steps toward the cabin. He paused to compose himself, then rapped on the door.

"Come in, lover. It's open."

Blake eased the cabin door open and stepped tentatively inside.

"Merry Christmas, baby." A blonde with a pageboy cut and hazel eyes, dressed in a black negligee, extended her arms for a welcoming embrace.

Blake staggered forward, and the room began to spin.

"Give me a kiss."

Impossible!

"What's the matter, lover? Aren't you glad to see me?"

Holly!

***

Bing Crosby was crooning "I'll Be Home for Christmas" as Blake blinked his eyes open.

Holly had her back to him, humming along to the music and swaying gently in front of flames blazing in a fieldstone fireplace.

Blake felt leather beneath his hands and arms. When he turned his head to either side, his view was partially obstructed. He was seated in a wingback chair.

He tried to lean forward to stand, but quickly dropped back into the seat. He didn't have the strength to push himself to his feet.

Holly slowly turned toward him, continuing to move to the music. She smiled. "Ah, you're back."

"Holly, how—"

She leaned forward and pressed a finger to his lips.

"Shh. All in good time. First we'll have a drink." She handed him a snifter of brandy from a side table. "I've got mine here." She picked up another snifter from the fireplace mantel.

Blake glanced around. On either side of the fireplace were bookshelves, holding a small stereo system, CDs and tapes, and several paperbacks. Above him was a pine cathedral ceiling. Looking down, he saw a polished hardwood floor. Rustic, but several notches above a rough-hewn cottage.

"Like it?" Holly sat on the floor in front of him and tucked her legs underneath her. "It's my parents' place. It used to be our cottage, but my folks spent a bit—more than a bit, I guess—to turn it into their retirement home." She smiled. "They're away on a Caribbean cruise, so they won't walk in on us."

She paused and raised her snifter. "Here's to the season. Drink up."

She kept her eyes on him as they downed their drinks.

Blake closed his eyes to savor the warmth of the brandy, but the comfort was short-lived—nausea swept over him and his aches renewed their throbbing.

This can't be happening. She can't be here.

But when he opened his eyes, she was smiling at him.

He struggled to rise again, but collapsed back into his seat.

He sucked in a breath. "What happened to Gabrielle?"

"Don't worry. She's here."

"I want to see her!"

"All right. She's upstairs." Holly jumped to her feet. "I'll bring her down."

***

"What's the matter, lover? Don't you recognize her?"

Blake was speechless. In Holly's right hand was a brown wig and in her left a contact lens case.

"I figured Holly needed a bit of a makeover to get you up here, so *voilà*, we have Gabrielle."

"But...but," Blake stammered, "H-Holly's dead. I mean, you're dead."

"You're right, Holly *is* dead," she replied, "but *I'm* not. I'm Holly's sister. Her twin sister. Ivy."

***

Blake felt a snifter being pressed to his lips.

"Here, take a sip of this. It's brandy."

Blake sipped, but a wave of nausea washed over him.

"Better?" She took the snifter back to the side table. "First you collapse when you get here, then you pass out just now." She chuckled. "You sure know how to show a girl a good time."

Ivy sat on the floor in front of him. She wrapped her arms around her legs and propped her chin on her knees.

"Holly and Ivy?" Blake croaked. "This some kind of joke?"

"We were born on Christmas Day. Thirty-one years ago tomorrow." She glanced back at a clock on the fireplace mantel. "At midnight, it'll be thirty-one years ago today."

She turned back to him. "Anyway, my mother always liked that carol 'The Holly and the Ivy,' so what else would she name twin girls born at Christmas?"

Blake swallowed back the bile rising in his throat.

"Why am I h-here?" he whispered, fighting to keep his eyes open.

"Christmas is for family and friends, right?" Ivy smiled. "So I'm going reunite you with your family."

***

Blake felt a hand on his shoulder tilting him slightly forward. He felt a tablet being pressed to his lips.

"Take this," Ivy said.

He hesitated.

"C'mon. Be a good boy."

Blake glanced at the pill she extended.

"Pweeze, pwetty pweeze," Ivy cooed in a little-girl voice.

He pressed his lips together and shook his head.

"Take it!" she shouted. She grabbed the back of his neck and yanked his head forward.

Blake closed his eyes. "Okay."

He gulped down the pill, then swallowed some water from a glass she handed him.

"What did you just give me?" he asked as he returned the glass.

"Just a little something to keep you going a bit longer. Free sample from work."

"You work in a hospital?"

Ivy laughed. "No, I'm a lab technician at a pharmaceutical company."

She had changed into a red turtleneck, hip-hugging jeans and snow boots.

"Y-you're leaving?" He made another futile effort to stand, only to fall back into the leather chair.

"*We're* leaving," Ivy corrected. "As soon as Rick gets here."

She sat back down cross-legged on the floor. "Rick's my older brother. My *big* brother. He wanted to play pro football. Tried out as a linebacker, but didn't make the final cut. Now he runs his own sporting goods store."

She paused. "I'll need his help the rest of the way. You were a bit of a load to drag from the door and prop up in the chair."

With his joints aching in protest, Blake shifted in his chair.

"I'm sorry about Holly. I never meant—"

"Spare me the crocodile tears," Ivy snapped.

"I didn't kill her."

Ivy sprang to her feet. "Yes, you did! You weren't driving the truck that hit her. But you killed her just the same. Holly was high-strung, suffered from depression. She'd fallen for you—hard—but you turned her away from your door. That pushed her into the street…and in front of that truck."

She paced for a moment, then turned back to him. "We all took Holly's death hard. My parents…well, you can imagine the shock. And Rick, he's very protective. He wanted to put the hurt on you, but I convinced him to wait for the right time."

Ivy paused. "She was my *twin*. She was part of me. When she died, something died inside of me."

She fixed her angry eyes on him. "You killed her, you killed part of me, but you also killed part of yourself."

Blake stared at her uncomprehendingly.

"Holly was desperate to see you, remember? She had something important to tell you." Ivy paused. "She was pregnant."

Pregnant. The word slammed Blake like a two-by-four.

"Impossible!" he gasped. "I believe in safe sex. I was careful."

"Yeah, I know. Holly told me. She didn't understand it, either. But condoms have been known to fail occasionally." Ivy's voice softened. "She was so excited, so happy she was going to have a child. Your child."

Blake hung his head. He wanted no part of marriage and kids, at least not until he'd climbed a little further up the corporate ladder. But...someone calling him Dad sounded good.

Ivy resumed her pacing. "I had to do something, didn't I? I couldn't let it go. You had to be punished. But how?"

She turned to the bookshelf, ran her finger along the edge of a row of paperbacks, then pulled one out.

"When I was up here last summer and looking for some light reading, I came across this."

She held the book in front of him. *The Pale Horse*, by Agatha Christie.

Blake shook his head. "Never heard of it."

"You can always learn something from Dame Agatha when it comes to poisons," Ivy continued. "This book had a real beauty—thallium."

Blake swallowed hard.

"Thallium's a white heavy-metal element, atomic number eighty-one." Ivy grinned. "Its salts are colorless, odorless, tasteless and soluble in water. Highly toxic, as deadly as arsenic."

She crouched down in front of him, clutching the book. "It doesn't take much to kill you, as little as a pinch of salt, and it works slowly. It can take ten to twelve days."

She rose and returned the novel to the shelf.

"W-what are...the s-symptoms?" Blake stammered.

"Let's see. There's headaches." Ivy started counting off on her fingers. "Abdominal pains, joint pains, nausea, lethargy, vomiting, delirium, convulsion. Sound familiar?"

Blake nodded. "Any-anything else?"

"Remember the stories about the CIA plots against Fidel Castro? Well, one says the CIA concocted a plan to poison him by putting thallium powder in his shoes. They thought it would make his beard fall off."

Ivy patted Blake's head. "That's one of the big giveaways of thallium poisoning, lover—hair loss."

Blake winced. "Y-you got this stuff at the lab where you work."

Ivy chuckled. "No, from the garage out there. Thallium used to be common in rat poisons, but not anymore. But I found an old stash out back, where my dad stores stuff. I took a bit in to work and put in some after-hours time at the lab to distill what I needed. The lab has the coat, gloves and goggles I needed to protect myself while working with it. I put it in a small paper packet so I wouldn't have to handle it again. Here, I'll show you. Let me get my bag."

A moment later, she returned with a tote bag and pulled out a small envelope. She pulled up the flap and held it open for him.

"That little bit of p-powder? That did this to me?"

"Not even that much. Less than a pinch does the trick. All I had to do was get it to you. I couldn't approach you, of course, but I figured you wouldn't be able to resist Gabrielle."

"That night at the piano bar? Th-that's when...?"

Ivy nodded.

"The wine?"

She nodded again. "A tiny tap from this packet while you went to the washroom."

"But why all this? Why bring me here?"

"It was a test."

"This is c-crazy!"

"Giving you the thallium was both a punishment and a test," Ivy continued. "You *will* die for what you did to Holly.

That's the punishment. But inviting you here was a test, to see if you had the strength to overcome all that the poison did to you. You could have died back at your condo or anywhere along the road. But you made it here, so you're worthy."

"Worthy of what?"

"Of being reunited with Holly."

"But I came for Gabrielle."

"Of course you did," Ivy said soothingly. "Gabrielle is your angel, the one who's going to guide you back to your family, to Holly and your unborn child."

"There is no Gabrielle!"

"Sure there is." Ivy put on the brown wig. "See? Here she is," she said, patting the hairpiece. "And when Holly tried to get past the concierge at your place in a wig, this was it. So in a sense, all three of us are here—Holly, Ivy and Gabrielle."

"You're sick!" Blake croaked. He stared at Ivy beseechingly. "Please, get me to my P-Pathfinder."

Then he heard the rumble of an engine and the crunch of tires on snow.

"It's too late for that, lover." Ivy stroked his brow as she set the wig aside. "That brandy I gave you when you got here? I laced it with another dose of thallium, so you don't have much longer."

Blake heard a vehicle door slam.

"That'll be Rick."

***

When he opened his eyes, Blake was lying spread-eagled on his back looking up at the night sky. It had started to snow again.

His cap was back on, and he groaned when he swiveled his neck to see what was on either side of him.

Snow, trees in the background and boots. Ivy's and Rick's, he guessed.

"Welcome back, lover," Ivy said, crouching over him.

"Where am I?"

"End of the line, pal," a man said. "Your new home."

"Now, Rick," Ivy said. "Be nice. It's Christmas, after all. I'll tell him."

She gazed down at Blake. "I don't know if you noticed on your drive up, but there are signs advertising lakefront lots for sale for people who want to build cottages. When she told me about the baby, Holly was also excited about buying a piece of land, something like this one, to build her dream home." She paused. "Never got around to it, though.

"Anyway, Rick and I thought what better place to reunite you with Ivy and our niece or nephew than here. They're waiting for you."

Blake's eyes darted frantically from side to side.

"It's peaceful here. You'll have passed on before anyone finds your Pathfinder in the driveway."

She dangled the keys of the SUV in her gloved hand and handed them to Rick. "Why don't you pitch these? You've got a better arm than I do."

Rick hurled them onto the frozen lake.

"P-Please, please don't leave me here," Blake begged.

"We have to, lover," Ivy said softly, "or Holly will be disappointed."

She looked at Rick. "I bet Blake thinks there's something we've forgotten that will connect him to us. That card with the directions. Well, it's a pile of ashes in the fireplace."

She paused. "Ready?"

"Ready," Rick replied.

They grabbed his legs and swept them in arcs in the snow a few times before bringing them together. Then they took his arms and swept them in arcs as well before placing them at his sides.

Blake moaned in pain. He couldn't muster the strength to scream.

Then Ivy lay down in the snow on his right and Rick on his left, and they swept their arms and legs in arcs. Then they got up and brushed the snow off their clothes.

"What was that all about?" Blake rasped.

Ivy smiled down at him. "Why, Blake, didn't you do this as a kid? We've just made snow angels." She looked up at the night sky. "Now, when Holly looks down, she'll see us."

"P-please, don't let me die," Blake croaked. "I didn't mean—"

"It's all right, Blake. Gabrielle understands. Holly understands. I understand," Ivy said softly. "We forgive you."

"But—"

"Hush, now," Ivy said. "Just listen."

Ivy and Rick looked up at the night sky and turned to each other.

"It came upon a midnight clear, that glorious song of old," they sang.

Blake couldn't lift his head to look at them. He couldn't move a muscle.

"The world in solemn stillness lay, to hear the angels sing," Ivy and Rick finished softly.

Ivy looked down at him again. "This is it, Blake. Holly will be here soon. Goodbye."

Ivy and Rick walked toward the road, singing, "Angels we have heard on high…"

"Wait…" Blake tried to raise his head, but it fell back in the snow.

"Sweetly singing o'er the plain…"

Their voices faded as Blake looked up at the night sky.

"And the mountains in reply, echoing their joyous strains…" he sang to himself.

The snow continued to fall.

Blake closed his eyes. He could hear the angels sing.

Ed Piwowarczyk is a veteran journalist who has worked as an editor for the *National Post* and the *Toronto Sun*, and as an editor and reporter for the *Sault Star*. A lifelong fan of crime fiction, he is also a film buff and wrote a weekly movie quiz for the *Toronto Sun*. He plays in the Canadian Inquisition, a Toronto pub trivia league. Ed lives in Toronto with his wife, Rosemary McCracken, author of the *Pat Tierney mystery series*.

"The Angels Wait" is his first published work of fiction.

Connect with Ed on Facebook.

The Ultimate Mystery

M.H. Callway

Editor's Note: Brilliantly unique and disturbing, award-winning author M.H. Callway bring us this fantastical journey into the subterranean tunnels of a world we can only hope is not our own.

"Mother, why is it always so hot in the tunnels?"

"Because that's how the Goddess made the world, Lily. Now get back to work." Maria resumed her digging.

Lily sighed. Her earliest memories were of shifting earth and rocks. Now, as an older child, her labors had become as automatic as breathing: she knew little else.

Luckily the guards had assigned her and Maria to the outer tunnels. To be sure, this meant they were the lowest level of digger, but it also meant that they mostly labored in solitude. The heat there felt less oppressive and they could steal time to rest. Except for the infrequent inspections, for the most part, the guards left them in peace.

These periods of solitude gave her and Maria time to talk. For Maria had always been there: large, forbearing, ever-patient under Lily's barrage of questions. Early on Lily had asked her: "Are you my mother?"

Maria sighed. "Not exactly. But, yes, for all intents and purposes, I am your mother."

"I don't understand. If you are not my mother, who gave birth to me? Where did I come from?"

"We all come from the same place. From The Centre at the heart of our citadel. We are all birthed there."

Lily had learned from the other diggers that all the tunnels of the citadel converged underground at The Centre, the place where the Authorities and their chief, the Supreme Ruler, dwelled. Only diggers of the highest rank carved and maintained the tunnels close to The Centre. Few, if any, of their companions, had seen it.

"But where is my mother? I want to see her. I want to be with her." When Maria replied that was not possible, Lily pushed down her fears and asked: "Did something bad happen to my mother?"

"Perhaps. I don't know. We are all separated from our mothers at birth. None of us will ever see our mother."

"Why not?"

"Because that is The Law of our world."

Maria warned Lily once more that she must never call her "mother". If the guards sensed the two of them had grown close, they would separate them. Their relationship must remain a secret.

Instinctively, Lily knew better than to press Maria for more answers. No one dared to question The Law. To do so meant a summons to the Authorities at The Centre, and those diggers never returned.

***

Miriam looked out her kitchen window, searching for Lucy. Where was that child?

"Lucy!" she called, striding onto the deck. The garden looked terrible in the summer drought: full of bare dirt patches, weeds and insects everywhere. A perfect match for the falling-down house they'd rented from the old farmer.

"Lucy, it's time for lunch."

She spotted her daughter's white blouse in the field beyond the garden. What was she doing? Digging again. Endlessly digging for buried kingdoms and treasure. What an imagination Lucy had! Well, no help for that. There was so little for her to do out here on the plains, having no one to play with.

"Lucy!" She watched her daughter toss away her stick and trail back toward the house. Almost eleven years old. Old enough to be told, her husband had said.

Miriam folded her arms. *I don't care if the Bible says I must obey him in all things,* she thought. *For all intents and purposes, I am her real mother.*

Lucy climbed onto the deck. "Mom, it's so hot. I hate this global warming. Why can't the scientists do something about it?"

"Because the scientists are wrong. They don't understand that God made our world. Even this awful heat is His will. Now, wash your hands and come for lunch, like a good girl."

***

Lily rarely saw diggers her size, since children fared poorly in the tunnels. Many died because they did not get enough to eat. During the frequent rock falls and tunnel collapses, children were more likely to lose their lives. Often, when she and Maria picked their way through the aftermath of a catastrophe, she'd see small limbs protruding from the debris.

More disturbingly, she'd heard stories about guards taking young ones to the Supreme Ruler. In the dark, the other diggers whispered that those children simply disappeared. The guards had their way with them. Then ate them.

She asked Maria if this was true.

"Of course not," Maria replied. "If we uphold The Law, the Authorities take care of us. That is the social contract our ancestors made long ago. We work to support the Supreme Ruler and the Authorities—and they feed us and keep us safe."

Which really means we dig and dig for nothing, Lily thought. Their food consisted of chunks of matter heavily processed at The Centre. On rare occasions it tasted sweet, but other times it tasted foul and bitter. Her fears multiplied.

"Is there meat in the food?" *Children?* she wanted to ask.

"No, not for diggers like us," Maria replied. "Only the privileged eat meat. Meat keeps them strong so they can take care of us."

In other words, the Authorities and the guards ate meat. But so did the hunters who left the citadel to forage for food. At the rare gatherings with other diggers, Lily heard exciting tales about the hunters' exploits. Rumor had it they did not always bring back all the food they found, even the precious meat.

"That means the hunters are breaking The Law!" Lily whispered to Maria.

"The hunters must sample their takings," Maria said, hiding a smile. "To make sure that the food is fit for the Authorities."

"I want to be a hunter."

"That is not your rank. You are a digger. The Authorities decided this for you when you were born."

"Why? And don't just say they obeyed The Law. Who made The Law anyway?"

"The Goddess made The Law and everything in our world."

Lily thought this over. Every digger knew the Goddess made the world, and that She had created the Authorities in her own image. Of course, no one had any idea what the Goddess looked like, or the mechanism whereby She passed on Her word to The Authorities.

"What if the Goddess got it wrong?"

"Enough! No more questions."

Not understanding the reasons for what happened in the world made Lily feel stupid. She longed to go to school, but education of diggers was forbidden. Learning was reserved for the privileged. Maria reminded her yet again that their low status was an advantage: to be overlooked meant to be safe.

"Are hunters allowed to learn?" Lily persisted.

"Only enough to navigate the Outer World, so they can bring food home to our citadel."

Now, more than ever, Lily wanted to become a hunter.

***

Lucy fidgeted on her kitchen chair. Every day Mom made peanut butter sandwiches for lunch, to save money, so Dad could have steak for dinner. To keep his strength up, Mom said. Because he was the one who travelled to earn money for the family.

"Time for your lessons, dear." Miriam gathered up their dirty dishes, clearing the way for Lucy's textbooks.

"Why do I have to learn at home? Why can't I go to school like other children? And don't just say it's God's will."

Miriam sighed. Lucy was always so full of questions. "Your father and I decided to home-school you the day you came into our lives. Public schools don't follow God's word, so the children there just learn about sex and drugs. I know you're lonely, but out here we're safe. And you'll stay pure."

***

The Outer World where the hunters searched for food remained a tantalizing mystery for Lily. She knew it only as a breath of fresh air gusting through a tunnel or a beckoning light at the end of a long passageway. She yearned to see it for herself.

"You would not like it," Maria said, in response to her pestering. "The Outer World is full of perils. Most hunters eventually die there. And they die horribly. At least as diggers we are protected inside the Citadel."

Except for the constant landslides and falling rocks in the tunnels, Lily thought. And the earthquakes and floods, cataclysms launched from the Outer World without rhyme or reason. One very old digger claimed that long ago a meteor pulverized the citadel, resulting in a huge loss of life. Rebuilding their home had taken her entire lifetime.

If I were a hunter, I would not suffocate in the tunnels the next time a meteor hits, Lily thought.

She bided her time until she and Maria reached their most remote working site. Maria had always forbidden her to venture into the tunnel with the glowing, faraway circle of light; she alone cleared that area. Lily's duty was to watch for the inspection guards. But Maria was older now and, often as not, Lily would spot her taking a snooze at the far end. This time, when she heard the soft whistling of Maria's snores, she ran into the tunnel, stepped over her sleeping form and looked out through the opening.

The light almost blinded her, but a stream of pure, dust-free air rushed through her body. Her energy surged, despite her nagging hunger. And as her eyes adjusted, the Outer World appeared in bewildering array of colors. All her life, she had known only shades of black and brown, so she had no names for these.

She gazed down the earthen wall of the citadel. So this was how their home appeared to the Outer World! The slope looked steep, but negotiable for someone as young and agile as Lily.

Maria stirred beside her. She did not berate her, only gazed at her in sad silence. "I tried to protect you. Now it is too late."

"You never told me how beautiful the Outer World is," Lily said, drinking it in. "What is that color?" She pointed down at the flat plain that stretched to the horizon.

"That is green, the color of grass." And when Lily pointed upward. "That is the sky. Its color is called 'blue'."

"In the grass I see thousands of colored spots. Some are blue like the sky, but what are the names of the others? And the scents—this is what heaven, the home of the Goddess, must be like."

"Perhaps. The grass is our hunting ground. Those spots you see are called flowers. Some of them give us food."

"Oh, why did the Authorities not make me a hunter? Why do they want me to suffer?"

"To suffer is our lot in life as diggers," Maria said wearily. "Now come away from the lookout. Remember The Law."

***

The air felt so humid and still, real thunderstorm weather. Miriam spotted Lucy by the kitchen door. In her hand, the girl held her father's rusty old tool box, the one she called her explorer kit.

"You'll have to stay inside this afternoon, dear."

While her daughter sulked in front of the television, Miriam took the remote and switched to the weather channel. A tornado warning for their area popped up on the screen.

"I want to play outside. I want to go to the end of fields," Lucy said.

"I don't like you wandering off where I can't see you. And, believe me, there's nothing to see out there. Just more fields that look exactly like the one behind our garden."

"That's not true. I want to find the blown-down house."

Miriam's glance drifted to the kitchen window. She silently cursed their landlord, the old farmer, for filling Lucy's head with lurid stories. Especially the one about the tornado hitting the neighbors' farmhouse, killing the mother and her baby.

She shivered. Their house didn't have a tornado shelter or even a basement. But God wouldn't send another twister here, would He? He wouldn't take another family. He couldn't be that cruel.

She closed her eyes and reminded herself to have faith.

***

Returning to the lookout became as essential to Lily as breathing. She coaxed and pleaded with Maria to work in the remote passage.

The sky was not always blue during their visits. Sometimes it had glorious tones of red and pink—and the large golden circle that Maria called "the sun" did not burn her eyes. Other times, though, dull grey clouds shrouded its beauty and torrents of water poured down from above, thundering against the walls of the citadel.

"That is rain," Maria told her.

Lily had always associated water with floods and death, but in the Outer World, it meant life. The flowers smelled sweeter after the rain, and the grass of the plains glowed a deeper and lovelier green.

"How far do the plains reach?" she asked. "What lies beyond them?"

"No one knows," Maria replied. "Twice in my lifetime, the Authorities have dispatched the bravest and strongest of our hunters to explore the far reaches of the plains, but only a few returned. We cannot afford to waste precious resources on mere curiosity."

"But the hunters who returned, what did they find?"

Maria looked thoughtful. "Wondrous things. Strange flowers and beasts, caches of food, sometimes in huge abundance. Even other citadels, such as ours."

"Where? Where are these other citadels?"

"Far away at the end of the plains. Citadels can only exist where the soil is dry and the flowers edible. But even where conditions are perfect, there is no guarantee you will find intelligent life out there."

"Tell me about the beings in the other citadels. Do they look like us? Do they speak our language? Do they obey The Law?"

"My understanding is that all citadels in the world are organized much like ours. In some, I hear The Law is much harsher."

"Or perhaps their Law allows diggers to be free."

Maria's shrewd eyes took her in. "Don't even think about running away."

"What if I am? Perhaps in another citadel I could be a hunter."

"Get that ridiculous fairytale out of your head! Even if you survived the plains and found another citadel, you would always be a foreigner there. And, if you're unlucky, the other beings will tear you to pieces simply because your color is different from theirs. I saw this happen with my own eyes."

Lily knew Maria never lied to her. "Were you…were you one of the explorer hunters?"

"Yes, long ago. I returned badly wounded and could no longer search for food. The Authorities wanted to retire me, but the Supreme Ruler spared my life. So now I continue to serve our citadel, but as a lowly digger."

Lily had a chilling thought. "What happens when you get too old to be a digger?"

"I will be retired. That is the Law."

***

Clouds covered the sky. A few raindrops pattered into the dry earth of the garden. Miriam gave up on the weather channel and turned on the radio. She strained to hear the local weather report over the blare of Lucy's television show.

Frustrated, she marched back into the living room and turned off the TV.

"Mom, you said I could watch it!" Lucy protested. "It's *Cosmos*, my favorite show. Dr. Tyson is talking about life on other planets."

"Your father doesn't like you watching TV. Especially that science show. God made the world. Science just explains His rules."

"Well, if God made the world, why did He make it so hot? Why does he make tornados? Why did he let that family get killed?"

"Because it's His will. Be quiet now." She picked up the telephone receiver and called the old farmer.

"Don't look too bad," he said in reply to her worries about the tornado warning. "But you're welcome to use our storm shelter. Drive yourselves on over."

The kitchen door slammed behind her. She turned to see Lucy race outside with her explorer kit and disappear into the field behind the garden.

***

Lily dreaded the thought of Maria growing old. Though Maria could still shift her share of dirt and debris, she tired easily and her secret naps lasted much longer.

I will run away and take Maria with me, Lily thought. She was an explorer hunter. She will find us a friendly citadel. We have to escape, or we'll die as slaves.

She longed for the Outer World with an intensity that frightened her. She waited until Maria crept into a side tunnel for one of her lengthy naps, then raced back through the maze of passages to her beloved lookout.

I'll never have another chance, she thought, and leapt outside into the brightness.

She slid and tumbled down the sloping earth wall of the citadel to the edge of the flowers. Gathering her courage, she wandered into the grass, reveling in the splendor of the plains and the intoxicating colors and scents of the flowers. From time to time she spotted strange beasts among the plants, some larger, others smaller than she. None spoke her language. They uttered only strange clicks, buzzes or roars.

Suddenly she heard the tread of footsteps: a troop of hunters on the march. She hid in the tall grasses until they passed out of sight.

She had dallied too long. The light was fading. Inky black clouds were streaming over the beautiful blue of the sky.

Halfway up the sloping wall of the citadel, the rain hit, a bombardment of water that sent rivers snaking through the dirt. She scrambled for footing as the soil beneath her melted into lethal mud. Using the last of her strength, she hauled herself back into the safety of the lookout.

Maria was waiting for her. "All your life I have tried to protect you," she cried. "Don't you understand anything I have told you? When the guards discover what you've been up to, the Authorities will summon you to The Centre."

"I was careful. Nobody saw me."

"You think of no one but yourself. You are throwing your life away - and mine as well."

"I would never do anything to hurt you. And the Outer World isn't full of horror. All I found was beauty. None of the beasts there did me any harm."

"You were simply lucky."

"I felt far safer in the Outer World than I do here in the Citadel. Let's run away together. So what if we die? We'll die as free beings."

"Don't romanticize death. Look at yourself: the rains nearly finished you off. Was that so wonderful and full of beauty?"

"At least when the next meteor strikes, I won't be buried alive in rubble."

"You think so? A meteor can strike you down in the Outer World just as easily. And a meteor is nothing compared to a comet, a pillar of fire that burns you alive."

"Another fairytale!"

"A comet nearly killed me. Unbearable heat and light crashed down from the sky and struck our hunting troop. I watched my friends burn and shrivel into charred husks. I only escaped because I'd fallen behind them. All I could do was pray to the Goddess to save them."

"And She did nothing, of course." In the face of Maria's horrified expression, Lily went on: "I think The Authorities just made up The Law so they get to eat all the good food. They say there's a Goddess so we'll do what we're told."

"Then how do you explain the sun and the rain? Who made the plains, the beasts and the flowers, if not the Goddess? Who made us?"

"How can I answer that, when I'm not allowed to go to school? Believe in the Goddess if you like. I don't! The Goddess is just a fairy tale."

"Heresy!" cried a voice behind them. The deep, implacable voice of a guard.

In a heartbeat, they were surrounded and placed under arrest.

***

The weather had turned strange. Dark clouds loomed on the horizon, while the sun beat down hotter than ever. In the distance, Miriam heard the ominous rumble of thunder. She fiddled with the controls on the radio, searching for a signal. Suddenly all the lights went out.

She tried to phone the old farmer again, but heard only static on the line.

"Lucy!" Where had the girl gone?

Miriam grabbed her car keys and ran outside. Clouds were streaming across the sky. The first splats of rain hit her skin.

***

The guards dragged Lily and Maria down into the depths of citadel. The air grew ever more hot and stifling.

"I'm sorry," Lily told Maria, only to be silenced roughly by a guard. *I should have let myself be drowned in the rain,* she thought. *I would have died free, and Maria would be safe.*

She looked desperately up and down the passages, but saw no chance of escape. Other diggers scuttled away in fear. Maria trudged ahead of her, head bowed. Fear ate through her belly like acid.

The tunnels grew wider. They had reached the heart of the citadel.

The Hall of the Authorities stretched before them, an enormous cavern stacked with food and trophies from the Outer World. Bodies of diggers and children lined the walls.

"Attention!" cried one of the guards. "Bow down! Show your respect to the Authorities and the Supreme Ruler."

Twenty or more figures strolled into the hall, glossy from meat and a life without labor. They surrounded an enormous being, larger than any digger, hunter or guard Lily had ever seen.

"The Supreme Ruler will do you herself," said the guard beside her. "Hope she's quick about it for once. I'm starving."

So the stories about the missing children were true!

A clamor of shouts and screams echoed down the tunnels. Lily's first thought was the other diggers had come to witness their execution. In the next instant, a noise beyond all description crashed down the roof of the cavern and she was drowning in earth. All around her she heard muffled cries of "Meteor!"

She struggled, battling a flood of soil and rocks, calling for Maria. Ahead she saw light. Using her youthful strength and every skill she had learned as a digger, she fought her way toward it. Miraculously, she surfaced into the Outer World.

She didn't hesitate. She dashed into the grass of the plain heedless of the water left by the rain storm. A huge force crashed past her, knocking her down: the Supreme Ruler in full flight in a crowd of guards, hunters and diggers.

Lily took refuge in the flowers, hiding the same way she had eluded the hunters. A giant beam of light streaked down from the sky.

"Comet!" shrieked a fleeing digger.

The comet struck down the Supreme Ruler in mid-flight. She writhed in agony. Her limbs began to shrivel and, as Lily gazed on in horror, fire burst from her abdomen and consumed her.

Lily crouched in terror, watching the deadly comet strike down again and again, burning the fleeing inhabitants of the citadel.

Abruptly as it had appeared, the comet vanished. More meteors crashed down from the sky, crushing everything beneath them.

She prayed to the Goddess to stop the mad carnage.

"Don't punish the others. I was the one who broke The Law. Please don't let them die. Please save my mother."

Finally the meteors ceased. Rain began to fall, but Lily no longer cared. She wandered through the grasses, calling for Maria.

"Lily?" It was Maria's voice. She was limping toward her through the weeds, wounded but alive.

"Mother!" Lily rushed over to her. "You're safe! Thank the Goddess!"

"Yes, She looks after her children. After all, She made us."

Together they made their way into the safety of the plains.

***

"Lucy!"

Frantic now, Miriam searched through the field. Lucy wouldn't have searched out that ruined house on her own, would she?

Overhead, the winds were making a strange pattern, blowing across each other. "Oh, God, please help me!" she prayed.

There! A few feet to her right, she spotted a faint trail of smoke.

"Lucinda!" She rushed over and snatched the magnifying glass from her daughter's hand. "How many times have I told you? You could start a brush fire and kill us all!"

Lucy glared at her. Her jeans and runners were coated with dirt from kicking over the large ant hill beside her.

"What you are doing is cruel! Ants are God's creatures. They have a right to live, too."

"They're just bugs."

Lucy could be so mean sometimes, so eager to hurt things smaller than she was. We know so little about her birth parents, Miriam thought. What if it's bad blood coming to the surface?

She grabbed Lucy's hand and pulled her back toward the house.

"My explorer kit! You forgot my explorer kit."

"Leave it!"

The winds hit them full force when they reached the deck. Miriam dragged Lucy over to the car which sat parked in front of the house.

She heaved Lucy into the passenger seat. The wind tore at her clothes as she struggled to climb in behind the steering wheel. She started the engine and pulled onto the highway, heading for the old farmer's place ten miles down the road.

"We must pray now, Lucy. Pray to God to save us."

Lucy's pale face stared at her. "Is that a tornado, Mom?"

Behind them, to the west, an ominous funnel cloud was taking shape. Miriam pressed the accelerator to the floor, praying her car would go faster.

"Don't worry, Lucy. God will save us. He looks after His children. After all, He made us."

M. H. Callway is the pen name of award-winning author Madeleine Harris-Callway.

Her short stories have been published in several crime fiction anthologies and magazines. Her debut novel, *Windigo Fire*, was published by Seraphim Editions in September 2014.

She and her husband, Ed, share their Victorian home with a sweet, elderly cat.

Visit Madeleine at
www.mesdamesofmayhem.com
Or on Facebook.

An Inexpensive Piece

C.A. Rowland

Editor's Note: Author C.A. Rowland explores a troubling look into the human psyche in this creepy, wonderful and strangely touching tale of one man's deep but misguided affection.

Sam leaned back in his chair and watched Jacqui approach. He liked the gentle sway of her hips and the way her long brown hair fluttered in the slight breeze.

He'd been six when his mother had died in the tornado that ripped away everything he knew and loved, but he'd never forgotten how she moved. It was one of the first things he noticed in a woman. That, and whether she wore simple or gaudy jewelry. He could tell a lot from a woman's choice. He always kept track of those little things.

As he observed Jacqui, he could see she was thinking about something. Normally she'd sense his scrutiny and her walk would become a bit more self-conscious. Today, she was distracted. He sighed.

Bouncing between foster homes, he'd learned a lot about women. There were the do-gooders–always trying to take care of him and be his mom. They couldn't replace his mother, and didn't seem to understand why he kept them at a distance until he'd had time to develop trust that they would stay.

Then there were the ones who were in the foster-care program for the state money and had no real interest in getting to know him.

As he got older, he found the women he dated fell into two slightly different camps. The first were the whores. Women who wanted someone to buy them dinner and nice things–and were willing to engage in sex in return. The second were the wanna-be wives. They longed for a relationship. They were willing to have sex after a few dates, if they thought things would develop further.

Jacqui fell into the second camp, and he had high hopes she might be the one for him.

As Jacqui drew near to the table, Sam stood and kissed her cheek. She gasped as he revealed the yellow rose in his left hand.

***

Jacqui hesitated to raise the subject during the meal. Sam bringing her a yellow rose was so romantic. Surely he cared for her, since he remembered details, like how much she loved roses, and especially the yellow ones. Maybe it wasn't too soon. She glanced up at his face—not classically handsome, but his boyish charm drew her. She took a deep breath, gathering her courage.

Sam took the last bite of his pie as Jacqui said, "We need to talk." She watched him choke his mouthful down.

"What's wrong?"

"Nothing's wrong. We started dating three months ago. I just thought we should talk about seeing each other exclusively."

"Whoa, babe. I told you when we met that I only wanted to date—nothing serious."

Jacqui's shoulders dropped. "I know, but you also said you were open to something more with the right woman."

"Sweetie, I like you but I'm not ready for anything close to permanent. I like things as they are."

"Well, you knew I wanted something more than dating. Are we even headed that way?"

Sam stared at her silently.

"Aren't you going to say anything?" Jacqui asked. "Guess I got my answer. You can get the check." Gathering her things, she made for the exit.

Sam didn't try to stop her.

***

Jacqui stared at the blank screen and willed the machine to remain dark. She wondered again if she should have listened to Sheila. Perhaps she'd pushed Sam too soon. She'd thought he would call her after the lunch, but he never did. They'd had such wonderful long conversations. She didn't understand why he didn't want to get closer.

Jacqui thought about calling him, but decided if she truly wanted a long term relationship, he needed to be the one to reach out. Now she wondered whether he'd ever taken her seriously. She looked back at the screen.

Jacqui would never forget her first conversation with Sheila—no matter what happened tonight.

She thought back to an earlier lunch, when she'd met Sam at a little outdoor café in Fredericksburg. She loved living thirty miles south of Washington, D.C. Close enough to take in all the cultural events in the metropolitan city, but far enough so the pace was slower and more relaxed. The weather had been warm and she'd worn her favorite chiffon flowered skirt.

Sam had slipped away from work for an hour. He had a demanding job at the bank—she wasn't sure what his title was exactly, only that he worked long hours.

"Great legs, babe. You should wear short skirts more often," Sam said.

After kissing Sam goodbye, Jacqui walked to the antique store to browse. The woman who struck up the conversation had seemed so nice, commenting on a vintage cut glass pitcher.

"I'm Sheila. Do you shop here often?"

"No. I was having lunch nearby."

"I think I saw you—weren't you at the café with Sam?"

"Do you know Sam?"

"Yeah. I dated him for a while. How long have you been dating him?"

Jacqui paused and stared at the woman. "About three months," she said. "Did you follow me here?"

"I did," Sheila admitted. "I know this will sound like I'm a bitter ex-girlfriend, or something worse, but I wanted to warn you. And ask if you will help me."

Jacqui's mouth dropped open.

"I don't understand."

"Sam and I dated for six months. I wanted to get more serious, but he just wanted to date. Sound familiar?"

Jacqui hated to admit it, but she'd been wondering lately whether her relationship with Sam was headed to the next level. She shook her head.

"We broke up," Sheila continued, "shortly after our conversation about a more permanent arrangement. A week later I discovered a necklace given to me by my late husband, Danny, was missing. I know, you're thinking I misplaced it. I didn't. The necklace is only worth a hundred dollars. We bought it in Hawaii when we got engaged, so it holds a lot of sentimental value for me."

"I still don't understand what this has to do with me," Jacqui said.

"Have you asked Sam whether he intends to get more serious?" Sheila asked.

"Not yet."

"But you're going to, aren't you? I can see it written on your face. That's what I wanted to warn you about." Sheila let her words sink in. "I met Sam at the gym. A class instructor introduced us. After our relationship ended, I was talking with the instructor one day and mentioned our breakup to her. She told me she had also dated Sam, long before I had, and a piece of her costume jewelry went missing after they broke up. She thought maybe she'd lost hers, and hoped it would turn up. It never did. Since hers was also inexpensive, she never reported the loss. Just like me."

"Are you saying Sam is a thief?"

"I don't know for sure, but it's quite a coincidence, don't you think? She broke up with Sam, and lost a piece of jewelry. I broke up with him, and my necklace went missing."

"Sure, but couldn't a housekeeper have taken it? Or you might have just lost it."

Sheila shook her head. "No. I used to hold the necklace every day. I know when it went missing. It was always in the same place in my jewelry case."

"Did you report the theft to the police?" Jacqui asked.

"Yes, but they're busy with 'real crimes'. Like I said, the necklace wasn't worth a lot in money. They said the same thing you did. If I hadn't talked to my friend, I wouldn't have suspected Sam. But I don't have any proof."

"I don't know why you're telling me this. Sam and I are fine. None of my jewelry is missing."

"It won't be. Not until you break up."

"Are you suggesting I break up with a perfectly good guy, just to prove your theory? I'm not willing to do that."

"No. What I'm asking is that you let me know when you're ready to press Sam to solidify your relationship. If he agrees, then I'll wish you the best. If he doesn't, and if you quit dating, I'd like to find out whether we can prove he's a thief."

"Or maybe he's not," Jacqui said.

"A possibility."

"I'll have to think about what you've told me," Jacqui said.

"Here's my card. If you decide to help me, I'll arrange everything. Although you might owe me lunch, if it turns out I'm right."

Jacqui wasn't sure what "everything" meant. She knew only that she wanted to escape from the woman. She walked away, thinking she'd never call Sheila.

She shook her head and checked the screen again. None of this made any sense. She'd never imagined she would be sitting in front of a monitor connected to a camera in her bedroom. The lens was hidden and was pointed directly at her jewelry box, which sat on her dresser.

Sheila's friend, Eddie, had assembled the equipment. Apparently he was a wiz at this sort of thing. The camera relied on a motion sensor, and recorded anything that moved. The system had been installed two days after Jacqui's awful conversation with Sam, when she'd realized he wasn't likely to call.

Jacqui participated in a Zumba class on Thursday nights. Sam knew her schedule, and she'd left her car in the YMCA parking lot, in case he checked.

Jacqui had to change her clothes in the bathroom if she didn't want the camera to catch her naked. She felt violated by the intrusion, by being restricted in her own home. She wondered again whether she was doing the right thing.

Years earlier, her apartment had been broken into by a group of kids. They'd taken some money and rummaged through her drawers. She'd felt unclean and unsafe for weeks afterwards. She hated feeling vulnerable, and if Sam was going to take something of hers, she wanted him caught.

Now they waited–Sheila, Jacquie and Eddie.

Jacqui jumped as her cell phone buzzed. She read the message: Alarm has been triggered at your address. Please call ABC Security.

Her attention was drawn to the computer screen, which had come to life.

Crap, Jacqui thought. *Sheila was right, and that asshole is gonna take something of mine. How could I have been so stupid as to let him into my home and life?* She looked up to find Sheila and Eddie's gazes moving between her and the screen.

"He's there," Jacqui said.

Movement on the screen. It was still dark, but there was just enough light from a lamp Jacqui had left on to make out a male form.

Turn around, Jacqui willed. *We want to see your face.*

The camera was angled down from a bookshelf, so there was a good shot of the jewelry case and the space above it. But since it keyed off movement, it hadn't captured the face of the burglar. If he didn't turn, they'd know what was taken, but would have no proof it was Sam.

Jacqui turned to Sheila. "What if he doesn't face the camera?"

"I don't know–any ideas?"

Jacqui dialed the number for the security company.

"I just received your text message. No, I don't have a pet that could trigger the alarm...I just broke up with my boyfriend...No, I don't think he'd be there...He's not supposed to be there...Please call the police to check on my house."

Jacqui hung up. "I'd love to confront him, but I'm not sure we can make it there quickly enough. Has he shown his face?"

"Not yet," Eddie said.

***

Sam lifted the catch on the jewelry box and carefully pushed open the lid. He loved the fact that each piece had lain next to Jacqui's skin. Why didn't they invent jewelry that retained the warmth of a woman's body?

Jacqui had been his twenty-first girlfriend. The number had always been lucky for him. He'd been sure she was "the one". He'd even allowed himself to hope they could plan a future together, but then she'd pushed things.

Didn't she realize that by doing so she'd emasculated him? He couldn't live with that.

Oh, well, it didn't matter. His perfect match was out there somewhere. For now, he would choose a piece to remind him of Jacqui.

He rummaged through the jewelry, much as he'd done with the rubble after the tornado, except this time he wore gloves. He'd been in Jacqui's bedroom before, but he wasn't taking any chances of leaving fingerprints.

A pearl necklace—too expensive and old fashioned—discarded. A rope of handmade beads—too ordinary and specific to Mexico—set aside. His fingers pushed the earrings and pendants from side to side. The case was disorganized, in the same way Jacqui was somewhat flighty.

He focused on a dull gold point that peeked up from one corner of the box. Gently, he cleared the area and brought forward a heart pendant on a simple necklace. The short gold strand rested in his hand, curled, and he could see she hadn't worn it in a while. His finger caressed its surface, relishing in the carved heart that mirrored the shape.

Perfect. Simple, inexpensive, and unlikely to be missed. He pocketed the necklace, taking one last swipe at the others to make sure he had chosen the right remembrance. He closed the lid, leaving everything as he had found it.

The necklace would be a welcome addition to his collection. He couldn't wait to see them all spread out, as he recalled each woman they represented.

He'd never told anyone how much it meant to him, finding something of his mother's amongst the bits of torn fabric, rocks and trash. He didn't consciously realize that he did the same with each ex-girlfriend—scouted for an inexpensive piece, the perfect remembrance.

He heard a door slam. He'd stayed too long.

***

They continued to stare at the monitor for a moment. The thief didn't seem to be worried about time. Jacqui watched him fondling a necklace with a pearl setting. A lovely piece she'd picked up as a souvenir during a trip to Santa Fe. She hated to lose the necklace, even though she didn't wear it often.

"I can't stand this. I want to be there," Jacqui said. "If they catch him, I want to make sure he doesn't talk his way out of this."

"I'll drive you," Sheila said. "Eddie, would you please stay here? Call us if you see anything helpful."

Ten minutes later, the women turned onto Jacqui's street and saw a police car parked in front of the house. As soon as they rolled to a stop, Jacqui was out and running.

"Ma'am, stop right there. You can't come any closer."

"That's my house. I received a call from the alarm company. Was someone inside? Did you catch him? Did he take anything?"

After confirming her name and that she owned the house, the policeman escorted Jacqui over to where another officer was talking to someone. Jacqui swung her head this way and that, trying to see who the man was.

As she approached, he looked at her.

Sam.

"Jacqui, I'm so glad to see you. I'm sure we can clear this up now," Sam said.

The second officer turned. "Is this man your boyfriend? He says he left something in your house and came back to retrieve it."

"We broke up earlier this week. He has no reason to be in my house," Jacqui said.

"I thought I'd left one of my shirts. When you weren't here, I didn't think you'd mind if I used your spare key," Sam said.

"You didn't leave anything behind. And you know full well I have Zumba class on Thursday nights."

The officer assessed Sam.

To Jacqui, he said, "We'll need you to check your house to see if anything is missing. And we'll need you to make a statement at the station. Can you come down?"

"Absolutely," Jacqui agreed. "I'll check my house. I don't have a lot of expensive things, but I do have some jewelry. Will you search him?"

"Yes, ma'am. We'll do that at the station."

Jacqui watched as the officers put Sam into the squad car. She pinched her arms to keep from reaching out to him when she saw the sad look of bewilderment on his face.

***

Jacqui and Sheila finished their lunch at the café.

"Have you heard anything about the case? Is there a trial date yet?" Sheila asked.

"No trial date. I heard from the D.A. and Sam has agreed to a plea bargain. So there's a hearing, but that's all. After they found the necklace, I reminded them about you and your friend. They searched Sam's apartment. They found a stash of jewelry. Once you and Cathy identified the pieces he stole from you, the matter was pretty much settled. Not to mention the video we made, which sealed his fate."

"I'll be glad when this is over and I can have my necklace back," Sheila said. "I miss the comfort of having it near me to hold. Always makes me feel closer to Danny. You know, if Sam had picked anything else, I'm not sure I would have ever approached you."

"I know. He took the necklace my mother gave me for my seventh birthday. I would have hated to lose it. I have other things of hers, but that one has always been special. I hope, one day, to have a daughter to pass it on to. Oh, well, are you finished? Wanna check out the antique store for new items?"

"Sure," Sheila said. "You getting the check?"

C. A. Rowland is an author, lawyer, speaker and teacher. She is currently working on short stories and a humorous mystery novel set in Savannah, Georgia. She's a member of Sisters In Crime, Society of Children's Book Writers and Illustrators and Virginia Writer's Club, Inc. Her short story, "The Gift", was a semi-finalist in the Bethlehem Writers Roundtable 2014 Short Story Contest.

A Locked Room Puzzle

Anne Barton

Editor's Note: Author Anne Barton brings us a mystery for the ages, made new and fresh by a master storyteller.

It was a lavish affair at the University's Faculty Club, a celebration for the country's leading forensic expert; an honorary degree and now a prize worth megabucks, which he'd donated to the forensic lab he had founded. When interviewed by the media, he was asked, "What was your most interesting case?"

"I've had many fascinating cases. You've been told of several of them in the address given by the president. Those have been widely reported in the media, so you know all about them. But the one I think would have been the most interesting was one I never got to work on."

"What was that?"

"It was a locked room puzzle that will be discussed as one of the most baffling of unsolved crimes—if indeed it was a crime—of all time."

"Why haven't we ever heard about it?"

"Oh, you have. But it is rarely thought of as a crime, and may not have been, but is still an intriguing unsolved puzzle."

"Do many people know about this?"

"Oh, yes."

"What was so mysterious about it?"

"It was something that couldn't have happened, but did."

"If so many people are aware of it, has anyone done anything to solve it?"

"Many theories have been offered, but most people merely go along with the standard line, which, by the way, was not the official explanation."

"Why not?"

"It was something the authorities, who had condemned the man, did not want to believe."

"Why?"

"Because they were afraid of what might be done by people who followed that line of reasoning."

"Okay. Let's end the suspense. Tell us about it."

"Very well. It occurred in another country, one with different ways of dealing with crime, where forensics was virtually unknown. It was never solved.

"The leader of a group that was considered a danger to the government was betrayed by one of his followers and executed, after only the most summary of trials. The authorities feared that if his followers got hold of his body, they would use it for propaganda. The room in which it was placed was guarded day and night by armed soldiers. But, in spite of the guards, two days later it was discovered the body had disappeared.

"The soldiers were accused of having gotten drunk, which they denied. And, in fact, they seemed sober and were not suffering from hangovers. The authorities then accused them of taking bribes from the man's followers. They denied this with equal vehemence. There must have been several changes of the guard over a two-day period, but none of the soldiers could be incriminated in any bribery scheme. But it was reasoned that dead bodies don't just disappear into thin air. Someone had to get into the room and remove the body.

"Furthermore, the locked door was found to have been unlocked, though it was definitely ascertained that it had been tightly secured when the body was put into the room. How could that have been done while the soldiers were on guard? There were two of them, right there by the door, all the time. Could they have just fallen asleep while on duty in the wee small hours of the night? But for both of the men on duty to do so at the same time was unlikely, and the commotion of opening the door and removing the body would surely have wakened them."

"Was there another way out of the room?"

"None. It was virtually airtight. There was only one door and there were no windows. The walls were made of solid stone."

"Did his followers have his body?"

"The man's followers did not, in fact, use his dead body for propaganda, and nothing is known of its whereabouts. Instead, they claimed that he was still alive and spending time among them! Very few people claimed to have seen him, and none of the authorities who had condemned him ever laid eyes on him. Yet his followers claimed that he had been seen by many of them, had eaten with them, and had given them instructions on how to carry on their work.

The authorities vehemently denied that he was alive, yet they couldn't produce his body or explain where it had gone. It was never found. The man's followers grew in number, eventually becoming more powerful than his oppressors."

"You say the case was never solved?"

"Never!"

"What would you have done, if you'd been in charge of the investigation?"

"I would have thrown the entire range of forensic science into this problem."

"You say you never had a chance to do so?"

"That's right."

"Why was that?"

"It was a matter of timing."

"Timing? How so?"

"I came along about two thousand years too late!"

Danger by Moonlight
Anne Barton

Editor's Note: A moonlight ride turns into a night of terror for two young boys in Anne Barton's taught and frightening tale.

"Hey, Derek, wanna go for a ride in the moonlight?" Chad asked.

"Sure! Sounds great."

Derek's parents were going to pick up Chad's and the two couples would drive into town to attend the Saturday night dance at the community hall, leaving the boys behind.

Derek was supposed to stay home and go to bed at a decent hour, but the prospect of getting out from under the parental thumb for once appealed to the 14-year-old. Derek's parents were a bit dubious about letting him hang out with Chad, a cunning thirteen-year-old who had urged Derek to try chewing tobacco, and who knew more than he should about things like sex. But out here on their farms, miles from town, Chad Monk was the only other person near Derek's age, and it was natural they should pal around together when they got a chance.

There was another reason for Derek's eagerness for saddling up his horse and going for a ride in the moonlight. The previous night, its bright glow had kept him awake, and he sat in the window of his loft bedroom looking out over the meadow, bathed in brilliant light of the nearly full moon. He had watched the cattle settle down for the night, a group of deer graze across the meadow, heard the owl with its plaintive hoot, and saw a coyote stalk one of the fawns before the deer sensed its presence and dashed away.

Sleepy, he had been about to end his vigil and climb into bed, when he heard the clop of horses' hooves and the jingle of bits. He watched Chad's older brother, Conner, returning home with his pack string along the road that branched off at a T-junction about a hundred yards up the one that went by Derek's home. They stirred up dust from the unpaved road forming a low cloud that obscured the horses' feet and making them look as if they were gliding on air.

Derek could recognize Conner by his typical slouch in the saddle, riding his dark chestnut horse, leading another saddle horse and two packhorses. The last horse in the string was a pinto, and its white rump shone in the moonlight. They clattered across the wooden bridge over the creek, now appearing to have feet like they should, breaking the spell. Derek stretched, yawned and headed for bed.

The memory was sufficient in itself to make a moonlight ride seem attractive.

Chad rode up while Derek was still saddling his horse. He swung a leg over his saddle horn, relaxing in the saddle, and bit off a chunk of chewing tobacco. "Hey! I know where there's pot being grown. I followed Con one day and found out where he got it. Cummon. I'll show you."

Derek was startled. He'd never had any contact with pot, had never thought about it, though he'd heard of the stuff.

"No. I don't want to do that! It's not right."

"Oh, don't worry. We're not going to get any. I just thought you'd like to know."

"Know what?"

"Where it's at! Then you never have to find someone to supply it to you. I know those guys who grow it, but they don't know I know. Con doesn't let me have any." This latter sounded like a grievance. "Let's go look."

But when they got near the place, Chad's mood had changed. "Let's tie our horses up here and sneak down there. I don't see no one around."

They cut across a ridge that separated the valley from the canyon of the creek where it came down out of the mountains. Derek wasn't sure where they were, but Chad seemed to know every game trail. They were following an old, unused logging road, grown over with brush.

When they came out above the site where Chad said the pot was grown, Derek recognized the curve of the creek away from the road, and the cabin at the upper end of a brushy meadow. He knew that two men who professed to be working a mining claim lived there.

The boys looked down from a steep hillside, traversed by the old logging road. The ridge where they stopped their horses was bathed in moonlight, but the canyon floor was as dark as the bottom of a well. Only vague outlines of the creek and the gravel road that ran along the near side of the meadow were visible.

"They grow it down there on that flat. The brush hides it."

"Do they do any mining? It's a claim, isn't it?"

Chad gave a snort. "Mining, hell! There's no gold here. Cummon."

They tied their horses among some trees and made their way down the old logging road on foot. They could see the cabin at the upper end of the flat, its door open, spilling out light, with two men sitting on the doorstep drinking beer. The sound of voices came to them, but they couldn't make out the words.

"They can't see us once we get down on the road. Cummon." The main road up the canyon followed the near slope of the hill, the meadow being on the other side.

The two boys slid down the bank above the road and ran across it to a grove of trees. They could no longer see nor hear the men at the cabin, but there was no indication that their nocturnal adventure had been spotted. Chad led the way along the edge of the grove until an expanse of grass separated it from the thick brush that covered most of the flat.

The grove of trees they had been moving through was still in shadow, but the moonlight now touched the valley floor. Chad signaled Derek to follow him across the open space, as bright as day in the light of the full moon. On the edge of the brush, Chad crouched and motioned Derek to do the same.

"There'll be some brush to hide the plants, but there should be some right in there."

"Chad, let's go back. I don't like this."

"Hey! Don't chicken out. No one's seen us."

"No! Let's go back."

"Tell you what. I'll just go nip a piece off the first plant I see, then we'll go. Can't go back empty-handed." He chuckled. He was obviously getting a kick out of the danger. Derek was petrified.

Chad crawled into the brush and was gone for a long minute. Suddenly there were shouts from the cabin and Chad scrambled out of the brush. "I tripped on a wire. Let's get out of here."

Not thinking of anything but speed, the boys made a mad dash for the road. Derek's longer legs put him in front and as he ran, he looked over his shoulder toward the cabin. Suddenly the ground gave way under him and he pitched headlong into a pit. Chad fell in on top of him.

They stood up. They were in a chest-high rectangular hole dug in the ground, mounds of dirt on either side, a shovel stuck into one of them. The bottom was soggy and made a sucking sound when their boots were pulled out of the mud. They rushed for the open end nearest the road, but the soft earth gave way beneath their boots as they tried to climb out. They fell back, panting.

"I'll boost you out, then you pull me."

Derek lifted Chad and gave him a shove upward to where the smaller boy could get hold of a bush and pull himself out. He turned and reached a hand down to Derek, who succeeded in scrambling over the lip of the hole. Then they ran.

Across the open, moonlit road, up the bank and onto the old logging road they had come down. There was brush along it and they threw themselves down flat, peeking over the top to see what was happening. Derek had been vaguely aware of the two men shouting to each other. Now he could tell that they had come down the meadow, one on either side, searching.

As they watched, the man on the far side started back to the cabin, but the one on the road below was too close for comfort. They dared not move. Then they heard him call out, and they got to their hands and knees and scurried up the old road, heading for better cover and for the horses.

Suddenly a light brighter than the moon flashed across the meadow.

"They have a spotlight on their truck," Chad exclaimed.

The spotlight covered the flat systematically, from one side to the other. Derek thought they should probably get a move on while the men down below were watching the brightly lit area, but the thought came too late. The light swung onto the road and then onto the hillside. It swept across them and moved away.

They started crawling on their bellies, but moving even faster than when they had been on hands and knees. When they reached the shelter of some denser brush they paused. The light swept past again, higher up.

"I hope they can't see the horses," Derek breathed.

"I hope the horses don't spook."

The searchers had apparently given up on the hillside and the boys got to their feet and ran, crouching, to where they had left the horses.

"We'll have to lead them over the hill," Chad whispered. "If your horse sounds like he might snort or whinny, hold your hand over his nostrils."

Derek had a different concern. He remembered how the pinto horse's white rump had shone in the moonlight and was afraid that if the spotlight shone on his horse's white blaze it would be clearly visible. He tried to hold his horse so that its head was turned away from the source of the light. The pickup had moved down the road and was traversing the area with its spotlight again.

Once they were over the top of the first low ridge, they swung into their saddles and turned down a faint game trail.

"We'll have to keep it to a slow trot until we're out of hearing," Chad murmured. "They can hear horses galloping."

"I hope you know the way."

Chad's laugh was a bit shrill. "Don't worry. We're in the clear now."

When they were certain they had put enough ground between themselves and the searching men, they hurried their gait, going at a fast trot or canter, depending on the terrain. The sure-footed ponies seemed to have no trouble seeing, in even the dark patches. They topped the final rise overlooking the valley and their homes. Here they stopped to see if it was safe to go farther.

"They're probably out on the road now, looking for us," Chad whispered.

They saw no light or movement, so keeping to the treed areas they worked their way down toward the road. The last few yards would be over open, moonlit hillside. Chad called a halt while they were in the last shady cover above the open space. Nothing seemed to be moving.

"Cummon," Chad motioned to Derek.

But just as the boys were about to step out into the open, Derek hissed, "Wait! Listen!" They heard the faint hum of a motor. Hastily, they backed their horses deep into the trees. Below, on the road, a black pickup truck rolled slowly by, its lights off.

"If they go on down the road, we can get to that next patch of shade," Derek said softly. He saw Chad nod.

They watched the truck ease around a curve in the road and disappear.

"Let's go!"

The boys dug their heels into their horses' sides, making for the shade of a huge cottonwood alongside the road. Derek doubted it would hide them if the truck came back. And at any time, the men in the truck might shine their bright spotlight into the shady spots along the road. But for now the truck was out of sight.

The boys looked at each other, doubt still holding them back. Then Chad grinned and barked, "Let's go before they come back." He shot out of the shade of the tree onto the road, with Derek right behind. They were near the T-junction. The truck had gone straight down the road past Derek's home.

They swung onto the other road, their horses at full gallop. They clattered over the wooden bridge, sounding, Derek thought, loud enough to wake the dead.

The boys wheeled the horses onto the Monk's driveway, rode past the house and right into the open barn. As they piled off the sweaty horses, Chad said, "Let's pull the saddles and turn them out in the corral with the others." They tugged at cinches, flung the saddles along the inner wall, and led their mounts by the bridles out to the corral, letting them loose on the far side of the other half-dozen sleepy horses.

Back in the barn, Chad grabbed his saddle and hung it by the stirrup on a peg on the wall. Derek looked for a peg on which to hang his saddle, but before he could, the sound of the truck came to them, close by.

"Get up here by the door!" Chad hissed. Derek flung the saddle down and ran for the end of the barn nearest the road. The boys flattened themselves in the shadow of the front wall, beside the open door of the barn.

The truck had stopped at the entrance to the farmyard. The boys hardly dared breathe. Then the brilliant spotlight flared up, illuminating the interior of the barn. Derek looked frantically back at the saddle lying in a heap on the floor. To him it looked as big as a boulder, a dead giveaway.

Slowly the light swung over to shine on the corral. The horses spooked at the sudden, brilliant light and crowded toward the rear of the corral. Would they see the sweat-stained backs of the horses the boys had been riding?

The spotlight made another traverse of the corral and barn, then switched off. But the truck did not move away. The boys stayed glued to the wall, wondering if the men would get out of the truck and come into the barn. Derek felt Chad inch slowly away. With an effort, he turned his head away from the dangerous mouth of the door to see what Chad was doing. He saw the boy grasp the handle of a pitchfork and ease it down off the wall. Not much of a weapon, if the men came in after them.

The motor sound deepened and began to move away. The boys stayed glued to the wall until the sound faded into the distance. There was no sound of anyone on foot near the house.

"Okay," Chad spoke softly. "Let's make a dash for the house."

"I've got to hang up my saddle. He moved back to where he had left it, trying to stay in shadow until he had to move out into the open to grab the saddle. Hastily, he hung it up.

"For Chrissake, hurry."

Derek scuttled back to their hiding place. They waited a few seconds, then when nothing happened, they made their dash to the house, going in the back door, which like most farm homes, was left unlocked. Without turning on any lights, they scrambled upstairs to a bedroom overlooking the road.

Chad moved to the window, but Derek grabbed him by the shirttail and pulled him down onto the floor. He had heard the truck approaching again. Now it was quite near. It stopped outside, but there was no spotlight this time. Saving their night vision, Derek thought, so they could see into the shadows. Would they see the sweaty horses this time?

After what seemed an age, the truck quietly rolled away, its sound muffled by that of another approaching vehicle, coming down into the valley from the direction of town.

"That's our truck," Derek exclaimed with relief. "I can tell by the sound."

The boys tumbled down the stairs, turning on lights as they went. The elder Monks were getting out of the truck. Derek dashed out of the house and dived into the back seat of his parents' truck.

"What are you doing over here?" Derek's mom asked.

"Oh, we went for a ride in the moonlight then came over here to play computer games," Derek answered casually.

"You were supposed to be in bed." But Derek could see that his mom was so sleepy, she didn't question his behavior further. His dad stifled a yawn. In the back seat, Derek was the one who didn't need sleep right now.

At the T-junction, Derek looked up the road in the direction the boys had come and saw the black pickup pulled over onto the side of the road, in the shade of the large cottonwood. The moon, swinging around to the south, now threw shadow over a portion of the road. His dad didn't even seem to notice it, but Derek ducked down out of sight.

As he got out at their house, the black truck drifted by. Derek was in plain sight and froze with fear, like an animal caught in the headlights of an oncoming car. But the truck rolled on down the road, and Derek realized that to be seen getting out of his parents' truck was probably the best thing that could have happened.

He scurried up the ladder to his loft bedroom and crept up to the window overlooking the road. Sure enough, the black truck ghosted by again, heading up the valley. He saw it stop at the T-junction for a long minute, then its headlights blazed forth and it rolled away at normal speed. Derek was still shaking when he climbed into bed.

***

It was Wednesday when the RCMP showed up. Derek was helping his dad split firewood. His mom was in the garden, but went out to greet the Mountie, a sergeant, who got out of the SUV they used for back-country work.

"Mrs. Taylor?"

"Yes. What's the matter?"

"We are looking for a missing person. A young man about 6 feet tall, slender, with long, blond hair and blue eyes. We are asking everyone who was in town over the weekend if they have seen anyone of this description. You were in town on Saturday, weren't you?"

"Yes. We went to town for groceries and stayed for the dance. But I don't remember seeing anyone of that description."

"He's a graduate student doing some environmental work. Conner Monk packed him into the mountains a week ago Monday, and brought him out again Friday afternoon. He apparently drove his car into town, then disappeared. The car is there but no one seems to have seen him in town."

"Well, he wasn't at the dance. I'm not sure I'd have noticed him anywhere else."

Derek and his dad had come up to the road.

"Mr. Taylor?"

"No. I don't remember anyone like that."

The Mountie looked at Derek, who shook his head.

"Derek wasn't with us in town."

"Have you seen any strangers around here?"

Three head shakes.

"Thanks for your time." The policeman started to walk back to his vehicle.

Derek faced an agony of decision. Should he mention the hole in the ground out in the meadow? When the boys were riding home that night after their adventure, Chad had said to him, "That's a grave, you know!" Derek had nodded his concurrence.

If he told about seeing it, he might have to explain the rest of the incident. He could put it over on his dad, who was easily fooled, but his mom was something else. Derek thought she could read his mind. But on the other hand, he could puff out his chest and brag about helping the police catch some bad guys. Pride won out.

"Wait!" Derek shouted. The policeman turned around, a quizzical look on his face. "I know where the body is buried."

"Derek!" his dad admonished. "He doesn't need to listen to any of your stories."

"But…"

"Go back to the house!"

The Mountie held up his hand. "No. Let's hear what the lad has to say."

"It's like this. Me and another kid went out for a ride in the moonlight Saturday night. He showed me a place where he says they grow pot. I dunno whether he knows what he's talking about, but he said that. We couldn't see any pot growing, but we did see a grave."

"Derek!"

"Go ahead, Derek," the policeman encouraged. "What made you think it was a grave?"

"Well, it was about that size and shape. I saw an empty grave in town once when we went to a funeral, and it looked about the same size. This one wasn't as deep, though."

"This was at night?"

"Yeah, but it was real light. There was a great big moon." That wasn't quite how he remembered it. They'd have seen it and wouldn't have fallen in if it had been out in the moonlight, but he wasn't about to admit that part.

"This was an empty grave?"

"Yeah. The shovel was still there."

Derek's mom then threw some cold water on the fanciful story. "But if this man left the area on Friday, even if this was a grave it couldn't be his."

"But that's just it!" Derek insisted. "Con didn't bring anyone out on Friday afternoon. I was sitting up looking out over the meadow on Friday night. It was real clear moonlight. That's why I wanted to go riding on Saturday night.

"Anyway, I saw Con coming home with his pack string, way late that night, and there wasn't anybody with him. He was leading the other saddle horse and his packhorses. I watched them for quite a while."

"Do you remember where this place was? Could you find it again?"

"Oh, sure! It's up the canyon where the land sort of levels out and the creek swings way wide out around a sort of brushy meadow. Two guys have a cabin at the upper end. They say it's a mining claim."

"Oh, that place!" Mrs. Taylor exclaimed. "That used to be my favorite fishing hole until those guys set up their cabin there. I took my Dad up there last summer when he came to visit. If you go way out where the creek bends around, it undercuts the bank and makes a deep hole. You can literally catch your limit in that one spot."

"But you quit going? Why?"

"When Dad and I were out there, one of those guys came down and told us to leave. He was wearing a gun and sort of had his thumbs hooked into the gun belt. We said we had a perfect right to fish there. We weren't interested in gold mining. He just stood there and watched us. It was sort of creepy, so we decided to go on down the creek and leave him alone."

"I don't know whether you realize how lucky you are to be alive," the policeman said. "Yes, we know that place, and Derek, yes they do grow pot there. Mrs. Taylor, if you and your father had stumbled onto any of their plants, you might be the ones in a grave up there."

"But neither Dad nor I would even know what marijuana looked like."

"The man who was watching you wouldn't have known that."

"Oh, my God!" She turned pale.

The Mountie turned to Derek. "Could you show us exactly where this hole in the ground was?"

"I think so."

"I'll take Derek with me. You folks can come also, if you want." Then seeing Mrs. Taylor's look of distress, he added gently, "It's perfectly safe. Those men have cleared out. I'll have some reinforcements out there, as well."

When they came to the meadow, Derek said, "It's near this end, not up by the cabin."

The Mountie drew his SUV off the road into the shade of a large pine tree. Derek's mom pulled up behind them. His dad had stayed at home, saying he had work to do and it was probably all a fancy daydream anyway. They got out.

"Now, can you show me where this hole was?"

"I think so, especially if I can go up on the hill. That's where we were."

"Okay, go on up."

Derek walked along the road for a ways, looking for the faint remains of a logging road, where they had made their way down, and where they had scrambled on their bellies back up. He spotted the area and pulled himself up the bank, hanging onto brush. It took him a lot longer to get up on the old logging road than it had done on Saturday night, when they'd had the devil on their tail. He stood up and looked back down toward the meadow.

Unable to spot the place where the grave must have been, he made his way up the faint road until he reached the clump of brush he remembered hiding behind. He looked down at the meadow, letting his eyes traverse the ground, trying to recognize some clear landmark. There was no sign of a grave.

I know it was there, because we fell into it, he told himself.

He moved back down, slowly, looking for the tracks he and Chad had made, climbing back up on the old road.

I wonder why they didn't look for our tracks instead of going up and down the road, he thought. He couldn't understand why the men who were looking for the boys had missed what seemed so obvious.

There it was!

From above, he could make out the oblong of disturbed earth, covered now by brush, which was beginning to wilt.

"Hey!" he called out. "It's right down there." He pointed. The sergeant moved up the road looking as he went. "A little farther. There! You're right opposite it."

Other policemen had arrived on the scene by that time, and Derek heard the sergeant giving orders. Two of the new men scrambled down from the road onto the brushy meadow and started moving away from the road at a right angle.

"A little to your left," Derek called. The men moved on. "You're about there."

A moment later, Derek saw them halt, move a few pieces of brush, and call back to the sergeant, "Yeah, there's a freshly filled in hole here all right. Better send some shovels down."

Derek sat on a rock, not willing to go near where the others stood and lose his grandstand view. The men dug away at the soft earth, sweating in the mid-day sun. Abruptly they stopped and began to brush dirt aside with their hands. One of them straightened up.

"Sarge, you'd better come down here."

The sergeant followed the trail the other men had made, stopping at the edge of the area that had been dug out. The two others continued to move dirt by hand.

Derek could see what looked like a leg, encased in blue jeans, the foot wearing a hiking boot. The men worked upward along the body. One started to uncover the head. The sergeant turned back to the road and walked to where Derek's mom was standing. Derek could hear his voice clearly.

"We owe it to your son! Actually this was not a graduate student gone missing. This man was one of ours, trying to get the low-down on this so-called mining claim. He has been shot in the back of the head."

Derek saw his mom grab hold of the door handle of the pickup to steady herself.

Suddenly Derek saw a movement out of the corner of his eye. Turning to look across the canyon to where the steep hill rose above the opposite side of the creek, he could see a man on horseback and recognized him as Con Monk.

Monk reined in his horse, studied the activity below and started to back his horse out of sight. He spun the horse around and trotted swiftly and silently back into the trees, just as the boys had done on Saturday night.

Derek had a sudden intense fear that Con might have seen him and known that he had been the one to rat to the police. He threw himself down the hillside and ran to the sergeant.

"Hey, I just saw Con Monk come down the hill over there. When he saw you, he turned his horse and rode away."

"Thanks, son!" The Mountie went to his SUV and could be seen giving orders over the radio.

There must be other police around nearby, Derek thought. The sergeant came back to where Derek and his mom were standing. He seemed to notice Derek's sudden fear.

"Mrs. Taylor, I think you should take Derek home now. It isn't going to be very pleasant here. We will be by later to get a statement from him. But we are really thankful for his powers of observation. We might never have found this grave."

Derek's mom nodded, still unable to speak. The two of them got into their pickup, and Mrs. Taylor carefully turned it around and started back down the canyon. When they had reached the big meadow valley, she found a spot and pulled over to the side of the road, shutting down the engine.

She turned to her son. The uncompromising expression on her face was one Derek knew very well. It was what Derek thought of as her dark look, and it boded no good to the boy.

"Now, young man. I think you have some explaining to do."

Anne Barton is a retired veterinarian and flight instructor. She has written eight mystery novels, one autobiographical book and numerous articles and short stories. Her short story was a co-winner of the Bloody Words contest in 2001 and is published in *Bloody Words, The Anthology*.

Born in Drumheller, Alberta, she grew up in Northern Idaho, returned to Canada, and now lives in the beautiful Okanagan Valley in British Columbia, where she is deeply involved with Habitat for Humanity and her Anglican Church work–that is, when she isn't riding horses or curling.

Leverage

Andrea Kikuchi

Editor's Note: Short, sweet and wonderfully vicious...Andrea Kikuchi delves into the mind of one disgruntled employee.

Mary discovered proof that Bill was having an affair.

Perfect. It was just the leverage she needed to save herself.

All through the morning, she'd watched people walk into Bill's office, and walk out a few minutes later, devastated because they'd been downsized. At least most of them were devastated, with the exception of a select few who'd been given generous severance packages.

Mary watched as her co-workers packed their belongings into Bankers' boxes, and were led to the door by security guards. Lives deeply altered, families let down, all for the sake of the bottom line.

"It's not going to be me," Mary said to herself. She had years of service to the company; time away from her husband and children, out of loyalty. Misguided loyalty to a company that believed it owed her nothing but an empty box and an escort to the door.

This was not going to happen to her.

She waited for her name to be called, fondling a photograph in her hand. She glanced at it from time to time.

After decades of being nice, it was her turn to be naughty.

Bill hung his head out from around the corner. At least he gave her the courtesy of calling her name, instead of having his secretary summon her. She slowly walked in and took a seat in the excessively large office, overlooking the ocean.

Bastard, she thought to herself. How could he keep all of this when people were losing their livelihoods?

"Mary, as you may know, we've been experiencing some financial constraints. Unfortunately, we can't keep everyone, and I know that you have a number of years of service here."

Mary's mind wandered. She heard only bits and pieces of what Bill was saying, "Hard work hasn't gone unnoticed, blaa, blaa, blaa...."

It wasn't until he said, "We have to let you go," that she started paying attention.

"Interesting," she said.

"Interesting?"

Mary placed the picture on his desk. It showed Bill and Judy, one of the accountants, at the staff Christmas party. There wasn't any mistletoe in the picture, but he and Judy were being extremely festive.

"Interesting," she repeated.

Bill was mortified, "Where did you get this?"

"Doesn't matter."

"What do you mean it doesn't matter?"

"Where I found this doesn't matter. What it *means* is what matters. It means I'm not going anywhere, Bill.

"In fact, I really like the view from this office."

Andrea Kikuchi lives in Saint John, New Brunswick, with her husband and two children. Her stories have been published by the *Tokyo Notice Board*, *Broken Jaw Press*, and most recently *Hard Times in the Maritimes*. She teaches creative writing classes and is the co-chair of the Fog Lit Readers and Writers Festival in Saint John.

Learn more about Andrea at her Blogsite:
http://andreakikuchi.wordpress.com/
and at her Facebook Page

Potluck
Lynne Murphy

Editor's Note: With her characteristic wit and delicious humor, Lynne Murphy offers a "treat" that is sure to delight readers, especially those who are young at heart.

When tiny plants started showing up in the flower pots at Golden Elders Condo one spring, everyone was intrigued. What could they be? Bessie Bottomley provided the compost for the pots and she didn't recognize the seedlings.

Bessie was known as the Worm Lady of Golden Elders. She collected fruit and vegetable scraps from her neighbors, fed them to the worms that she kept in containers on her balcony and gave back the rich compost the worms produced. She knew the seedlings weren't tomato plants because she refused to take any bits of tomato. Those seeds passed through the worms unscathed, sprouted in planters and annoyed people.

The strange little plants were the main topic of conversation when several ladies gathered for coffee on Bessie's balcony one June morning.

"They look a bit like tiny shefflera," Bessie's friend Charlotte said. "But I've never grown shefflera from seed so I'm not sure what the seedlings look like."

"It might be a kind of cleome. All those leaves around the central stem," said Olive, another of the experienced gardeners. "I think we should just wait and see what they turn into. There are so many of them growing in all our pots. Maybe we could plant a nice border of cleome along the walls."

The talk turned to Maisie, who was at her physio appointment. Maisie had been suffering from terrible pain in her shoulder, which made it impossible for her to play cards. Since Maisie played euchre or bridge (badly) at least four evenings a week, the problem was curtailing her social life.

"The doctor told her it was deterioration of the spine that was causing the pain," Bessie explained. "There isn't anything they can do about it except strengthen the muscles with physio. That will help her move her arms a bit better."

The ladies all shivered at the thought of what might lie ahead for them and went on to more cheerful topics. The tiny plants continued to grow, unmolested.

***

It was the more worldly-wise Isobel who enlightened her friends.

"Lord tunderin' Jasus girl," she said, after examining the planters on Charlotte's balcony a few weeks later. She was not a gardener herself, so she hadn't used any of the compost. "That's marijuana. You girls are growing pot in your pots."

"Marijuana?" Charlotte said. "Oh, my goodness. That's against the law. I'll have to pull it right out. And tell the others to get rid of their plants. I wonder how many people in the condo are using this batch of Bessie's compost."

"Now, hold your horses, Charlotte. This could be a good thing. Let me think about it."

"But what if the police find out?"

"The cops are not going to come inspecting planters in a seniors' condo, unless somebody calls them. Remember how long we've been selling liquor at parties without a permit, and no one's ever caught us? 'Cause no inspectors ever think we might be breaking the law in a place like this."

"Well, we only charge two dollars a shot," Charlotte said. "But I won't pull the plants up till we tell Bessie. Since they came from her compost."

Isobel called 'round to the nucleus of the Sisterhood and asked them to come for coffee the next morning. Maisie was the first to arrive, hunched in on herself with pain. Since Maisie was under five feet tall at the best of times, this meant her head was in the vicinity of Isobel's bosom.

"Not getting any better, is it?" Isobel asked.

"They keep telling me when the muscles get stronger, they'll make up for the deterioration of the bone, but nothing seems to work. Sometimes I want to give up."

"Just you wait. I might have something that will help."

The other ladies started arriving, and everyone had to be seated and served coffee. Then Isobel stood up and called them to order.

"Ladies," she said, "I want to tell you them little plants you're growing, well, they're marijuana."

She was unable to continue because a chorus of surprised comments broke out.

"We're growing pot?"

"So that's what marijuana looks like!"

Bessie was loudest in her disbelief. "How can that be? I distinctly told people not to put seeds in with their scraps."

"I don't think they did it on purpose," Isobel said, when she could be heard.

"Did the seeds go right through the worms like tomato seeds do? Wouldn't it make them high?" Maisie asked.

"How could you tell?" Olive said.

"Girls!" Isobel banged on the table to bring them back to order. "Now Charlotte wants to get rid of the plants, but I have a better idea. You know you can get a prescription for the stuff from your doctor for pain. Margaret got one when the chemo was making her so sick."

They all paused for a moment to remember Margaret, who was no longer with them.

"Well, here's Maisie in awful pain. Why don't we just bypass the doctor and give Maisie what she needs?"

Olive, who was usually the most law-abiding of the group, spoke up, surprising everyone.

"I vote we go ahead. Maisie needs help right now. It would take her months to get Dr. Wilson to agree to it, if he ever did. The old stick in the mud."

Many of the people in the condo went to Dr. Wilson because his office was close.

There was a flurry of comment, then Maisie said, "It's a good idea, but I wouldn't want to smoke it. The smell's pretty easy to recognize."

"Brownies!" Charlotte said. "Gertrude Stein used to bake it into brownies."

"Did she use to live here?" Maisie asked.

Charlotte, the reader of the group, said, "Oh, you know Gertrude Stein, Maisie, 'Pigeons on the grass, alas'." Which didn't enlighten Maisie at all. "She was a writer. She had a friend, Alice Toklas, who wrote a cookbook with this recipe in it. They were lesbians."

"You mean like June and Dorothy on the fourth floor? The ones that are always golfing?"

"Like them. I'll go to the reference library right away and look up her recipe. Better not go on the internet looking for it. They can track you if you use the Google."

"While you're gone, the rest of us should go through the borders and see if there's any pot growing there," Bessie said. "If there is, we can transplant it into our own planters. We may need quite a bit."

"I want to help," Maisie said, "but I can't kneel down because of my knees. And I wouldn't be able to pick out the plants anyway." Her eyesight was very poor.

"You can bring your bundle buggy and collect the pots with the plants in them," Isobel said.

"I'll tell Roger we're going to do some weeding," Bessie said. Roger was their friendly concierge, who liked to be kept informed. "But he mustn't know what we're really doing. We have to keep this to ourselves."

The ladies all said, "Yes, of course, Bessie."

Charlotte felt a pleasant nervous frisson when she requested *The Alice B. Toklas Cookbook* at the Toronto Reference Library that afternoon, but the librarian didn't even raise an eyebrow. The recipe was called Hashish Fudge. It wasn't really for brownies, more like an unbaked fruit and nut concoction. It seemed vaguely familiar, and then Charlotte remembered.

"For heaven's sake," she said to herself, "it's like those Chinese Chews mother used to make at Christmas. I wonder if she got the recipe from this book. Leaving out the cannabis, of course."

The recipe said to dry the leaves after the plant had gone to seed, but while it was still green.

"Maisie needs it now. We don't want to wait till it goes to seed," she told the other ladies when she got home and showed them the recipe. They had found quite a number of marijuana plants in the borders. Luckily, the hired landscapers, who were supposed to keep the borders tidy, were allergic to weeding. They never pulled anything up till it got to be at least two feet tall.

"That old fart, Reverend Carp, came by while we were weeding and said, 'Doing God's work, I see,'" Isobel told Charlotte. "I nearly laughed in his face."

"Well, it is a good deed we're doing for Maisie."

"I met him when I was taking the pots up to my place, and he looked in my bundle buggy and he said, 'Those look familiar.' I told him it was shefflera," Maisie said.

The Reverend Carp was not popular with the other condo residents. He had a nasty habit of taking over the condo information meetings, asking pointless questions until everyone got fed up and left. And he wasn't even an owner, just a tenant. Furthermore, there were some people who claimed he was not really an ordained minister at all, just a graduate of a mail-order Bible college.

"We can chop up some of the bigger leaves and dry them in a very slow oven," Bessie said. "Olive, you do it because you're on the top floor. The smell won't drift up to anyone above you."

"I'll fry some onions while I'm doing it. That'll mask the smell if there is any. The rest of you get going on chopping the figs and dates. We could try the bars tonight instead of playing bridge."

***

That evening, at seven o'clock, the Sisterhood arrived in Olive's apartment, where a pleasant smell of fried onions hovered in the air. Charlotte was first. She had chopped the fruit and nuts and combined them with sugar and butter. She was carrying the mixture in a covered cake pan.

"I met Reverend Carp in the elevator and he said, 'Feeding the hungry?' so I said. 'We're having a potluck at Olive's.' That man is the worst snoop in the building."

Isobel, Maisie and Bessie arrived together. Maisie was carrying bags of chips and Cheesies. "I've heard pot gives you the munchies," she explained.

"Good thinking," Olive said.

Charlotte put her cake pan on the kitchen counter and demonstrated. "We have to dust the dried leaves over the mixture, and then roll it into balls about the size of a walnut, like this. The recipe says not to eat more than two." The others joined in until they had a whole plateful of neat little balls. Charlotte eyed them proudly and said, "Maisie, you go first since it's supposed to help your shoulder."

Maisie obliged. The other ladies watched her closely and, when nothing happened immediately, they each took one. Their reactions varied from, "Not bad," to, "I never did like dates," to, "I wonder why they called them Chinese Chews. There's nothing Chinese about them."

"Should we play bridge?" Olive asked. "While we're waiting for results? It may take longer than with smoking, because smoke gets into your blood stream faster."

They got out the cards and assembled around Olive's dining room table. Maisie pulled up a chair and sat, watching. The game proceeded normally for about half an hour. Then Charlotte picked up her hand, sorted it, and said, "I bid four spoons."

The other ladies stared at her.

"I'm starting to feel a little odd," she said and giggled.

Maisie got up and moved over to the chesterfield.

"I feel just lovely," she said. "My goodness. But it feels more luxurious here."

"I guess it works for her," Bessie said. "I don't feel a thing."

Olive walked over and closed the door to the balcony. Then she moved back, clinging to the furniture until she was as far from the balcony door as she could get. She sat down in an armchair and gripped the arms tightly.

"Nobody go out on the balcony. It's not safe out there."

"Do you think we'll try to fly?" Charlotte asked. She giggled again. "You look absolutely beautiful, Maisie. I love that blouse on you. It shimmers."

"Shimmers. Yes, it does. It shimmers. Where are those Cheesies?"

Charlotte handed her a bag and ripped open another for herself. They began shoveling snacks into their mouths in a very unladylike way.

Isobel, who had been quiet up till now, suddenly stood up.

"Shimmers. That reminds me of a poem we had to memorize in high school back in Come By Chance. 'The Lady of Shallot', I think it was. 'Aspens shiver.' Not shimmer. I'll have to start from the first. 'On either side the river lie, long fields of barley and of rye—'"

"The stuff is definitely working," Bessie said. "How is your shoulder, Maisie?"

"It feels lovely, just lovely." She smiled beatifically.

There was a knock at the door.

"Don't answer it," Olive said. "It might be the cops."

The knock came again, and then the unctuous voice of the Reverend Carp was heard.

"Mrs. Graham? Are you there?"

"We have to answer it, Olive" Bessie said. "He'll have the whole floor wondering where you are."

"You go, Bessie. I can't get up."

Bessie went to the door and opened it.

The Reverend Carp said, "May I come in?" He was a stout little man and Bessie towered over him, but she found herself stepping back. The Reverend advanced, his nose twitching like a beagle's.

"Ladies," he said, "I have reason to believe that something illegal is going on here."

Charlotte and Maisie giggled. The Reverend looked at them coldly. As the only rational woman in the room, Bessie felt she had to take control.

"You girls keep quiet," she hissed at the others, and turned to the Reverend. "We're just having a potluck supper." Then, inspired, she took the plate of cookies off the table and offered it to him. "Have a cookie."

The Reverend, who was known to be greedy, took one and popped it into his mouth. He went on talking as he chewed.

"I didn't recognize those plants at first when I saw them in Mrs. McClain's bundle buggy, but when you said 'potluck,' Mrs. Manners, it triggered my memory. Those cookies are very good."

"They are," Charlotte said, and Isobel and Maisie chimed in, "Very, very good."

"Have another," Bessie said.

"Thank you. I was not always the person I am now. In my youth I experimented with the softer drugs." He continued at length to describe those experiments. At some point Bessie sat down. The Reverend, being used to preaching, stayed on his feet. Bessie stopped listening. She didn't pay attention until she heard, "And those little plants looked to me like marijuana."

Bessie stood up so that she could loom over him. "That's crazy. Where would we get marijuana?"

"I do not know. But if you're running a grow operation here, I would like to be included. Or I will be forced to report this to management. Could I have another of those little cookies?"

Bessie hesitated. The recipe had said to eat no more than two. What if the Reverend suffered an overdose? Then she decided it would serve him right. And, while he ate, she would have time to think.

"Here," she said. He managed to take two more cookies. "Reverend Carp, you are seriously mistaken. Those are shefflera plants, which we were rescuing from the borders. We are all respectable women. We would never—"

But the Reverend wasn't listening to her.

"Mrs. Bottomley," he said, "I never realized before how beautiful you are. You're like the Goddess Juno. So tall. So stately." He suddenly clutched her around the waist. His nose was buried in her bosom.

"Reverend Carp!" Bessie said, like someone in a Jane Austen film. "You forget yourself." She tried to remove him, but he was clinging to her like a baby monkey to its mother.

"I think you had better go," Olive said, suddenly coming out of her catatonic state. "I can't have this sort of thing in my apartment."

Bessie finally detached the Reverend, using both hands, and opened the door.

"We can discuss this later, when you're more yourself," she said. She pushed him outside and shut the door behind him. Then she turned to the other ladies and said, "What do we do now?"

Charlotte and Maisie were stuffing their faces with chips and Olive had gone rigid again. Bessie looked to Isobel for some sort of reply.

"'That clothe the wold and meet the sky, and through the field a road runs by to many-towered Camelot,'" Isobel offered.

"Oh, for God's sake," Bessie said. She wanted to take another cookie so she could get some of that happy feeling, too. She must need more to take effect because of her larger size. But perhaps it was just as well that someone was thinking straight, in case the Reverend came back. "I'm like the designated driver," she thought. She sat down on the chesterfield and put her head back. In spite of Isobel's chanting, (it was a very long poem), she slept.

When she woke, it was dark outside. The dining room light was still on. Maisie was asleep on the chesterfield beside her and Charlotte was curled up in an armchair. Isobel had fallen asleep with her head on the dining room table. Only Olive was still awake, sitting in her armchair, staring straight ahead. Bessie went back to sleep.

***

The next morning, Olive was roused by loud knocking. She struggled out of her chair and went to the door.

"Who is it?" she asked.

"It's Roger, Mrs. Graham. Could I have a word with you?"

Olive looked around at her friends, who were all trying hard to come awake and sit up.

"Just a minute, Roger," she said and turned to the ladies, "Are you all okay?"

"Wonderful."

"I have no hangover."

"My shoulder doesn't hurt like it usually does in the morning."

Only Olive was dubious.

"I didn't like the way I felt. Something else had control of my mind."

"You just had a bad trip," Maisie said. "I'm so thankful something worked for the pain. We have to keep growing those plants."

"We'll have to deal with the Reverend Carp first," Bessie said.

Olive opened the door and peered around it.

"Roger, is something wrong?"

"We had an incident," he said. "I wanted to make sure you're all right."

"An incident? What happened?"

The other ladies had finally risen and joined Olive at the door.

"I understand the Reverend Carp was feeling a little—well, not himself. He came down to the security desk early this morning and made improper suggestions to the night guard, Sophie."

"Sophie? The one who looks like a female impersonator?"

"Yes. She locked him in a cleaning closet and phoned me at home. When I got here he was raving about cookies and goddesses and pots and all sorts of things I'd rather not talk about. We finally called an ambulance and they took him to the hospital. I also called the owner of his apartment. Apparently he did quite a lot of damage there. He won't be back here to live, if the owner has anything to do with it."

"How shocking! But why have you come to me about this?"

"Well, he was also raving about you and Mrs. Bottomley. I got to thinking—maybe he had been up here, too. Acting crazy."

"Thank you for telling me, Roger, but there is no need to worry. Mrs. Bottomley is just fine. So am I."

"That's all right then. I'm relieved. I'll leave you to get on with your day." He looked around at the disheveled ladies. "Having a breakfast meeting, are you?"

Maisie came up with the perfect answer.

"We're planning our next potluck party."

Lynne Murphy is a retired journalist who has been reading and writing mysteries for many years. She helped found the Toronto Chapter of Sisters in crime, which led to her joining a writing group, which led to her becoming one of the Mesdames of Mayhem. Her short story, "Saving Bessie's Worms", was published in the Mesdames anthology, *Thirteen, an anthology of Crime stories*. (Carrick Publishing, 2013) Her story "The Troublemaker" appears in the Sisters in Crime anthology, *The Whole She-Bang*.

Lynne lives in a condo in Toronto and she has found life there to be an inspiration for her stories.

Easter Aches

Jayne Barnard

Editor's Note: Frightening...Jayne Barnard brings us vulnerable characters and a desperate plot in her riveting story of ambition and deception.

"You'll poison me."

It was Artie Rusnak's usual complaint. He wasn't the only poison-obsessed Kimberly Acres resident. Half the sweet old ladies in this seniors' home were convinced the other half would kill them for their lunch seat next to the Acres' most eligible widower, whoever they thought that was.

"Not today, Mr. Rusnak," said Darlene. "But if you don't want it...." He snatched the chocolate egg as she trundled the cart towards the reception desk to ask me, "You want tea?"

"Leave the pot," I said, shoving aside stacks of candy confiscated from residents. Didn't relatives didn't realize all those sweets played fast and loose with elderly digestive systems? "My throat is killing me."

"I hope you're not getting that flu." Darlene peered past me to view her reflection in the office window, fluffing up her straw-blond hair. "Shelby Todd's coming in, but she looks like death. Or it might be her screaming fight with Remi in the parking lot. Over his new truck, I bet." She caught my look. "I wasn't spying. I saw them through the window of *Pere* Bonneau's room."

Right. When she was in there smoking. The comatose old priest couldn't squeal on her, but her clothes reeked and his room would too. She off-loaded the tea urn, pocketed a chocolate bunny and trundled away just as Shelby appeared. The senior nurse kicked off her soggy snow-boots in the front entrance, flung her jacket at the office coat rack and dropped into a chair. As she bent to put on her nursing shoes, gray roots were visible on the top of her head, creating a skunk-stripe. How to look all of your fifty-whatever years.

"Excuse me?"

I looked up, square into the eyes of the handsomest man to walk through these doors since, well, ever. I did a quick shoulder-check for Darlene. Kapuskasing's dating pool for over-thirties is barely ankle-deep. She wades in amongst the bottom-feeders on occasion, but I don't. Thus, I haven't dated in a couple of years. I wasn't about to let her blow my chance of reeling in a handsome stranger.

I offered my warmest smile, but to no avail. All Handsome wanted was to talk to Artie Rusnak and others of that era. He showed a letter from our head office, authorizing him to hang around asking local-history questions, so long as he didn't disturb the residents. I was only staff, but when he smiled at me, I was so disturbed I almost drooled on my purple scrubs.

"First you sign in. And hand-sanitize." I pointed out the sani-stand and the pen, watched as he first printed, then scrawled, "Richard Delaney" in the appropriate boxes. "Artie's having his tea. Would you like a cup?"

When Richard sat down, Artie told him, "They poisoned my old friend Gil for his money. I know. I used to be with the OPP."

Richard, unfazed, said, "You know about every crime that happened on your watch."

I left them to it and started collecting teacups at the far end of the corridor. By the time I had worked my way back, Artie was happily, and almost accurately, recounting the case of the body in the bush.

Richard prompted, "And it had been there all those years?"

Artie nodded. "Since 1977. Those Andrews boys, they didn't tell a soul, because their double-still setup was near the body. Well, that and Robert's long-haired wife. Her folks were Air Force, soon moved on, but she stayed. She went with Davie Andrews before Robert came home for the summer from university. Some said after that, too, but I never believed those rumors. Spiteful women's gossip, and Helene, Robert's mom, was the worst. Always with the knife edge on her tongue. Who'd blame a girl for running off rather than share a roof with Helene? We all thought Robert had gone after his wife, turned his back on his family. Until the body was found." He paused, looking sad, and then returned to his theme of the day. "They poisoned Gil, you know."

"I'm afraid that's all you'll get from him this time around, Mr. Delaney," I said. "Artie, are you ready for Family Feud?" I helped him to his walker and he clomped toward the TV lounge.

As we strolled the other way, Richard said, "He talked about the Gaudette family like they were the Kennedy clan."

"Gilbert Gaudette was a Joe Kennedy figure fifty years ago, except he had five daughters and only one son. Gil made a fortune in lumber, but he lived out his last years here in Kimberly Acres like anyone else. He and Artie were thick as thieves until last fall's epidemic. Norovirus and a respiratory. We lost three residents, and some of the others never fully recovered, Artie being one."

"He seemed lucid to me, mostly."

"He spins a good yarn, but he garbles bits of them together now. If you want to hear the originals, I taped them when he first moved in." Hah! Something Darlene couldn't cap with her bigger, better, tighter, or brighter assets.

Richard glowed like he'd seen the Grail. "I'm sure you wouldn't lend them, but could I copy some? Or listen to them at least?"

"They really are tapes," I said. "Unless you have an old cassette player handy, you'll have to use mine." I capped it by offering him candy eggs. He capped that by offering to buy me lunch tomorrow in the staff cafeteria, if I'd bring my tape player and Artie's tapes. He'd be working out of the staff conference room and could listen there.

Later, as I spoon-fed mashed potatoes, wiped chins and coaxed Artie to eat his peas, I privately gloated. A date! Having that to anticipate almost made up for Shelby spending the dark hours in *Pere* Bonneau's dim room, her forehead resting on his bed. Whether she was snoozing, praying, or sobbing over her wastrel husband—the spoiled only son of the oldest Gaudette daughter—she wasn't needed on the floor for a change, so I left her to it.

The next day, toting a bag of Artie-era tapes and my battered portable cassette player, gussied up in my good street clothes—because who wants to do a first date in hospital scrubs?— I arrived early at the conference room. Richard was huddled over a laptop and I took a moment to appreciate his dark curls and strong, clean-shaven jaw. Being seen with him wouldn't hurt my reputation any.

I took him down to the caf and made my best effort at small talk, but he kept bringing up Gilbert Gaudette.

"His son's murder is unsolved, right? They know where now, but not exactly when, or by whom. Think of the cover copy."

Whom? No man from Kap could say that without sounding fake. I've always been a sucker for a vocabulary.

"Uh, yeah. Artie talks about that on his tape." I looked around. The lunch crowd had all but vanished. "We can listen to it now, if you like."

While Richard refilled our mugs, I fast-forwarded through the third-hand description of bitter arguments between Helene, Robert's mother, and Joanne, his young wife, that led to Joanne hopping the next bus south, with Robert presumably following her a couple of weeks later. Once Richard was ready with his notebook, I hit 'Play.'

Artie's voice, slightly fuzzy, said, "They should have posted a reward, but Helene didn't want anyone saying she drove her son away. So they hired this detective, but all he found was a speeding ticket Robert got near North Bay a couple of days after he left Kap. Got, but never paid. Helene hoped to her last breath they were out there somewhere, raising sons to carry on the name. Gil left everything to Robert."

I remembered that day, how Artie made me shut off the tape to hear about Gil's will: everything to Robert, then Robert's children, and then, only if none of the above survived, a share-out to his daughters and their kids. Gil didn't like his sons-in-law, and hoped those bozos wouldn't see a dime, but Artie wouldn't say that on the record.

He went on, "When the body was tripped over by those kids out hunting last fall, Robert had been gone so long that the OPP couldn't trace his movements, or even tell for sure when he died. He might have left town and come back a few years later, or never left the area at all. Of course they interviewed the Andrews boys, what with the body being found a mile or so from Mrs. Andrews' farm. Yes, I said a mile, missy, and don't you correct it to kilometers."

I smiled at the memory as my voice on the tape said, "I won't. I assume Davie Andrews denied all knowledge of the body."

Artie gave a yappy laugh. "Not on your life. Davie claimed he and his brother found it on the road near their still. The head was shot half off, but they knew Robert and his car was right beside him. Figured why should a hunting accident by persons unknown force them to move their rotgut operation? So they dragged the body into the woods, took his wallet, and sold the car to a chop shop in North Bay. Donnie was interviewed in Monteith jail, arson charge that time, and he told pretty much the same story. Either they rehearsed it, or it was the truth."

Richard leaned over the tape recorder as if Artie was in there, and could hear him. "He was right by his car, and shot? Could he have killed himself?"

"Shh," I said, and let the tape play on while Artie discussed forensics, the likely range of the shot, then a hopeless foot-by-foot search for a thirty-year-old shell casing and any other evidence.

"I was retired by then," Artie was saying, "but I got this report straight from a young OPP who came to ask me if the Andrews' boys' tale could possibly be true. I said you had to know them back then to believe it. They thought moon-shining whisky to pipeline camps was gonna make them rich, get them out of Mitchell's Corner forever. Instead they went to jail, been in and out ever since. If they killed him, they'd claim it was a hunting accident anyway, that they just covered it up. Nobody could prove different, and the worst they'd face is another few years." Artie digressed, and I turned the tape off.

"You get anything new out of that? Richard? You're really pale."

He blotted his forehead with a paper napkin. "Yeah, must have eaten something that disagreed with me. How much more is there?"

"Long as you're not contagious, I won't have to kick you out. There's about five hours of Artie's stories, not all about Robert or the Gaudettes, but they're sprinkled through the rest." I caught sight of the clock above the salad fridge and jumped up. "I'll be late for work."

"Can I keep these tapes for the afternoon?"

"Sure. Drop them at Reception when you leave. I'm on until eleven tonight." I hurried off to change. Richard followed to chat with Artie, or rather to mine the old man for every last scrap of memory.

I was changed and at the desk when he came back, wearing my zany blue flowered scrubs today, although I usually saved them for the final day of my rotation. Hey, they're good with my eyes, and a girl needs every edge, with Darlene and her full frontals in the vicinity. I doled out chocolate eggs to keep him there, and suggested other residents he might interview.

We were bantering along nicely about post-work drinks when, behind me, there sounded an almighty crash and clatter. I turned to see Shelby, whiter than the ceiling tiles, clutching the office door frame to stay upright in the midst of strewn files, a broken coffee mug, and a slew of metal barf pans. I ran to help her to a chair, barely aware of Richard waving as he trotted back to Artie's tapes.

"Shelby, you shouldn't be at work if you're sick."

"I'm–I'm fine," she said. "I just need to lie down."

"At home. I'll call Remi for you."

"No!" She took a deeper breath. "I'll rest in the break room for a bit." I helped her creep as far as the front counter, where she leaned a while before heading down the hall. If I had to cover both our jobs all shift, I'd be a wreck by eleven. I grumbled over the cleanup until Darlene came along with the tea trolley and sloshed me out a cup.

"Anything good in the files today?" she asked, rifling the chocolate boxes for nutty ones.

"*Pere* Bonneau moved his toes."

"Nice for him. Where's Shelby?"

I explained, adding that I wished she would go home so I could call in a casual to cover her work.

Darlene tutted. "And catch Remi with some woman? Who'd risk that?"

"You're kidding!"

"What rock do you live under, hon? Since the kids moved out, he's always trying to get women home with him when she's working evenings or nights. Even me, his own daughter's best friend. Slime-bucket."

"Why would anyone go home with that creepy old fart?"

"Because he's Gil Gaudette's grandson, and going to be rich soon." She closed one chocolate box and opened another. "Can't come too soon for Shelby, I'll bet. She'll divorce his ass the day after the inheritance is settled. Only way to get out without taking half his debts. That new Ford F150 he's driving? Bought in Timmins. Nobody here will sell to him on credit. His big, new Bayliner boat that he keeps out at Moonbeam marina? About to get repossessed. They're way behind on their mortgage, too. Gil finally died, so they're safe for now. No banker in town wants to piss off Kap's next millionaires."

"Old Gil would be turning in his grave."

"Yeah, all the class went out of that family a generation back, when Robert Gaudette ran off after some low-rent base brat. Or died, or whatever. That's what's holding up the inheritance. The lawyers have to make sure Robert didn't have kids before they can split up the pile. And nobody knows his wife's maiden name any more. *Pere* Bonneau married 'em, I think, same year as Shelby and Remi. But he can't tell anybody anything now, poor old coot. Just lying there drooling year after year. My time comes, I don't wanna go slow like him."

A yell and a clatter came from the TV lounge. Darlene scuttled away before she could be sent to help. I went along to the lounge to restore order, feeling sorry for Shelby. A high school star, provincial biathlon champion at sixteen, and look at her now. It was the typical small town story: got pregnant by her first boyfriend, married too young, stayed too long for her children's sake, and was working herself to death while he played around. She needed the break the inheritance offered.

If the only delay was finding Robert's wife's maiden name, *Pere* Bonneau's tape might have it. I'd just have to drop by the conference room on my break and ask Richard if I'd brought that one along. Thoughtful of my co-workers, that's me.

Shelby came back before the supper rush, looking a bit better. She was friendly, too, asking about Richard: how old he was, where he came from.

I told her about the book project and his interest in Robert's death.

She shook her head.

"No good raking up that old past, now that Gil and Helene are gone."

"Don't you want to see justice done for Robert?"

She shrugged. "I'd rather see that money so I can pay off my kids' student loans, get them off to a good start in life."

Some start. They were my age, give or take, and had been out of college for years. If they weren't started by now, they were as lazy as their old man.

I said, "Well, I'm going to listen to my *Pere* Bonneau tape for Joanne's maiden name. Maybe that will speed things up."

She smiled. "An excuse to visit your new friend? You can go right now. Take him some tea while you're at it. But hurry back. Supper's up in ten minutes."

We found *Pere* Bonneau's tape, but Richard was halfway through another of Artie's digressive memory dumps and said he'd listen later. I didn't linger. Suppers to serve, chins to wipe.

Once the residents were in bed, Shelby went to lie in the dark for another hour. Richard hung around the desk for most of that time, chatting and sampling Easter candy, lightly flirting until

I was pretty sure he was angling for that post-work drink to be at my place. He even stacked chairs in the TV room while Shelby and I did our last rounds. A basic nice guy. When the night nurse clocked in, I didn't bother changing back to street clothes. I just headed off with Richard to pack up the tapes and carry them, and him, to my place.

Except the tapes were gone.

The tape player sat on the table, mouth gaping, but *Pere* Bonneau's tape and every one of Artie's had disappeared. Apart from Richard's briefcase and my tape bag, there was nowhere they could hide. All the same, I crawled on the floor, checking under the chairs.

Richard watched, at first without comment. Then he said, "Don't any of your residents wander at night? They could have walked off with these. And does it matter if the memoirs of an old priest are missing? Anything interesting he knew would be under the seal of the Confessional."

"It does matter. *Pere* Bonneau is the only lead to Joanne's maiden name."

He knelt beside me. "I know her last name."

I stared at him. "You do? Then why...?"

He grinned. "A beautiful woman invites me home late at night, and I'm going to say it's not necessary?"

I sort of smiled back. "I guess not. You got it from the newspapers, huh? The lawyers should have tried there."

"I got it from here." He pulled out his wallet and put his laminated birth certificate into my hand.

I read: Richard Delaney Gaudette, born Kingston, Ontario, December 12, 1977.

"Then you're..."

"Robert and Joanne's son, yes." He sighed. "I'll tell you all about it. But off the floor, please."

I let him raise me, rather than scramble clumsily up on my own, and took a chair. And a minute to let the whirl in my brain settle. He thought me beautiful, but he had lied to me by omission about something as basic as his real last name. And there was something fishy about those tapes vanishing, just when there was a lead to Robert Gaudette's wife and son. But he'd been with me, so he had not hidden them himself.

Besides, there were so many other ways he could have distracted me from listening, especially if he smiled at me the way he was doing now, only in my dimly lit living room with soft music playing in the background. Ahem....

"I don't think a resident took them," I said. "When they wake up at night, it's for the bathroom, and most of them ring for help getting there. But who besides us would care about the tapes all of a sudden?"

The answer came to me in one of those blinding flashes.

"Oh, God. Shelby. I told her *Pere* Bonneau might have said your mother's name on my tape. If the lawyers found Joanne, and then you, Remi would inherit nothing. As long as the estate's in limbo, the bank won't foreclose on her family. But how would she know you existed? Until today, when I guess she recognized you and darned near fainted from the shock. You must look like your dad."

"So it is the same Shelby." Richard perched on a corner of the conference table. "When she realized she was pregnant, my mother called a woman named Shelby. Her only friend in the family, she told me. She pleaded with Shelby to ask Robert to phone her, so they could talk about what to do next. He never called.

"She tried the house a few times, but chickened out whenever Helene answered, and then Shelby hung up on her. That's when she figured Robert didn't want anything to do with her or the baby, and went on with life by herself. Pre-child support laws. Nobody would walk away nowadays. All it takes is a DNA swab and a court order to force payment."

I grabbed his hands. "He didn't call because he was already dead, I bet. Shelby must have told Remi, who she was either already married to or about to marry, about your mom's call. Shelby was pregnant when she got married, so she'd be looking for a secure future with Remi, and that meant cutting out Robert's wife and baby. Remi must have gambled on Joanne not coming back if Robert wasn't around to ask her to. I bet he lured your father out to Mitchell's Corner and shot him. He expected to become the official heir as soon as Robert's body was found.

"No internet then, no 24-hour news cycle. One dead body in the north might never be reported in any southern Ontario paper, much less one your mother would see regularly. Nowadays, she could easily set a Google alert for any mention of Robert's name. But not then. So the Andrews brothers got rid of Robert's body, and the family hung in limbo all those years, until it was found. They never knew you existed."

"If you're right," said Richard, standing up, "and Remi learns we're looking into the murder, what he's going to do next?"

I pushed back my chair. "He'll silence *Pere* Bonneau, and maybe Artie too. Come on. I need to know those old men are okay before we do anything else."

We crept along the night-dimmed corridor, our footsteps mingling with the light jazz the night nurse played while she charted. Artie's snores were shaking the giant Easter bunny taped to his door, so I only peeked in to make sure he was alone. Peering around Pere's half-open door, I saw Shelby kneeling by the bed, hands clasped and head bent. A soft murmur reached my ears. Richard looked past my shoulder, then pulled me away.

"Catholics," he muttered. "Always thinking confession solves anything."

"Does it count with God if the priest is in a coma?"

My mind flashed back a few steps to Artie's room. I hurried in for a second look, and came out holding a box of chocolates.

"These were behind Reception at lights-out."

"I told you they wander at night." Richard opened the box. "Rum-butter centers. Irresistible."

As he plucked the first chocolate from the box, some part of my brain registered a déjà vu. A box of chocolates was found in Gil Gaudette's room when he died. Why? He had a stomach virus. Vomiting and diarrhea for three days before his heart quit. No eating chocolates then. In the midst of the twin epidemics, with people coughing, barfing, shitting, and dying, I hadn't given the box a moment's thought beyond setting it aside for the nurses' station. Shelby had emptied the box into the garbage instead.

"Don't eat that," I snapped, snatching it from his fingers, and ran toward Reception.

In good light, the freshly melted seam around three chocolates' bases was easy to see. I cracked one open and found an assortment of chopped pills pressed into the rum-butter filling. I held it out to Richard.

"Remi couldn't have done this without being noticed coming or going on the floor. Shelby must have doctored them in the break room when I thought she was lying down."

"And if she doctored these chocolates, she might have poisoned my grandfather the same way. Maybe Artie's mind isn't so far gone after all."

We both looked down the corridor to *Père* Bonneau's half-open door. I thought of Shelby, all those years ago, young and fit from her winter biathlon training, a provincial champion with the long gun. She was dating Remi, who, as everybody knew, was second in line behind the Gaudette crown prince. Maybe she was even pregnant already.

And there was Robert, deserted by his wife, unsuspecting and alone on a back road, meeting his wife's best friend for what he probably thought was news of Joanne's whereabouts. Did Shelby use his shotgun, or bring her own competition rifle? Did it even matter now?

Whatever Shelby had done back then, whatever she might have whispered to the old priest in those dark hours by his bed, was lost in the mist of time and the mystery of the confessional. So much pain and uncertainty for the Gaudette family, so many years of Richard believing his father had refused to acknowledge him.

All those heartaches because of one woman's ambition, or her desperation.

Easter, a time of redemption. But not for Shelby. What we held in our hands was hard evidence of attempted murder.

Time to call the OPP.

Jayne Barnard lives in Calgary, Alberta, in the angle between the Bow and Elbow Rivers, in a solar-powered urban cottage with computers, cats, and many books. When not writing, she can often be found promenading in Steampunk gear or Edwardian costume with others of her tribe.

Connect with Jayne on Facebook
or at her Blogsite
http://laceymccrae.blogspot.ca/

The Peace of Mind Thief
Alex Carrick

Editor's Note: We began our carousel of crime with an exploration of secrets, and it's fitting we should end with a tribute to those "imps of evil." Alex Carrick shares his exceptional wit and wordcraft, as we join him in the bucolic town of Quiet Bay.

***

Secrets!
Sugar sprinkled on candy or arsenic mixed with nightshade.
Are you in the know or flying blind?
Delicious seductive power or unpredictable happen-anytime pain.
Who to bring into the inner circle?
Who best left excluded?
Where to extend the intimacy?
An implication of purity that's non-existent.
Most secrets aren't.
Obscuring the truth, they rarely reveal.
Rather standing in the way of a conclusion.
Birthing misconceptions, resentment and anger are their twin companions.

Still, this was a secret she knew she'd take to her grave.

What surprised most was her certainty she could carry through with intent.

Her resolve was usually less firm. In this, there were reasons to stay the course.

What she had done turned out so well. She'd rolled the dice and won the treasure.

No more tempting fate. Cash in her winnings. Accept the good and dare not look back. And never, ever share.

Thankfully, she had an advantage, a secret within a secret.
She was the only person who knew what she was hoarding.

***

Most of the townspeople of Quiet Bay were upset.

The source of the disharmony had been festering for more than a year. At first, it was viewed as a joke, but matters had progressed beyond that stage.

Plenty of meetings had been held on the subject. It was a constant topic of conversation.

Some were holding their emotions in check, hoping that legal action would solve the matter, although so far that had proven ineffective. A victory in the courts one month led, upon appeal, to a setback the next.

The source of the problem was only a five minute walk out of the center of the village along the beachfront.

A certain Mr. Gary Willikers was in the process of building an enormous structure on land that most people had taken for granted was public property.

Mr. Willikers was one of the community's few celebrities. Not because of anything he'd done to earn the acclaim. Instead, his notoriety derived from his profession.

He was in the real estate business. True to what he'd seen in his travels to southern environs, he'd adopted a simple marketing ploy, blitz advertising.

He'd seen the signs elsewhere. "Live like a Hilton when you Buy with Milton" was his favorite.

He tweaked the message and plastered his picture everywhere with the caption "Sell with me and say, 'GEE WILLIKERS, THAT WAS EASY!'"

Lately, though, his business had been in a tailspin. He'd pulled some deals judged to be questionable by his neighbors and fellow residents.

Through no fault of his own, some properties he'd helped move were now worth a good deal less than they had been a year or two ago.

Taking advantage of the downturn in the market, he'd also made a purchase for his own use that violated what some thought was fair play.

Exhibit number one, Miss Hook. Shortly before she died in a care facility, Mr. Willikers bought her home down on the lakefront.

The word around town was he'd picked it up for a song. Ms. Hook needed money for medical expenses and he'd stepped in as a sugar daddy, with a hidden motive. Or so the story went.

The reality was he'd struck a fair bargain, what with prices dropping as quickly as they were.

The cost of gasoline was going through the roof and vacation homes were falling out of favor, given the long drive from major cities.

Mr. Willikers had a specific plan in mind for Ms. Hook's land. His real love, and another reason his real estate business was withering, was astronomy.

He built a permanent wooden deck over the sand in his new backyard from which he could gaze at the stars.

That alone would have been bad enough. The shoreline had always offered a free and open stroll along its entire length.

It was phase two of his project that really set everyone's ire to jangling.

In keeping with his theme, he was well along in constructing a giant wooden rocket ship on top of his new patio, with a set of stairs ascending to the top. At the summit, he planned a flight deck to serve as his astronomical look-out.

In the earliest stages of his projectile project, the ridicule began. The townspeople turned nasty. They were upset over the disruption to their routines.

They started to speak of Mr. Willikers as a space alien. Maybe he came from the stars, was the joke. He should go back where he came from, was what a lot of them thought and said.

For a certainty, something must be done to stop work on the aberration. Extraordinary measures were justified and needed.

***

Chester Nails was the owner of the local hardware store.

He ran an independent operation affiliated with a big corporate chain.

The locals weren't pleased with him either. Whenever he was asked what he thought of the "monstrosity", his response was always measured.

He wasn't sure it was so bad. Maybe it would be a case of unintended consequences.

He was aware it might change the town.

A giant wooden spaceship on the water's edge could be a tourist attraction.

Had anyone thought of that? Not likely. Not among the mental heavyweights who were his staff and customers.

Whenever he talked about the possible benefits, he received looks that suggested he might be the one from Saturn.

That morning had been a perfect example.

Mr. Nails was as loyal to his wife and family as a steak-and-onions man could be. It didn't make him a monk, though, did it?

He had no control over where his wanton imaginings might take him. He wasn't ever going to act on them, but the journey provided most of his daily joy.

At least he could cultivate his pleasant imaginings. And where better to plough a furrow than in Herzinger's Drug Store, four retail outlets down the street from his own.

That's where, on any given day, he'd run into Holly Hoody, prettiest girl in town and full-time cashier.

Balding, middle-aged and of average height, Mr. Nails was unaccountably a dandy in one area. He was the proud owner of a dozen pairs of high-end sunglasses.

If he tried on enough "shades" and got the timing just right, Holly, would come over and help him with his choice.

She'd give her opinion about how he looked. It cracked open an opportunity to converse in other areas.

Ah, the sweet delight of talking with an intelligent young woman. Mr. Nails would leave the store ecstatic.

It would be the highlight of his day. He'd often walk back to his own emporium with a secret smile so big it would have been nice to push it in a shopping cart.

He barely acknowledged to himself what he was doing.

If he thought it went unnoticed by everyone else, he was sorely mistaken. Small towns hold few secrets. Few and far between were those who weren't aware of his silly infatuation.

Holly had a boyfriend, the local leader of the town's questionable element. All such small ponds have a "bad boy", someone who finds their own particular niche by being a little wilder than others.

Sex appeal was the desirable spinoff from being on the outs with the law.

Sydney Steeler may have been a renegade, but he was also smart. He knew his charisma was enhanced by dating Holly, the daughter of the police officer who headed up the local constabulary.

Young Mr. Steeler was becoming a problem for Chester Nails. Not only was Holly obviously attracted to Syd, but there were rumors Chester's own son had become a disciple as well.

Socially-awkward hero-worshipping teenage boys gravitated to Syd like he was a drumstick.

As a consequence, Chester's son had become increasingly disrespectful while also growing careless about keeping up his studies and other duties.

One inscrutable teenager at a time, Chester thought as he turned his mind back to Holly.

That morning, during another harmless dalliance, Holly brought up a distasteful subject. She'd been talking to Syd and it was his opinion that someone should blow up Gary Williker's rocket ship.

Chester uncharacteristically went ballistic.

"That's a ridiculous notion. The man has a right to do with his property whatever he likes. We can't be taking matters into our own hands."

He was immediately sorry. The crestfallen look on Holly's face's made him feel miserable. He briefly tried to smooth things over, but his efforts fizzled and he soon took his leave.

His mood remained out of sorts long into the workday.

Chester understood where he'd gone wrong. Syd's "leit motif" was the roar of his Kawasaki motorcycle. Chester's was the sound of the garage door opening and closing when he drove off and returned in the family van.

He was still distracted at dinner that evening. Even later, as he climbed into bed with his wife, a surprising series of speculations poured out of him.

He explained to her, hypothetically of course, how he would deal with the matter of Mr. Williker's pet project.

He'd simply do it. It would be risky, maybe a 50-50 proposition, but it was the only way it might work.

He'd find an excuse for being out at night on a regular basis so she would become used to his absences and sleep through them.

He added a playful embellishment. He'd claim he was going for a moonlight skinny dip.

Then one night he'd sneak down the beach through the water and launch a Molotov cocktail.

He'd make sure it was untraceable, something like petrol and a fuse in a large plastic baggie.

There were risks. Somebody might spot him. And he certainly didn't want to hurt anyone who might be in the vicinity.

He'd have to count on luck.

But if the cards fell right, it was do-able.

Mrs. Nails listened to his story. This wasn't her husband as she knew him.

She was astonished by his inner resolve.

Most of all, she was surprised to learn he was so upset about the matter. It had never surfaced before.

When she finally coaxed out the reason for his annoyance, she was impressed by the simplicity of his explanation.

"Gary Willikers may not have done anything wrong in a strict legal sense, but the truth of the matter is he's stolen the town's peace of mind."

***

One tumultuous week after the town's problem had been fixed, permanently and emphatically, Phoebe Nails, Chester's wife, was sitting in her living room when her teenage son came in after school.

She knew Benji was simply checking in before stepping out with his buddies. She'd only see him again next morning at breakfast.

He never seemed to do homework. He was showing up for classes, at least as far as she knew, and for that she was grateful. She hadn't heard anything to the contrary from the school's principal, who also performed double-duty as Quiet Bay's long-serving mayor.

Whenever she saw the village's top authority figure, she was sure to inquire.

Benji came in through the back door and after a brief violent fridge-raid in the kitchen, walked in to say hello to his mother positioned strategically on his exit route.

He'd have been pleasant enough in appearance save for a scowl that now often skewed his countenance.

At first, Phoebe assumed her son might be having girl trouble, but she was coming to entertain a different conclusion. She switched to worrying that Benji was disappointed by his parental examples. That wasn't fair. It would have to stop, she decided.

"Hi Ben," she said. "How was your day?"

"Boring. Same as always," was his uninspiring response.

"I'm sure it was better than that?" she answered cheerily.

"No. It was really lame. Nothing decent to say about it at all, really," he said with no enthusiasm.

Phoebe was becoming fed up with her son's moods. There was being a teenager and then there was immersion in the persona of a surly cur. Maybe they were the same thing. Still, this wasn't how she'd imagined her family would turn out.

She wasn't willing to lie down and take it.

Benji had been such a fun-loving and sparkly child. She had no idea where things had gone wrong. She and her husband often talked about it. He had even less of a clue.

Maybe it was TV, or video games, or peer pressure, or something in the local water supply.

Maybe he was simply a "bad seed". No, his whole generation seemed to be comprised of snarly malcontents. They couldn't all be rotten. That was too easy an answer.

Had she and Chester been lax as parents? Possibly. She'd known a much harsher discipline in her own upbringing and had resolved not to impose the same on her kids.

Maybe the reality is that children need a firm hand, even if it has other undesirable consequences.

As much as it was hard to endure personally, it was Ben's lack of respect for his father that grated her most. She knew, by tone of voice and offhand comment, that Benji thought his dad was a stick-in-the-mud.

"Ben, come and sit down. I have something important I want to discuss with you."

"Not now, Mom, I have to meet Syd and the guys. And I want to be out of the house before dad gets home."

"I'm mystified, Ben. What's so great about Syd?"

"Are you kidding? You know what he did about the rocket pad, right? The whole town was in an uproar and he came up with the solution. He's a hero."

"The sherrif doesn't think so," she offered.

Benji remained firm in his admiration. "Yeah, well Syd told us guys what he did. He's the man, right?"

"And you don't suppose he's lying?" she couldn't help but ask.

"No way. You adults – dad, the mayor, the sheriff – you all just sat around talking. You didn't do anything. Syd took action."

Phoebe nodded her head. She looked at him with a serious expression. "I have a problem with your father I'd like to discuss."

That spun his attention in another direction. "A problem with dad?" he responded.

For the first time in a long while, Benji looked puzzled. He wasn't used to his mother having any issues with Chester. They were a team. They presented a united front when it came to dealing with him and his foibles.

In his experience, they didn't have setbacks of their own.

He did some quick mental math and figured he could spare a minute to listen to what his mother had to say.

He sat next to her on the orchid-patterned couch. It was a plush affair with doilies on the arms, something that would have fit more appropriately in his grandmother's house.

He'd once come across the word "antimacassar" in a book and looked it up in a dictionary. Sticky-note fashion, he'd attached its meaning to his brain.

It was his proclivity for doing such things that informed him he might be a little smarter than most, as if that would ever get him out of this place.

Benji was one of those kids. There are a million of them. He was sure the people he was living with weren't his real parents. He must be adopted. There could be no other explanation.

His true lineage was royalty, but he'd been separated from the king and queen at birth, for some reason having to do with palace intrigue.

Someday, an envoy would come and rescue him, but for now he'd have to put up with far less than was his due.

Phoebe studied her son and then began to tell him about a possible alternative explanation for what had occurred seven days before, with Benji's father as the chief protagonist.

First, she made it clear he was never to mention any of this to anyone.

Especially, he must never let it slip to Chester that he was aware of what had transpired.

Soon, during pauses, she could hear a jaw drop.

***

A short distance away, Adriana Willikers, Gary's spouse, was also reflecting on the events of the past week. It had been a discordant seven days.

Alone at her ornate dining room table, she was drinking a second cup of cappuccino.

Adriana was a quiet woman who cherished her dignity. Given that her husband was so flamboyant, most people concluded she was mousy.

They had it backwards. She could reach down and find enough resolve to startle anybody.

Maybe it was her Italian background. A heritage of ruling the world, albeit two thousand years before, was coursing through her blood.

She'd met Gary at university. His flame of confidence was too often blanketed by a lack of drive. Her personality was kept to a simmer by a strong will that feared a dangerous burn.

As a couple, their combined thermostat sometimes swung to one extreme or another, but most often it was set at just the right temperature.

In this most recent instance, burdened by the distress her family was experiencing, she'd lanced the boil.

She'd spotted her chance and taken appropriate, if attention-grabbing, action.

A week before, Gary and their son, Bud, had driven fifty kilometers to the one cinema in the vicinity, located in Springdale – that mecca of urbanity – to see another of the horror movies they liked so much, something about the evil dead.

Besides, it was her night to have fun with the ladies. This was a recent departure from her usual reclusive ways.

Phoebe Nails, aware of Adriana's increasing isolation on account of her husband's obsession, had invited her into an arts and crafts group and been surprised to receive a speedy "Yes!"

This was the night of her inauguration, when she received the loose-knit violet-hued scarf that all the ladies wore around their necks while they were working together on their projects.

As the "newbie", it was her turn to supply the food. She'd spent the afternoon preparing shells and cream-filling according to her mother's impossible-to-botch cannoli recipe.

Halfway through the evening, she retired to the kitchen to arrange her culinary contribution on a tray in an appealing arrangement.

Henceforth, she'd never be sure to what degree she had actually planned what came next or whether it was simply a matter of the stars coming into fortuitous alignment.

Alone in the kitchen, hearing the buzz of conversation in the living room, and knowing the other women would soon be engrossed in gossiping about her husband's carpentry work, she slipped out of the house.

The Nails' lived five doors east along the beach from her own abode. She walked quickly along the shoreline and onto her rear grounds. The sound of gentle waves washing in and meeting resistance from the ill-placed deck might have been soothing under other circumstances.

That afternoon, Gary had told her about his newest outside-the-box idea. He'd purchased an old propane barbecue and was keeping it in the shed.

He planned to modify the unit by removing the lid and taking the gas lines out of the casing. He hoped that if he placed the modified contraption under his pet project and turned it on at night, he could simulate a jet-fired launch.

Or maybe spike up the flames for an after-burner effect.

This was all becoming too much for her. Her husband was being ostracized by the rest of the community. Bud's answer was to escape into the trouble that was sure to arise from hanging around with Sydney Steeler's gang.

Satisfaction of Gary's fantasy was costing them dearly.

This latest scheme of his was dangerous to boot.

Better to rid the family of the festering sore in a controlled deliberate manner.

She went to the shed, pulled out the barbecue and rolled it under the looming wooden structure.

She stepped into her home briefly to locate a long-stemmed lighter. She also went to a cupboard where she'd been keeping solidified bacon grease from earlier frying efforts in a large can.

Afterwards, she realized this did indeed indicate a measure of premeditation.

Back outside again, she smeared some of the grease on the lower superstructure. The rest, she spread across the grill of the barbecue.

She turned a valve and pulled the trigger on the lighter. Initial small flames almost immediately roared up ominously.

She stepped back quickly. The flames were angry. In no time, Gary's pet project began to burn.

She wheeled the barbecue back to the shed and sped back to her social gathering.

Re-entering the living room with a tray full of goodies, no-one appeared to have noticed her slightly extended absence.

As for subsequent speculation about who had done the shocking deed that night, Sydney Steeler provided a convenient diversion.

To embellish his own villainous image, he'd insisted on stealing the spotlight.

Adriana could never admit to her husband what she'd done. It was important for him to believe his ambitions had been thwarted by at least one member of an angry mob.

How let down would he feel to discover it was his wife who had perpetrated the crime?

Just the same, she knew it was time to make important changes in her life. Mix in with the other members of the community with a firmer commitment.

The quilting bee was the obvious entry point. She'd already established a beachhead.

She was sure their undeclared leader, Phoebe Nails, was a woman of substance.

Her fanciful designs stepped outside the norm. Most people were oblivious to their quirkiness.

Phoebe's pictures were fraught with subliminal messages.

She specialized in barnyard scenes. If one looked carefully, one could see that different species were giving each other "come hither" looks.

While there was nothing overt taking place, Adriana knew there was a sub-text.

She was dying to ask Phoebe if her suspicion was correct.

But that wasn't the sort of thing one could do cold.

There had to be a build-up of familiarity.

It was all very intriguing to say the least.

***

Two weeks had passed since the notorious event and Phoebe Nails was taking her usual afternoon break from her household chores.

Incapable of sitting idly, she was sketching a pattern for another blanket project to go in the spare room. Or maybe she'd sell it at the upcoming church bazaar, as she often did.

It was a cozy thought, speculating on how the various outputs from her nimble fingers were warming people all over time. Especially since so few of her friends and neighbors seemed aware of what was really captivating about her craftsmanship.

As it always did these days, her mind bounced back to a more potent wellspring of interest.

What she'd done in telling Benji that fanciful story was far outside her comfort zone.

It had required a measure of imagination and even a level of acting skill she'd previously not known she possessed.

The look of incredulity on her son's face as the narrative unfolded was worth everything.

It was good that he begin to see things differently. For his own survival, he had to realize the world isn't as straightforward as he might suppose.

There were nooks and crannies of truth that one could spend a lifetime spelunking without ever reaching the back of the cave.

Look at her. Who would ever figure she'd know the meaning of the word spelunking? She and Benji shared affection for vocabulary.

Maybe that's what would eventually convey him from their sleepy stream to a swifter-flowing river.

He could be an English teacher or a reporter somewhere south in one of the large cities.

She chuckled about the skinny-dipping reference. What had inspired Chester to add that pinch of spice? It had been years since he'd actually done anything so bold.

When they were kids, the chemistry between them had been sufficient to strip away inhibitions. A moonlit naked romp in refreshing waters had been one of the adventures that bound them together when they started dating.

As for her husband's role in taking care of the town's problem, she really had no idea whether he'd set fire to the spaceship or not.

Nor did she care. Non-fiction or false, the imagery had apparently ignited a spark under Benji.

Both she and Chester were incredulous when he'd descended the stairs for breakfast that morning and said he'd like to spend more time helping out around the store after school and on weekends.

He graced them with a shy smile.

His essence was more assured, as if warmed by an incredible secret.

"Will wonders never cease?" she whispered to herself.

Now if she could just get the goat in her latest barnyard scene to look at the sprightly young cow in a lascivious manner, her day would be complete.

It wouldn't do to make the randy intent too obvious.

Nor the returning leer too welcoming.

"Barely discernible" was her guiding credo.

It was the sort of challenge she really enjoyed.

Her mother-earth face glowed.

***

Towards the end of the business day, Gary Willikers came into Chester Nail's hardware store.

Unsure how his approach would be received, but driven by innate decency, Chester went up to Gary and said, "Too bad about your building project. I thought maybe you had something there."

Gary was mildly surprised to be openly addressed on the subject. "Yes, well dreams rarely come true, but I do regret the way things turned out."

Chester was puzzled by Gary's calm. "You don't seem too upset."

Gary gave Chester a cock-eyed look. His expression turned reflective. "You know what, you're right. I thought I'd be horribly upset. Before there are momentous changes in our lives, we imagine them with all kinds of reservations.

Then they happen and you realize it was the build-up that was so stressful. The aftermath might be anything. It's almost certain not to be what you expect.

How do any of us cope with life? What a struggle. I just wanted to do something different. It was the kind of thing my father would have done. He liked grand gestures.

But clearly, it was upsetting a lot of people. I tried my hardest. Now it's been taken out of my hands."

Chester jumped in, "In effect, you've been provided with an excuse."

"You're a wise man, Chester. In short, yes".

"So what can I help you with today?" said the shopkeeper.

"Well, I want to spend more time with Bud. He says he'd like to go camping with me. Sounds like an excellent idea. What can you show me in the way of equipment?

Chester's response to such a question was always near at hand. "We have everything you'll ever need to have a great time. Where are you thinking of going?"

Gary didn't hesitate. "No place special in mind. I don't suppose it has to be very far. We're pretty remote right where we are. Savage, one might even say." A grim smile captured his face.

"True." Chester chuckled.

"I just want to find a clearing where Bud and I can set up away from any artificial light. Then we can get out the telescope and look at the stars."

"Yes, I've heard that's a hobby of yours," said Chester.

No doubt about it, Gary was warming to Chester. He'd always thought of him as just another fixture around town.

Maybe he'd been hasty in his judgment. And hadn't Adriana spoken highly of Phoebe Nails lately.

He'd share some humor with him. "Actually, I have an ulterior motive."

"Yes?" Chester intuitively picked up that a punch line was coming. He was prepared to smile.

Gary rose to the occasion. "I want to point out the quadrant of the sky where Bud's grandfather was born."

***

Three weeks after the shocking event that had his tiny community back on a more serene keel, Sheriff Hoody was on pedestrian patrol past the shops and cafes along Main Street.

He was well aware everyone in town was awaiting an arrest in the mysterious case of the rocket-ship fire at the Willikers' place.

Okay, maybe he wasn't the smartest man hereabouts, but there were certain things he couldn't do.

Before he'd lost his hair, he'd been a good-looking guy. His formidable size made him a local high school sports hero.

He'd been grateful for the advantage when he was younger. It helped him woo and win his ex-wife.

Their union had produced the extraordinary creature that was on display every day at the local pharmacy.

He wasn't at all happy that every self-deluded stud in town circled her like she was a candy bar.

That was life. He presumed it would ever be thus, a male-female dynamic that even crossed genders and always set the agenda.

Thursday night, three weeks prior, the former Mrs. Hoody contacted him and asked him to check on their daughter in what had once been their marriage bastion.

He generally didn't like going over there, since it reminded him of his reduced circumstances, living in a mobile home on the edge of town.

But he couldn't ignore his duty when it came to his darling child.

He arrived at 29 Shady Lane at 9:30 p.m. and used his old key to let himself in.

There was no evidence of Holly in the front rooms. He walked down the hallway that connected to the bedrooms and pushed open her door. Big mistake!

There were two figures uncovered and entwined on the bed. The one on top was startled by the movement behind him and looked up in mid-thrust.

A naked Sydney Steeler stared into the shocked eyes of Sherrif Hoody. Fistfuls of crap were about to overload the shredder.

Holly, still in the throes of pleasure, was at first oblivious to what was transpiring.

Harlan Hoody's frame shook with rage, but before his anger took wing with harsh words, a call came over his walkie-talkie. All three occupants of the room could hear the distress message.

"There's a fire at the Willikers' place. You'd better get over there right away, Sheriff."

Harlan looked at the pair and knew a great divide had been crossed. Relations with his little girl would never be the same again.

He rushed out of the house to do his duty, but his thoughts were preoccupied.

Worse, in the days that followed, he realized he shared a secret with the devil.

Syd was never boastful about his sexual conquest. He did, however, have immunity when it came to talking up his role in the great conflagration.

Harlan's hands were tied. He couldn't arrest the individual who was apparently the prime suspect in the case. He was well aware "said individual" had an iron-clad alibi.

Whenever anyone asked why he hadn't taken legal action against Syd, given the rumors that were circulating, Harlan would say he didn't have enough proof, but he was keeping an eye on the boy.

Besides, in his own mind he was conflicted. Where was the crime?

He knew Adriana Willikers was the culprit. She'd burned down her own property, a misdemeanor at best, since she didn't have a fire permit. He'd checked already.

He'd deduced Adriana's culpability on account of her carelessness. Fibers from her purple scarf had caught on some railing that escaped the blaze.

Being aware of the inner practices of all the social gatherings in his preserve was part of his job description.

If he arrested her, he'd only be tearing a family apart, one that was attempting reconciliation.

He knew what it was to live through a breakup. Best to be avoided if there were smoldering remnants of affection.

For the sake of his community, this was a case that should remain unsolved on the official blotter.

The townsfolk had a better Sheriff in Harlan Hoody than they would ever know.

"What a life," Harlan thought for the thousandth time that day. He paused in his walk through the beautiful little village where he'd always resided.

A lesson from the yoga class he sometimes watched on television surfaced unbidden.

"Oh well, on the plus side, it's great to breathe deeply and be here in this special space."

Harlan was becoming almost "new age" in his spirituality.

"That's a joke," he thought. "Wasn't it 'space' that got us into this mess in the first place?"

Alex Carrick obtained his undergraduate degree at the University of Western Ontario (London, Ontario, Canada) in 1969. His M.A. in Economics was earned at the University of Toronto (U of T) in 1971.

After finishing the courses for a doctorate while living at U of T's Massey College, the lure of the job market proved too great and Mr. Carrick was hired by the Canadian Institute of Steel Construction (CISC).

In 1985, Mr. Carrick became employed as Chief Economist with CanaData, a product line of Reed Construction Data, based in Atlanta. He is frequently quoted by major news outlets. His online video analyses are a popular feature with the *Daily Commercial News* and *Journal of Commerce*.

Alex is also an award-winning short story writer. He has twice received Honorable Mention in the international *Lorian Hemingway Competition*. In the summer of 2012, his personal blog was chosen Writing Website of the Week by *Writer's Digest*.

Carrick Publishing, which Alex manages jointly with his wife Donna, has published nearly 100 anthologies, fiction and non-fiction works by a variety of talented authors.

Visit Alex at his Website: www.alexcarrick.com .

Visit us at

http://www.carrickpublishing.com/

We hope you've enjoyed this crime anthology

brought to you by

CARRICK PUBLISHING.

We're always happy to hear from our readers.

You can reach us through our Facebook Page,
on Twitter @CarrickPub,
or email us for information about
any of our titles:

CarrickPublishing@rogers.com.

All rights reserved, 2014
e-Copyright 2014
Print Copyright 2014
©Carrick Publishing

Made in the USA
Charleston, SC
06 November 2014